TANGLED WEBS

Margaret Tessler

ACKNOWLEDGMENTS

Warmest thanks go to my family and friends for their encouragement and faith in me. To name them all would take another book. I would especially like to acknowledge Jerry Aguirre, Mel Eisenstadt, Damon Fay, my comadre Merlinda Sedillo, my sister Louise Gibson, and my daughter Mary Behm, for their expertise in various fields. Also, thanks to members of my writing workshops: George Anderson, Mary Blanchard, Edie Flaherty, Jeanne Knight, Betsy Lackmann, Jan McConaghy, Ronda Sofia, and Mary Zerbe. Most of all, thanks to my husband, Howard, for always being there.

Cover art by Mona Meyer

CHARACTERS

Sharon Morgan: Attorney with MacDougal & Martínez; now living in San Antonio, Texas

Ryan Salazar: Sharon's childhood sweetheart; a high-school teacher in Zapata, Texas

Erica Montoya: Sharon's childhood friend; Head Start coordinator; now living in California

Laura Velásquez: Sharon & Erica's childhood friend who died under mysterious circumstances

Abuelita: Laura's grandmother

Aunt Amanda: Sharon's mother's maiden aunt

MELENDEZ & SALAZAR FAMILY:

Alana & Beto Meléndez: Ryan's sister & her husband

Miguel Meléndez: Their 16-year-old son

Gabe Meléndez: Their 14-year-old son

Carlos Meléndez: Their 7-year-old son

Leo Salazar: Ryan & Alana's brother

Ysela & Ricardo Salazar (Amá & Apá):   Ryan, Alana, & Leo's parents

OTHER RECURRING CHARACTERS

Tina & Johnny Quemado:	Leo & Laura's friends and neighbors; teachers
Mac MacDougal & Vince Martínez:	Senior partners at Sharon's law firm
Dave Martínez:	Vince's nephew; associate at law firm
Mrs. Pirtle:	Elderly manager of Los Mareados
Ray & Emma López:	Friends of Erica and her family; co-managers of Los Mareados
Bernice Peralta:	*"La fea"* ("the ugly one"); troublemaker
Patty & Tony and Marisa & Luis:	Ryan's friends harassed by Bernice
Andy Estrada:	Lawyer who counsels Meléndez family
Julio Gallegos:	Zapata County sheriff
Billy Archuleta:	Sheriff's deputy
Sara & Jimmy:	Carlos' friends
Percy Smithers:	Vice President at bank
Elmer Smithers:	Percy's son
Dora & Viola Trujillo:	Ryan's students

For my daughter Valerie,
who fell in love with my characters

CHAPTER 1
January, 2000

"Don't tell anyone you're a lawyer, Sharon. Pretend you're a bird-watcher or something."

The warning would have sounded comical if not for the desperation in her voice. After ten years of little more than hastily scribbled Christmas notes, I'd gotten an unexpected call from my girlhood friend, Erica Montoya. But she was so upset I could hardly make sense of what she was saying.

"Erica, I haven't even said I'll come down there yet." Though I already knew I would.

"You have to, Sharon! You just have to! Please. I know you think it's crazy for me to call you like this after all these years...."

That was the only part of this conversation that *wasn't* crazy. As kids growing up in Zapata, Texas, Erica and I had been practically inseparable. We'd spent every summer together since we were seven, and had even gone through two years of junior high together. Although we'd both moved away and our correspondence had gradually dwindled, our friendship never wavered.

"After all these years, Erica, you know I'll be there."

"Thank God, Sharon." A sigh of relief mingled with the sound of muffled sobs. She paused in an effort to regain her composure. "And thank *you*. You can't imagine."

I looked at my calendar, then closed my eyes. "Will tomorrow be soon enough? I can come down now, but...." But it would leave a lot of people in a bind. Still, Erica came first. I began mentally rearranging my schedule.

"Tomorrow. Tomorrow's fine." Her voice sounded less frantic, but still ragged. "It—it helps just to know I'll see you tomorrow."

"Till then, try not to worry." What an idiotic thing to say, but all I could think of at the moment. "Let's go over this again so we can make plans."

Erica was staying with friends and was convinced their telephone was bugged. She wouldn't even give me a name or number, having made her call to my office from a pay phone. We'd barely agreed to meet tomorrow evening at 6:00, when her voice suddenly sank to a whisper. "I have to go now!" Then a click, followed by a dial tone.

CHAPTER 2

If you travel Texas Highway 16 from San Antonio to Zapata, it becomes increasingly lonely, marked by mile after dusty mile of deserty vegetation—mesquite, thorny blackbrush, prickly pear, and the like.

Sometimes you can spot a scissor-tailed flycatcher rocking back and forth on a telephone wire. More often your only company is an occasional caracara hunched over his fencepost like some gloomy sentinel who's assigned himself the job of discouraging trespassers.

And trespasser I was. I hadn't been in Zapata since Erica's quinceañera, her fifteenth-birthday celebration, twenty years ago. To tell you the truth, I wouldn't have ventured down that lonely road even now if I'd felt I had a choice. And I couldn't help wondering, for that matter, why the caracara chose to patrol there on such a dreary January day. Although this proud Mexican eagle fascinated me, he was still a bird of prey, and pickin's looked pretty slim to me.

Maybe we both needed the solitude. For me it offered a chance to mull over everything Erica had told me. I couldn't imagine who would want to murder Laura Velásquez. But I couldn't imagine her committing suicide either, which had been the official conclusion. Sweet Laura, with her angelic smile.

I'd never been as close to Laura as to Erica, but I'd always liked her. The three of us were a study in contrasts. Erica, with her dark eyes and long black hair, seemed unaware of her natural beauty. I was never satisfied with my blond curls, hazel eyes, and skin that tended to freckle easily. If not for Mrs. Montoya, I probably would have ruined my skin trying to get a tan, but she was fanatic about sunscreen and constantly assured me that I had a beauty of my own. As for my curls, they'd recently been hacked off in a disastrous encounter with a snooty and very expensive hair stylist.

I'd always thought Laura exotic. Her almond-shaped eyes were light blue, thanks to some Castillian forebears; otherwise she was dark, her short black hair framing a delicate face.

In temperament, Erica and I were much alike—down-to-earth kids with a streak of mischief. Laura, on the other hand, had an ethereal quality, a dreaminess, that set her apart.

I found it inconceivable that Laura had died from an overdose of prescription drugs, and felt my legal instincts kick into overdrive. Who was Laura's doctor? Why had he prescribed barbiturates in the first place? Could the pharmacy have made a mistake? How I'd like to question a few people! Probably the very reason Erica wanted me to keep a low profile.

Erica said it was a "hate crime" but was too distraught to explain her reasons. It seemed unlikely to me. People who commit hate crimes usually make a big production of them and like to see their names in the paper. Bombing things and torturing people was more their style. Poisoning didn't fit the picture.

Erica had also rambled on about how Laura's grandmother—Laura's *Abuelita*—had "upped and moved back to Mexico" six months ago and hadn't been heard from since. But that was as incoherent as the rest of her outpourings. I couldn't make the connection. Besides,

Abuelita had been talking about going back to Mexico ever since I'd known her.

And how long had *that* been? How long since I'd let myself think of the past, the way I was doing now? I had tried so hard to develop the habit of never looking back. I certainly didn't want to dredge up any romantic memories of Ryan.

Back to the problem at hand, I told myself sternly. And what exactly was the problem? Although Laura's death seemed to be the immediate concern, I sensed there were deeper issues at stake.

Highway 16 ended abruptly at El Tigre Exxon, where I pulled in for gas, a Dr. Pepper, and a package of Tom's peanut-butter crackers. The attendant, a nice-looking kid whose nametag read "Enrique," studied me with a mixture of nonchalance and curiosity. Strangers around here aren't unusual if they're elderly and/or gray-haired. A 35-year-old blonde doesn't exactly blend in.

"Trece cuarenta y cinco," he quoted innocently, his gaze fixed on the computer.

"'Tá bueno," I answered, looking him in the eye as I handed him the thirteen dollars and forty-five cents.

He grinned. "Thanks. Come back now."

I smiled back at him. "Thanks. I will."

From there I crossed the street to find myself on Farm Road 496, which continues another three miles to the Rio Grande and Los Mareados Motel and Apartments, where Erica wanted me to stay. It was a small L-shaped complex consisting of twelve units with kitchenettes. Most of the tenants, older people on fixed incomes, had moved in permanently.

The manager, Mrs. Pirtle, was an elderly woman with fuzzy gray hair. Her eyes appeared gray and fuzzy too, but that could have been because her glasses were so smudged.

"Hello, I'm Sharon Morgan. Do you have a vacancy?" Rhetorical question, since there was a large sign by the office proclaiming "VACANCY."

"Well, I might have," she said grudgingly. "And I might not." She peered at me over her useless glasses. "We don't usually have young folks here, and my tenants want it quite. None of that screechy music. No BOYFRIENDS with motorsickles and like that."

"Gracious, no. I spend all my waking hours watching birds. I'm quite quite. I mean, quiet." Flustered is what I meant. I've never been very good at lying and I felt my insincerity prickling me like heat rash in summer.

Mrs. Pirtle looked—naturally—unconvinced and more suspicious by the minute. "You mean a young person like you don't have employment? You just set around watchin' birds all day long?"

"Oh no. I'm a photographer for a new wildlife magazine, and I've been assigned to, uh, take pictures. Of birds." The photographer bit was a stretch; I was doing well to know the difference between a tripod and a lens-cap. I could only hope Mrs. Pirtle wouldn't ask to look at my "professional equipment," which consisted of one pocket-sized camera.

But since the Rio Grande valley was well known as a haven for rare birds and not-so-rare bird-watchers, my fabrication calmed her. She dug around for some registration forms, which she shoved at me to sign.

Now that I'd been accepted, I felt bold enough to ask how the apartment complex had gotten its name. This finally brought something like a smile to her face.

"It's Spanish," she told me importantly. "Spanish is such a pretty language."

"Oh yes, very pretty. Is Mareados a family name?"

She laughed at my ignorance. "No, dearie. Well, I don't know EXACTLY, but it's to do with the sea. '*Mare*' means 'sea' in Spanish."

Mar, I corrected mentally, but didn't interrupt.

"We're actually on the river, or the '*ree-o*,' as they say around here."

We're actually on Falcon Lake, a reservoir that was created decades ago from the Rio Grande, stretching some thirty miles as the crow flies. But some of the older residents, like Mrs. Pirtle and my Aunt Amanda, continued calling it the river; I had picked up that habit myself.

"When they were choosin' names for this place, they wanted somethin' kinda classy," Mrs. Pirtle explained, "and Mr. López suggested 'mareados.' It has such a nice sound, don't you think?"

I agreed, wondering who the humorous Mr. López might be, but decided not to tell her the word means "seasick."

Mrs. Pirtle fished out some keys and led me to #12, diagonally across from her unit, #1. I shivered involuntarily. Erica had told me that—up until her presumed disappearance—Laura's grandmother lived in "the last apartment, the one on the end."

This must have been her apartment. I pulled my jacket tighter around me, telling myself this might be a real break if it meant I could find out something about Laura. But at the moment, I felt more chilled than lucky, and the chill had nothing to do with January.

CHAPTER 3

If I'd hoped to find clues about Laura's death or her abuelita's abrupt departure to Mexico, my hopes were quickly squashed. When Abuelita had lived with Laura's family, her room was crammed with garish statues and sad-eyed pictures of every saint imaginable. Thinking about it now, I could almost smell the votive candles she placed everywhere.

Abuelita was very tiny and, I used to think, incredibly ancient, though she probably wasn't more than 60 at the time. Laura told us she was a *curandera*, a healer, and I was sure she possessed magical powers.

I supposed she'd moved into Los Mareados when Laura's parents moved to Laredo. But there was no sign of her presence now—not even a drop of candle wax. I poked half-heartedly in all the drawers and crannies and found the apartment as sterile and impersonal as the picture of the dogs playing poker. I even looked behind the picture, but found both wall and picture intact.

A slight feeling of depression replaced the eerie sensation I'd experienced earlier, and I still had three hours to kill before meeting Erica. I had a theory I wanted to check out and decided to begin my charade.

I hadn't come entirely unprepared. Before leaving San Antonio, I'd stopped at Goodwill to buy khaki shorts, unmatching shirt, frumpy hat, and oversized binoculars—the standard bird watcher's uniform. I already owned a scruffy pair of hiking boots to go with it. I paid more than I would have liked for the binoculars, so to counteract my extravagance I picked up some wire-rimmed glasses for $7.95 at the H-E-B.

Now as I donned my spiffy new outfit, sans binoculars, I thought of Mac MacDougal's warning: "Sharon, you're not Perry Mason. You work with indigent people, not 'suspects.' Promise me you'll be careful."

I'd given Mac an edited rundown of my conversation with Erica and my need to take a few days off from the firm of MacDougal and Martínez. They were very accommodating, even staying late with me to iron out last-minute details, which was one of the many reasons I liked working for them. Moreover, I appreciated Mac's fatherly concern for me.

"I'll be careful, Mac. I promise."

I'll be careful, I repeated to myself as I headed into town to buy a few groceries. The wind chapped my knees, which I hoped worked in my favor by aging my skin in a few short minutes.

Ramirez Minimax was now the Super S; otherwise the store was startlingly familiar. The aisles were clogged with shopping carts where people had stopped to hug the friends and relatives they hadn't seen since day before yesterday at Mass.

My theory was panning out. Nobody paid attention to the dowdy *huera* puttering along peering at labels, supposedly studying them. After spending countless childhood summers here, I'd learned the lingo—a mixture of Tex-Mex and a Spanish dialect unique to Zapata—and could readily pick up the gossip. And mucho gossip there was.

A pertinent scrap caught my attention. I edged closer to the two women who'd mentioned Laura's name, hoping my ears hadn't visibly perked up.

"It was that whore, that Bernice."

9

Now my ears were quivering in earnest. Unfair. There had to be more than one Bernice in town.

"I don't know...."

"Of course it was Bernice." A third woman had joined the conversation. Apparently I wasn't the only eavesdropper. "She's always making trouble. Always after other people's husbands." Hearing the acid in the woman's voice, I could almost picture her expression. I wished I dared to look at their faces.

Out of the corner of my eye, I saw the second woman shake her head. "No. Laura would not have taken her own life. Not because of Bernice. Not because of anything."

They were silent, and for a moment I wondered if I'd lingered in the aisle too long. Turning toward another shelf, I glanced at their faces and realized their troubled thoughts had nothing to do with me.

"Pobrecita. Poor Laura," the first woman whispered. The others nodded, and they moved on.

CHAPTER 4

Where was Erica? She'd promised to come to Los Mareados at 6:00. By then it would be dark, and she thought everyone would be home eating dinner.

When she hadn't shown up by 7:00, my imagination had concocted such unbearable scenarios, I couldn't sit still any longer. I drove down Mockingbird Avenue, as if I could make her materialize by driving past her old house. The lights inside reminded me that someone else was living there now.

As I slowed down, dogs began barking, setting off a chain reaction for six blocks around. Someone came to the door to see what had agitated them. Since my little white Honda wasn't going to turn dark and blend into the night, I slouched down as far as I could without slipping below the steering wheel and drove on.

I figured I might as well swing by Laura's old house too, although it was several blocks away. Unlike Erica's, Laura's house was totally dark, and there were no watchdogs to care whether I came or went.

I considered driving down Ryan's street. Come on, Sharon, act your age, I chided myself as I pushed that thought from my mind.

I circled by the plaza instead, then drove back to Los Mareados. I hoped Erica might have arrived while I was gone. Instead I found a note from Mrs. Pirtle Scotch-taped to my door:

"SOMEBODDY was snooping around your
place, so I called Mr. Lopezz. Bafore he got
here, they left. Mr. L said it was only Ernie
GRIEGO, but I don't know why HE'D be
sneeking around. I thout you said you din't
have any boyfrends."

Well, Mrs. Pirtle was plainly miffed. I walked over to her
apartment and found her glued to the window, binoculars
pressed to her face. I wondered if she felt it her duty to
keep track of all her tenants night and day.

I knocked on her door and waited.

"Go away. I ain't home. Come back in the mornin'."

"I don't have any boyfriends," I told the closed door, "and
I was worried about the prowler you saw."

"It wasn't any prowler. It was Ernie Griego. He won't
come back."

"How do you know?"

"Don't bother me now."

And what will you do if I keep bothering you? I muttered
to myself as I walked back to my apartment. Conk me with
your binoculars? Call Mr. López, whoever he is? Kick me out
of this classy establishment?

Erica had called while I was out and left the briefest of
messages on my cell phone: "Sorry about tonight.
Tomorrow, same time."

I kicked myself for not taking the phone with me instead
of leaving it on the night stand. We had agreed before I
came down here that it would be safe for Erica to use that
number as long as we kept our conversations brief and
innocuous. I wished more than ever she'd left a number
where I could reach her.

Nothing to do but wait another day. Erica, where are you? I hope that was you Mrs. Pirtle mistook for a burglar.

* * *

The next morning I dressed in a gray no-nonsense sweatsuit and stomped over to the office. The sky was overcast and gloomy. I had slept poorly and was hardly in the mood to play games with Mrs. Pirtle. I was definitely not in the mood to watch birds, much as I might have enjoyed it otherwise.

I banged on the door more loudly than necessary and wondered what idiocy awaited me today.

Mrs. Pirtle hadn't cleaned her glasses since yesterday, and they were almost opaque. She pushed them to the end of her nose and glared at me. "What do *you* want?"

What happened to "dearie"? I took a deep breath, tried a different tack. "I came to apologize for knocking on your door so late last night." *If 7:40 was unreasonably late.* "You must have been upset."

She nodded, pursing her lips. She pushed her glasses up, then down again when she realized she still couldn't see me.

"There was quite a commotion, Missy."

"I'm sure there was. I'm sorry Mr. López had to be called. Is he the sheriff?"

"Ha! Mr. Raymond López, sheriff? Ha! No, that's Julio. Julio Gallegos, to be exact, but ever'one just calls him Julio."

I hesitated, wondering how far my tact could stretch. "You must have had a good reason for calling Mr. López instead of Julio."

She bristled. "Those were his orders."

"Mm."

She reached under the desk, pulled out a box of Kleenex, took a tissue and wiped her glasses, spreading the smudge around. "He tells me, always call him first. That old weasel."

"You don't like Mr. López?"

She fussed with her glasses again.

"Is he the owner?"

"No, he just thinks he is. I use to like him. But not after last night."

"What exactly happened last night?"

"He tells me there's no need to call Julio, that it's just Ernie Griego. Well, let me tell you, it was NOT Ernie Griego. He thinks my eyes ain't good enough to tell the difference. Well, maybe I got poor eyesight, but I ain't stupid, and I know Ernie Griego, and that wasn't him."

"Mr. López should give you more credit."

She leaned forward. "I always mind my own business, but this ain't the first time. Somethin's goin' on. Wicked things." She shook her finger at me. "I could tell you—"

The door creaked open and she switched gears. "Mornin', Mr. Bigelow, can I help you?"

"No, no. Just came in to pay my rent."

I was wondering if I should outwait Mr. Bigelow, but he didn't seem in a hurry to leave. Darn the luck—just when Mrs. Pirtle was on a roll.

Mr. Bigelow studied me without blinking. "Don't I know you from somewhere?"

"I don't think so." But I had the same vague impression. A not very pleasant impression. I searched for some childhood memory, but nothing came. All I saw now was a balding man with purplish skin, a large nose, and bulgy eyes.

"You look familiar," he persisted.

"Really? Must be someone else. I've been told I look like Meg Ryan."

"Nope. Not her. She's much prettier."

And I wasn't even in my disguise. Which reminded me, I needed to get back to Plan A. I went back to the apartment and set up my laptop on the kitchen table. There were too many loose ends floating around in my head, and I needed to commit them to my computer's memory before they got any looser.

First on my list were my worries about Erica. What was she so afraid of? And where was she?

Then of course there was Laura. Judging from the conversation I'd overheard at Super S, Erica wasn't alone in disbelieving the suicide verdict.

And who was "that whore Bernice" the ladies had been discussing? I felt the hackles rise on my neck, and rose to get a Dr. Pepper. I poured it into a glass and watched it fizz. I hadn't thought of Bernice Peralta since we were kids. After all this time my dislike seemed childish, and I was surprised I still felt so much resentment.

For years I'd spent every summer visiting my great-aunt Amanda, who lived next door to Erica Montoya and her family. Erica and I became fast friends during that very first visit, when we were only seven years old. Every summer after that we simply picked up where we'd left off.

In fact, since she had four older brothers and I was an only child, we'd declared ourselves to be sisters to each other. Apparently her brothers considered it a package deal and enjoyed having both of us to boss around.

I loved Erica's parents, who were like second parents to me. Mrs. Montoya even became my godmother—my *nina*—when I was confirmed. And it was Mr. Montoya who presented me at my swearing-in ceremony after I passed the bar ten years ago. The whole family had flown in from California for the occasion—including Erica's brothers, their wives and children—which made it all the more special.

The only fly in my relationship with Erica had been Bernice Peralta. She was one of Erica's "year-round" friends up until seventh grade. By then Bernice had become more interested in boys than in us, and we ran with different groups.

Up till then she constantly tried to drive a wedge between Erica and me. She won over Aunt Amanda with her phony good manners, and loved to drop hints of misbehavior on my part. I could hear my great-aunt now:

"Sharon, don't give that nice Bernice such dirty looks. What an impolite child you can be!"

This lasted until the day Aunt Amanda caught Bernice unawares and realized she'd been smirking behind her back all along. After that I never had to hear any more comments about how nice Bernice was.

Laura's abuelita had never been conned by Bernice or anyone else. Abuelita made the sign of the cross whenever she caught sight of Bernice, and insisted that Erica, Laura, and I wear garlic around our necks in case Bernice "*les haga el ojo*," should give us the evil eye. Aunt Amanda put a stop to the garlic, saying it was a silly superstition. I wonder....

The last time I'd seen Bernice had been at Erica's quinceañera 20 years ago. My mind veered. That memory could stay buried.

Well, this wasn't getting anywhere. The question wasn't whether or not *"esa puta Bernice"* of Super S gossip was someone I knew and disliked, but whether or not she had something to do with the mystery surrounding Laura.

I finished my Dr. Pepper and resumed my list. Who is Mr. López, and why did he brush off Mrs. Pirtle's report of a prowler? Why did he insist it was Ernie Griego, when Mrs. Pirtle seemed so sure it wasn't? Who IS Ernie Griego? What was Mrs. Pirtle about to tell me before Mr. Bigelow came in? Why does Mr. Bigelow look familiar? Does it matter?

I stood and stretched, rubbing my neck. Maybe Erica would show up tonight. In the meantime, I'd go crazy if I didn't do something constructive. I made a quick change into rose-colored sweater and slacks, then swiped a comb through my butchered hair. As I stepped out the door I saw Mrs. Pirtle waving me down. Good. Maybe Mr. Bigelow had gone home and she was ready to continue airing her grievances.

No such luck. "There's a young man askin' after you," she sniffed. "Fella from up to the Axion."

"The Axion?"

She glared at me. "The Axion gas station up to the crossroads."

Oh, the Exxon station. Not that I was any less confused.

"I thought you said you din't have any boyfriends."

"I DON'T have any boyfriends."

"Why not? You're not one of them Libyans, are you?"

"No, I can honestly say I'm not." *I'm not even a lesbian, Mrs. Pirtle. Are you a homophobe?*

"Did this person leave a message?" I asked.

She flung a scrap of paper at me. The cramped handwriting and poor spelling matched the note she had left last night. "Call RYAN imedeatily at the Exon—756-9504."

I could think of only one Ryan, and thinking of him made me smile. Ryan Salazar was the first boy I'd ever loved—and a part of me would always love him. It had been so many years since I'd given myself permission to think about him, I'd even avoided driving down his street last night. But suddenly his memory danced before me, and the memory was sweet.

Of course he was probably married by now with a house full of kids. No need to get my hopes up. Besides, the person who called me could be someone else named Ryan.

Whoever it was, why would he want me to call him at a service station? I was reluctant to use my cell phone, figuring Mrs. Pirtle probably used a scanner along with her binoculars. Gosh, I was getting paranoid along with everyone else. Maybe it was contagious.

In any event, I preferred to go "up to the Axion" to find out what this was all about.

CHAPTER 5

The only person I saw manning the checkout at the Exxon convenience store was a dumpy boy bent over a copy of *The National Instigator* that he'd spread out across the counter.

"Excuse me," I said, drawing him reluctantly from his immersion in some juicy scandal.

He placed his finger on the point in the page where he'd been interrupted and looked in my general direction.

I wanted to knock on his forehead and shout, "Anybody home?" Instead I stepped into his line of vision and smiled sweetly. "I'm looking for Ryan. Is he here?"

"Ryan?"

"Yes. Ryan. Does someone named Ryan work here?"

He blinked as if registering that a real live human being was standing before him. He scrunched his face into a puzzled frown. "Ryan? Nope." He apparently considered the matter closed and returned to his reading.

"But I had a message to call him here," I persisted, raising my voice in annoyance.

Dumpy rolled his eyes, then yelled over his shoulder, "Oye, Rique, esa loca quiere saber...."

Enrique, the boy who'd waited on me earlier, sprang with the alacrity of Superman from behind the Slurpee machine that he was cleaning. Wiping his hands on a paper towel, he reached the counter in a few quick strides and squelched Dumpy with a look.

"If this NICE LADY wants to know something, let's see if we can help her."

A pretty brunette about my age or a little older appeared beside Enrique. "Ms. Meléndez—asst. mgr." according to her nametag. Something about that name rang a bell— something just beyond my reach.

"Yes, Oscar," she said. "Helping customers *is* our job."

I marveled at her ability to speak so softly and still sound so icy.

"Glad to hear that," said a customer who'd come in to pay for his gas.

Enrique stepped behind the counter to take over for Dumpy, who was trying rather unsuccessfully to fold up *The Instigator*.

Ms. Meléndez sighed resignedly and turned to me. "Let's sit down over here." She led us to a small eating area near the Coke machine.

"This place has everything," I said, glancing around.

"Some people like to grab their breakfast burrito and run. Others like a place to sit."

"It's nice to stop awhile."

"But you didn't do that yesterday."

I realized she was studying me and not just making conversation.

Her face was impassive. "You don't remember me, do you," she said.

She looked so familiar, just on the edge of memory, but out of context. I couldn't connect her with someone I'd known over 20 years ago. "No. I'm embarrassed to say I don't."

She smiled then, her eyes crinkling at the corners. "I'm glad you're honest. To be truthful, I didn't recognize you either. But my brother did."

Her brother. Ryan Salazar. Of course. "You're Alana Salazar," I blurted out.

She smiled. "Meléndez now."

"You married Beto?"

She nodded.

"I'm glad. I always liked him." Beto and Alana seemed completely unmatched when they started going together in high school. Alana, "the Salazar twins' big sister," was pretty and popular and could have dated anyone she wanted. She was still attractive, her once-long hair now short, curving gently around her oval face, emphasizing her deep brown eyes.

I wondered how time had changed Beto. I remembered him as wearing "high-waters" and owlish glasses. He wrote poetry and probably couldn't have caught a football if it was rolled to him. A lot of people considered him nerdy, but I thought he was nice because he was nice to us younger kids.

"You remember after all," she said.

"Yes, but I'm confused." Getting back to the reason I was here. "How come...?" I stopped, trying to think of Dumpy's real name before asking why he'd never heard of Ryan.

"How come Ryan was able to recognize you?" she asked, misinterpreting my hesitation.

"Well, that too. I've only seen him once since eighth grade. I'd like to think I've changed since then."

"You had your 15 minutes of fame around here when you graduated law school and got your picture in the paper."

Aunt Amanda. She would want everyone to know her great-niece had amounted to something after all. But that was 10 years ago, and even then I suspected there were no more than a handful of people who'd been remotely interested. On the other hand, Ryan had noticed.

I wasn't sure how to take Alana's teasing. I'd held her somewhat in awe when we were growing up. The difference

21

in our ages seemed so much greater back then. I wondered if she knew about all the smooching that had gone on between her brother and me in the park behind the Dairy Queen.

"I'm sure my fleeting fame was quickly forgotten." I waved my hand, banishing my 15 minutes into thin air. "But I can't understand why what's-his-name doesn't know who Ryan is."

"Ryan's a high-school teacher. He's *Mr. Salazar* to these kids."

"A teacher!" All I could imagine was a skinny 14-year-old with braces on his teeth teaching high-schoolers to play a drum. Obviously I wasn't very good at visualizing my old boyfriend as an adult.

"What does he teach?"

"Spanish and Freshman English."

"I wish I'd seen his teacher-picture in the paper."

Alana laughed. "You are at a disadvantage."

"Why would he want me to call him here?"

"I doubt that he did."

"But this message...." I pulled Mrs. Pirtle's illiterate scrap of paper from my purse and handed it to Alana.

She bit her lip, dimples appearing in her cheeks. "My, my. How quaint. Well, God only knows what this person thinks he...she?...heard."

"She."

"Ryan was probably trying to explain that he'd seen you here, but the number he left is his *home* phone. And I also doubt that he wanted you to call him 'imedeATily.' Though he clearly wanted to get in touch."

"If I had only called 'imedeATily' instead of simply showing up here, I could have saved you a lot of trouble."

"No trouble. Actually, it was nice to see you. But I do have to get back to work."

I looked at my watch. "Ryan's probably still at school right now."

"Probably. Try calling him around 3:30."

* * *

A few blocks northwest of El Tigre Exxon was the Catholic Church. A larger church had replaced the original building since I'd been here last. The new church, graceful in its simplicity, reminded me of mission churches from an earlier era.

I knocked on the rectory door and was greeted by Father Lucero, a middle-aged man with intelligent eyes in a gentle face. Once seated in his office, I explained that I was an old friend of Laura Velásquez and was distressed to learn she had died. "I've heard rumors," I said truthfully, "that don't make sense, and I was hoping you could shed some light on things."

Father Lucero seemed to turn this over in his mind before speaking. "Laura Velásquez. Yes. You say you were a close friend of hers?"

"*Old* friend is more like it. We were friends when we were kids, but we'd lost touch over the years. I just found out about her death a couple of days ago."

"I see. And you're here now because you're concerned about the rumors you've heard." Father Lucero shook his head sadly. "I'm afraid I haven't been here long enough to be of much help."

"You're new to this parish?"

"Yes, I came here in November after Fr. McNaughton retired."

"I don't suppose Laura—I know you can't break a confidence, but can you tell me if she ever came to you for counseling, or if you had any reason to think she was depressed?"

"No. No to both questions. If she was disturbed about something, I regret that I didn't pick up on it. Unfortunately, I simply hadn't gotten to know her very well. And I didn't meet Mrs. Velásquez—Laura's mother—till she came down from Laredo to make funeral arrangements."

"Do you think Mrs. Velásquez had any—I mean, did she say anything about Laura's state of mind?"

"It's interesting that you ask that. Ordinarily I wouldn't say anything myself, but...I believe you *are* a friend, 'old' or not. To answer your question, I thought at first it was just something a mother would naturally want to believe—a defense mechanism perhaps. Mrs. Velásquez vehemently denied that Laura took her own life."

"Laura did get a Catholic burial then?"

"Oh yes. Even if it were suicide, the Church would give her the benefit of the doubt. There's always the possibility— probability really—that a suicide victim is acting irrationally."

"You say 'even if,' Father. You aren't sure it was suicide yourself, are you."

Father Lucero shifted uncomfortably. I waited.

"Rumors can be so ugly. But maybe some gossip does bear repeating," he said at last.

"Yes?"

"From what I hear, a lot of people—not only her family, but others—thought it out of character for Laura to do such a thing." He paused. "Also, nearly everyone seems to have loved her."

"*Nearly* everyone?"

His kind face was troubled. "I wish I could help you. But I'm afraid there's nothing more I can say. I hope you find what you're looking for."

"Father, I'm sorry, but if I keep trying to read between the lines, I might come up with the wrong conclusions."

"Or the right ones. But I've said enough. No more cross-examination."

His words caught me up short. "I'm sorry. I didn't mean to put you off."

"You didn't, my dear. Not at all. I like your straightforward approach. But if you're going to be asking anyone else questions, it would be wise to be less direct. In fact, you need to be very careful."

I wished he would be *more* direct, but perhaps he'd said all he felt free to say.

I rose to leave. "Well, thank you, Father, for your time and your patience. I would follow your advice about being careful if I knew where to follow it. Right now, I'm not sure where to go from here."

Father Lucero led me to the door, then stopped before opening it. "Have you talked to Laura's husband?"

Her husband! Why hadn't Erica mentioned anything about a husband?

Father Lucero nodded. "You look surprised. I wondered. When you called Laura by her maiden name, I wondered. Still, it's natural to call someone by the name that's more familiar. Especially someone you haven't seen in a while. I knew her as Laura Salazar."

If he was trying to put me at ease, it wasn't working. "Salazar!"

No wonder Ryan had been trying to call me. How could Erica have failed to tell me this!

Strange that Alana didn't mention anything either. And why had Laura's mother been the one to make funeral arrangements?

The more answers I got, the more questions I had. And the more unsettled I felt.

CHAPTER 6

"You are at a disadvantage." Alana's words rang in my ears. I had tried to keep my worry over Erica at bay by keeping busy. Now my frustration was colliding with my anxiety.

I sat in my little Honda, arms folded across the steering wheel, and cradled my head on my arms.

Erica, you asked me to come down here, but I still don't know what it is you expect of me. You've given me NO, as in ZERO, information. Okay, a little information. Damn little. I don't even have your phone number.

You don't want me to tell anyone I'm a lawyer, but everyone in town has seen my lawyer-picture. Okay, not everyone; just Ryan Salazar. And keeping quiet is probably the one particle of wisdom you've dispensed. People don't like being grilled.

But if I don't ask questions, what is it you want me to do? Am I supposed to wander around town in funny glasses hoping I might overhear something to do with Laura? Better yet, should I stalk Bernice Peralta? And what am I supposed to say when I call Ryan? "Hi there. Long time, no see! Oops, didn't know you were in mourning. Must have slipped Erica's mind."

My frustration vented, the anxiety clamored to be heard again. I needed some fresh air. The sun was flirting with the clouds and the wind had spent itself for the time being. I left the car in the parking lot and walked catty-cornered to Los Pasteles Bakery. This building was new to me too, but the fragrances were sweet and familiar, setting off a pang of nostalgia. As well as a pang of hunger. I'd had nothing for breakfast and only a Dr. Pepper for lunch.

I settled down with a warm concha and a steaming cup of coffee, and made a conscious effort to savor each mouthful instead of wolfing it all down. When I'd finished, I called Ryan from the pay phone outside.

"Sharon!" His voice sounded deep and warm. "I was hoping you'd call. Where are you?"

"Los Pasteles."

"Sounds inviting. Maybe I could meet you there."

"Okay. I could probably go for another concha." It occurred to me that I'd really like a good salad instead. I couldn't just sit around eating sweet rolls all afternoon.

"I'll be there in five minutes—más o menos."

I could picture him giving the back-and-forth hand gesture that signified he'd be here anywhere from the specified five minutes to a few hours.

"Good. I'll wait here five minutes—más or menos."

He laughed. "Ándale pues."

Well, he certainly sounded in a good humor. Not exactly the grieving widower. Maybe it would help to see him in person. Among other things, I'd sure like to know how he'd found me at Los Mareados.

On impulse, I opened the phone book and looked up Bernice Peralta. No luck. Probably married by now and listed under another name. Next I looked up Mrs. Pirtle's nemesis, Mr. Raymond López. Ah, what have we here? The address of one "Ramón López" was listed as 237 Mockingbird Avenue— the Montoyas' old address! The very place I'd driven by last night, disturbing all the dogs. Curiouser and curiouser.

* * *

Ryan showed up within a few minutes and slid into the booth across from me. Whatever other changes had taken place, he still had the same deep brown eyes I remembered.

He reached across the table and took both my hands in his, then released them gently and stood up again. "I need an empanada and a cup of coffee. How 'bout you?"

"Another cup of coffee is all."

The cashier regarded Ryan flirtatiously and he grinned in return. They exchanged a few words I couldn't hear. Apparently they were pretty amusing, because the two of them began laughing. His nonchalance grated on me.

Ryan returned with our coffee and two apricot empanadas. "In case you change your mind."

Before he could say anything else, I leaned over and touched his hand. "Ryan, please accept my condolences. I'm so sorry about Laura."

He gave a start, then looked down. I couldn't read his expression. "It's been hard on all of us."

I drew my hand away. "I know. But on you especially."

"Me? Why me especially?"

"Well, it just seems natural...."

"Am I missing something here?"

"I was about to ask the same thing. Weren't you and Laura married?"

"Where did you get that idea? Never mind," he added as comprehension dawned. "You got the wrong twin." His jaw tightened.

I felt I'd hit a raw nerve but didn't know why. There had never been any competition between Ryan and his brother that I knew of, but maybe this was different.

In both looks and personality, Ryan and Leo were the most un-identical twins I'd ever known. Leo looked like the husky football star he was. Ryan, small and thin, had enjoyed sandlot sports, but never took them seriously. He'd preferred playing drums in a rock band with his friends.

"Well, I feel pretty stupid," I said. "But if I don't jump to at least one wrong conclusion a day, I consider the day a waste."

Ryan laughed, and his eyes became warm and friendly again. His smile was attractive too—the braces had done a great job. He was still slim, and nicely built. Not very tall. That was okay. I could settle for short, dark, and handsome.

He moved the plate of empanadas toward me. I shook my head, and he moved it back. He ate a few bites before breaking the silence. "What did you do to your hair?"

So much for romance. "I cut it." And so much for idle chit-chat. "How did you find me?"

"From the beginning?"

"Yes, I'd appreciate that."

"I was born to Ysela and Ricardo Salazar in the year of our Lord...."

"You know what I mean!"

"Sorry. I thought this conversation needed—never mind. Let's see. I stopped at El Tigre to go to the ATM."

"Didn't you have school?"

"Teacher's conferences. Mine were in the evening. Anyway, you were busy at the checkout, and I thought you looked familiar. Then when I heard you talking to Enrique, I was pretty sure. So then...." He looked up at the ceiling. "So then, I followed you."

"You *followed* me!"

"I wondered where you were staying. I was kind of surprised. I mean, why not the Best Western or the Executive Inn?"

"That's *my* long story. But go on with yours."

"Then I thought maybe I was wrong, that it wasn't you after all. And even if it was, it might not be such a good idea to drop in without warning."

"Very diplomatic."

"But I couldn't get you off my mind, so today I decided to go ahead and call. Strange lady that runs the place."

"I'm dying to know what that conversation was all about!"

Ryan grinned, then took a few swallows of coffee before continuing. "I asked for you, and she asked if I was a photographer. Now that intrigued me. When I said no, she started babbling about your boyfriends and how you weren't supposed to have any. That intrigued me too. She seemed worried that I was going to come over on my 'motorsickle' and play loud music. I almost thought the hell with it. But, well, I left a message anyway."

"I'm glad you did."

"Yo también." He clasped his hands behind his head. "Now it's your turn."

"My turn?"

"To tell me *your* long story. What brings you here?"

I toyed with my coffee cup. Although the bakery wasn't crowded, I realized I didn't want to talk about "my story" where anyone else could overhear. "It's complicated. I'd rather not talk about it here."

Ryan gazed at me seductively through half-closed eyes and slipped into his pachuco accent. "I could follow you to your place in my peekup and serenade you weeth my drums. Your manager lady, she would like that, no?"

I couldn't help laughing. "Ryan, you're impossible."

31

"I try. Well, we could go to my place then. Or somewhere else—you name it."

Before I could answer, two teenage girls who'd been giggling in a nearby booth wiggled over to our table. They greeted Ryan, watching me out of the corners of their eyes.

"Bueno, Mr. Salazar. ¿Cómo 'stado?"

Ryan stood. "I'm fine. And you?"

"Okay." They answered and giggled in unison.

"I'd like you to meet my friend Sharon Morgan. Sharon, these are two of my students, Viola and Dora Trujillo."

They seemed oblivious to the formality and the fact that Ryan was still standing.

"It's nice to meet you," I replied.

"Same here." One of them ventured to look at me. "You look like Téa Leoni."

"No she doesn't," said the other one. "Más como Kathryn Morris."

"Pos, todas las hueras se parecen lo mismo," the first one replied.

This began another series of giggles.

Ryan turned red and his eyes narrowed.

"No le hace. It's okay," I said, smiling. "I don't think we all look alike, but I'll take it as a compliment anyway."

The girls had the grace to blush.

"Excuse us," Ryan said pointedly, "but we were about to leave. I'll talk to you two tomorrow."

CHAPTER 7

I realized it would be getting late soon and I didn't want to miss Erica again. My anxiety had returned, but at least I was no longer annoyed. Ryan and I had barely gotten out the door when a red Porsche screeched into one of the few parking spaces in front of the bakery.

"Oh God," Ryan groaned. "It's Bernice Peralta."

Bernice-Thorn-in-My-Side-Peralta. I could feel a headache coming on.

"Let's hope she doesn't see us," Ryan said, echoing my thoughts.

Fat chance. Bernice leapt from her Porsche with as much agility as one can leap in 5-inch heels and a tight skirt. She made a halfhearted attempt to straighten her skirt as she undulated toward us. I had to hand it to her. I'd have toppled over, but Bernice still managed to slink. Now that she was only a few feet away, I could smell the alcohol on her breath.

I would never have recognized her. Her hair, cut Cleopatra-style, was a peculiar shade of orange, the result of a bleach job gone wrong. It was hard to tell what she looked like otherwise, because her makeup was so heavy.

"Ryan," she purred, "what a surprise!"

Ryan mumbled something I couldn't hear.

Her eyes narrowed as she took in the fact that I was still standing next to him.

"Well now, Ryan, aren't you going to introduce me to your friend here?"

"This is Téa Leoni. Téa, Bernice."

She squinted as if trying to get me into focus.

"Been nice chatting with you, Bernice, but we're running late." Ryan took me by the arm and propelled me down the sidewalk.

"What are we late for?" I whispered.

"Finding your car," he whispered back. "Where are you parked?"

"In the opposite direction. Across the street."

We made an abrupt 180 and whisked past Bernice again.

"Why did you park over here?" he asked as we reached my Honda.

"I stopped in to see Father Lucero."

"Oh? Is that part of your long story?"

"Kind of. I'll explain tomorrow. I hope. Will I see you tomorrow?"

"Call me. We can make plans." He touched my cheek with the back of his hand, then bent down and kissed me lightly.

As he started to open the car door, we were interrupted by the sound of Bernice's red Porsche barreling into the parking lot. She stopped within a few feet of where we were standing.

She rolled down her window and drawled in a husky voice, "Well, well, isn't this just like junior high again?"

Neither of us said anything, but Ryan's face had turned to steel.

"Isn't that little Sharon?" Bernice slurred.

Ryan took a step forward, as if to shield me. "What do you want, Bernice?"

"Don't be so testy. I just want to talk to you." She gave him a sidelong glance that I suppose was meant to look sexy.

Ryan looked at Bernice with such pure loathing, I shivered. Only someone like Bernice would be too self-absorbed to notice. I'd never seen Ryan like this. People change of course, but this seemed extreme.

Bernice continued sitting there, revving the engine.

Ryan turned to me, his face suddenly drained and tired. "Get in your car," he said in a low voice. "Go back to the motel. But don't go straight back. Go down 83 for a while, then take a side street. I'll take care of Lady Dracula."

CHAPTER 8

I followed Ryan's instructions, driving south till I'd passed the Super S. I turned right for a couple of blocks till I reached the library, then turned north again. When I came to 496, I headed toward Los Mareados, glancing in my rear-view mirror more often than usual. If Ryan could find me and follow me there, I was sure it wouldn't take Bernice long to figure it out. And I'd had enough of her for the day.

The whole episode had left me shaken and queasy. I didn't know how to interpret Ryan's remark about "taking care of" Bernice. It sounded so sinister. Don't be melodramatic, I told myself. It's just a figure of speech.

I arrived at Los Mareados in time to fix some soup and a salad. But my stomach was still tied in knots, and I could barely force down a few bites. Funny. Toughing it out through law school was a piece of cake compared to having my emotions turned inside-out.

The clock dragged toward 6:00. A few minutes later, Erica drove up in a Ford Taurus rental car. I opened the door before she even had time to knock. I could see Mrs. Pirtle silhouetted in her window across the way and assumed she had her binoculars in place. I was glad Erica was wearing a skirt—no mistaking her for a boyfriend. I slammed the door behind us for good measure.

Erica and I looked at each other for a moment, then threw our arms around each other and began crying. Like a mother who fears for her children's safety when they're out late, then scolds them when they walk in the door, I started in on Erica.

"Where have you been? I've been so worried!"

"I'm sorry. My supervisor called yesterday about some nitpicky thing just as I was getting ready to leave, and I couldn't get her off the phone. She just went on and on and on...." Erica closed her eyes. "And here I am going on and on and on...."

Erica seemed listless, her mood entirely different from when she'd first called. She had always been beautiful, with glossy black hair and luminous brown eyes fringed by long thick lashes. But now her hair lacked its usual luster and hung limply to her shoulders. She was pale and drawn, with dark shadows under her eyes. I was sure both of us were short on sleep. My heart went out to her, and my need to scold evaporated.

"You're here now. That's all that matters." I gave her another hug. "How would some hot tea sound?"

Erica nodded and followed me into the kitchen while I sorted through the limited cookware looking for a teakettle. Finding none, I filled a small saucepan with water and set it to boil. I found two cups that weren't cracked and put a chamomile teabag in each.

After we were seated comfortably on the faded couch, we sipped our tea for a few minutes before Erica spoke. "I'll try to fill you in on why I asked you to come here, but it's hard to know where to start."

What I wanted to do was flood her with questions. But seeing her distress, I heard myself say, "Take your time."

When she still hadn't responded after a few minutes, I said, "Why don't you start with Laura."

"Maybe it would make more sense if I started with why I came here to begin with. Not that anything makes sense. But if I hadn't been in the wrong place at the wrong time...."

I waited.

"You know how involved I've been with Head Start."

I smiled to myself at her modest self-appraisal. She was not merely "involved"—she'd been instrumental in getting Head Start programs off the ground all across the southwest.

"I know."

"We wanted to implement some new ideas we were excited about, and some people here in Zapata asked if I'd come out from L.A. and work with them. I was so pleased they'd invited me, and I came down all gooey and sentimental."

"When was this?"

"Around the second week of January. I flew into Harlingen, rented a car, drove over here, and checked into the Best Western." She glanced at me with a trace of her old impishness. "And you must be wondering why I put my best friend up at 'The Seasick Manor.'"

"What are friends for? It's okay. Go on with what you were saying."

Erica took a few sips of tea, then set her cup on the coffee table. "Well, after I'd gotten the new program underway and had a little time of my own, I decided to look up old friends. The first person I thought of was Laura. I'd heard she and Leo were married about a year ago, so didn't have any trouble finding them in the phone book."

"But then...." Erica held out her hands in a gesture of helplessness. "Laura was always a little otherworldly, but this time she was even more so. She was just so *strange*. They both were. It was eerie." She paused, shaking her

38

head. "The whole evening with them seemed a little surreal. I'd thought of calling them again, to see if maybe my imagination was working overtime. Two days later, Laura was dead."

"Oh god, what a shock that must have been!"

"You can't imagine! It was hard to believe she would commit suicide. On the other hand, she had seemed so unlike herself, I thought maybe it was possible after all."

Erica clasped her hands together to keep them from shaking. "Then about a week after the funeral, the phone calls started. Every night about midnight I'd get a call from someone—I couldn't even tell if it was a man or a woman—threatening me. The first two nights it was just this garbled voice telling me to go home. The third night the call was full of obscenities, and I was told if I didn't leave town I'd end up like Laura."

I felt my flesh prickle. For once, I was glad Los Marcados was too cheap to install a telephone in each room.

"Besides being scared for myself, all I could think was, it hadn't been suicide after all, that Laura must have been murdered. And I couldn't even begin to guess who would do such a thing." Erica's sense of horror filled the room.

I shuddered, then reached for Erica's hand. "No wonder you were terrified." I thought about what she'd said, but something didn't connect. "Erica, even if that's true—that Laura was murdered—I don't understand why *you'd* be threatened."

"That's what's so bizarre—on top of everything else that's weird. I couldn't think of anything I'd done to agitate anyone, and I felt so alone. The only people in town I could think to call were Ray and Emma López. They'd bought our home when we moved to California, and had remained friendly with my folks. Of course by then I wasn't sure if I'd be welcome there either.

"They were kind enough to ask me come stay with them. They're very nice, but I could tell they thought I was overreacting to 'kids making crank calls.' Maybe that's why I didn't even mention the calls when I phoned you. I just needed a friend. I needed you."

"Now I wish I'd come the minute you called!"

"Believe me, just knowing you'd be here made all the difference."

"Have there been any more calls?"

She shook her head. "So that helps too. That and Emma's Valium."

"You're not still taking that, are you?" I asked, alarmed.

"No, Mom." She smiled, her eyes lighting up briefly. "Now that you're here, can't you see how I've got it all together again?"

"Goofy. How 'bout another cup of tea?"

We went into the kitchen, refilled our cups, and sat at the table. Sitting opposite her, I noticed once again how haggard she looked.

"Okay," I said gently, "let's backtrack. When you went to see Laura and Leo, what exactly happened that seemed so weird?"

"It was like—like talking to well-mannered robots. They never said one thing that wasn't superficial. And they didn't seem—I don't know how to put it—they didn't seem all that much in love. And yet, they never left each other's side. Sounds contradictory, doesn't it."

"Hmm. Do you think Laura could have been jealous?" I asked doubtfully.

"Because Leo used to be my boyfriend? But that was way back in junior high." The impish look returned. "Remember those summers? You and Ryan, and Leo and me?"

We both laughed then, thinking of the innocent kisses we'd enjoyed behind the Dairy Queen and how we'd tried to escape the watchfulness of Erica's brothers.

Erica started crying, soft splashy tears. "Oh Sharon, it feels so good to laugh," she said, even as she continued crying.

I retrieved a box of Kleenex from the bedroom and moved my chair beside hers. I held her hand and waited quietly till the tears subsided.

"I'm okay now, I think," she said, wiping her eyes. "Now where were we?"

"Could it have been jealousy that made Laura act so strange?"

"No, I'm sure it wasn't—I didn't get those vibes. Besides, it's just too far-fetched. No, it was something else."

"Do you think they were on drugs?"

"That crossed my mind. It seemed probable. At the same time it seemed so un-Laura-like. Remember how we all thought she was going to be a nun? She was so shy around boys. And though she obviously changed her mind, I never would have pictured her with Leo, but...."

"No, I don't see them together either. Even though Leo was sort of a late bloomer too."

"Dear Leo. Remember how pudgy he was when he was a little boy? Back in fifth or sixth grade, some kids called him a big fat pansy or something. And then this P.E. coach ridiculed him into getting into shape and going into sports."

"Sounds like a hateful way to do it, but at least Leo found he had a natural talent for athletics."

"I know. He was so sweet-natured, it seemed strange to see him so aggressive on the football field."

"Maybe he had something to work out."

Erica's shoulders drooped again. "Well, getting back to the present, I went to the funeral of course. What happened next is almost as hard to comprehend. Things kept getting stranger." She shook her head, as if to shake the strangeness away. "This is hard to explain. Afterwards, after the funeral, everyone went over to the Salazars'—the parents, I mean—and it was like I was invisible. I'd say something to them, and they'd just stare right through me. Even Laura's mother barely spoke to me."

"Surely it wasn't intentional."

"That's what I tried to tell myself—that they had a lot on their minds. But I didn't notice anyone else being treated that way. I felt kind of ashamed that I was even thinking of my own feelings at such a time. But, Sharon, it hurt so much!"

I gave her hand a squeeze, not knowing what to say. Erica's family and the Salazars had been friends forever. Whatever could have caused them to treat her so badly? A possibility came to mind, so nebulous I almost hesitated to voice it. Still, it was the only thing I could think of.

"Erica, tell me, when you were looking up old friends, did you happen to look up Bernice Peralta?"

CHAPTER 9

Erica looked puzzled at this off-the-wall change of subject. "Did I look up Bernice?" She shrugged, wrinkling her nose in distaste. "Not exactly. I'd considered it, but she's been married a number of times, and I didn't know what name she was going by. Then I happened to run into her at the Family Center when I went over to buy some Cokes. She looked so different, I wouldn't have recognized her if she hadn't told me who she was."

Different. Nice understatement.

"Anyway, I was so glad to see someone I knew, I guess I'd forgotten how...unpleasant...she could be. She suggested getting together at Eloy's Cantina for a drink, and in my goopy nostalgic mood it sounded like fun."

"So then what?"

"It was awful. She got drunk—was probably drunk before I got there, and all she was interested in was finding some guy to pick up. I had part of a margarita and left after about 30 minutes."

"Was this before or after you saw Laura and Leo?"

"Between, I think. After I'd made plans with them, but before I'd gone over. In fact, after spending time—if you'd want to call it that—with Bernice, I was looking forward to seeing them both—to seeing someone *normal*. Ironic, no?"

"Did you see anyone else you knew at the Family Center or Eloy's?"

"Mm. Not that I noticed. I probably wasn't in the grocery store more than five or ten minutes. Eloy's? Could be. Why all the questions?"

I told her about seeing Ryan, and about the ugly episode with Bernice. And though I wasn't sure how reliable it was, I told her about the conversation I'd overheard at the Super S linking Bernice with Laura. "Maybe I'm putting two and two together and coming up with five, but it sounded like Bernice was trying to break up Laura's marriage. Maybe Bernice and Leo were having an affair." I mentally gagged at the thought. "Anyway, it might explain everyone's hostility."

Erica looked skeptical. "In other words, anyone they think is a friend of Bernice's automatically becomes an enemy of Laura's."

"Something like that."

She mulled that over, then gave a short laugh. "You're probably right, because it's just as illogical as everything else."

We moved back into the living room and curled up on each end of the couch again. Erica went on to explain how she worried that I might be threatened too if someone saw us together, which was why she'd been so secretive. Los Mareados, despite its faded appearance, was the safest and most out-of-the-way place she could think of for me to stay. "Ray López is the property manager and I trusted his judgment."

"Mrs. Pirtle seems to take a dim view of Mr. López. He didn't take her seriously when she reported a prowler last night."

"Oh." Erica started laughing. "That was me."

"You! We must have passed each other on your way over. I couldn't have been gone more than 30 minutes or so."

"Figures. You missed about five or ten minutes of pandemonium. What a fiasco! Even though I was running late, I came on over. I was trying to be inconspicuous, so I parked across the street. I knew #12 had been the only vacancy, so I knew that's where you'd be. When you didn't answer my knock, I peeked in the window, and that's when all hell broke loose."

"Yes. Mrs. Pirtle informed me there was quite a commotion."

"A commotion she caused. She began yelling out her door at the top of her lungs and ringing a cowbell or something. So naturally everyone else came pouring out of their rooms to see what was going on. I went around the back way while everyone was milling around in front, got to my car and took off."

If this was the way Mrs. Pirtle usually handled disturbances, I could see that Mr. López was wise to suggest she not call the sheriff each time. But I still wondered who Ernie Griego was and why he'd been blamed.

Erica made circles with her index finger and pointed to her head. "Ernie's harmless, and sweet. He wanders around a lot, so maybe Ray—Mr. López—thought suggesting Ernie would calm Mrs. Pirtle."

Our conversation turned to our respective careers and family news. Soon it was well past midnight and we both were tired and talked out.

"Pretend I'm your mother and give me a call when you get back to the Lópezes," I told her as she was leaving.

Erica laughed, giving me a hug. "Sharon, you are good medicine!"

* * *

Once I knew Erica was safely home, my thoughts returned to Ryan and the confrontation with Bernice. I wished I'd given him my phone number too. I tossed and turned for an hour, and finally got up and scrounged through my purse for his number.

Forget it. You'll just wake him up and he won't appreciate it one bit, I told myself as I picked up my cell phone from the night table and punched in his number. The machine picked up after several rings. Why hadn't I figured on that? I hate people who hang up, so felt compelled to leave a message.

"It's Sharon," I half-whispered into the phone, wondering what to say next.

I heard the clunkety-clunkety-clunk sound a receiver makes when it's knocked from its cradle. My heart jumped to my throat. Next I heard some unintelligible muttering.

Then, "Sharon? Are you still there?"

I closed my eyes in sheer relief at hearing Ryan's sleepy voice, then sank to the edge of the bed.

"I'm here."

"Are you okay? What's wrong?" The drowsiness had left his voice.

"I'm fine. Listen, Ryan, I'm sorry I woke you up."

"You don't sound fine."

I cleared my throat. "Well, I was worried about you. That's all."

He was quiet for so long I wondered if he'd fallen asleep again.

"Good night, Ryan," I murmured.

"No, wait! Sharon? Don't hang up. I was just thinking over what you'd said." There was another pause, then, "I probably wouldn't tell you this if you hadn't called me tonight."

"Tell me what?"

He took a deep breath. "I was afraid you'd think I was, I don't know, overprotective, overbearing, over-something. Anyway, I sort of followed you home again."

"Sort of. What's that?" I laughed.

"I just meant I drove by your place later. I had to get rid of Bernice first."

I was sure it was just a poor choice of words, but after seeing Ryan's anger earlier, his remark unnerved me. "How did you do that?"

"Well, I argued with her for a few minutes—long enough to get you on your way. Then I told her to wait for me at Hugo's Lounge, that I'd meet her there. It's on the other end of town—across the Veleño bridge. And no, I didn't push her into the arroyo, though it was tempting."

"How could you be sure she'd wait for you?"

"I'm sure she didn't wait. I figured she'd find someone to buy her a drink and forget why she'd gone there in the first place."

I didn't feel so sure myself. I didn't think Bernice was one to be so easily deterred. Too late now. I'd just have to go along with Ryan's assumption.

"I watched her head toward Hugo's," Ryan continued. "And that's when...."

"That's when you sort of followed me."

"I needed to see your car there and know you'd gotten home safely."

"I'm glad. I guess I needed to hear your voice and know the same about you. I hope you don't think I'm over-something for waking you up in the middle of the night."

He laughed softly. "Any time."

"Well, I guess I'd better say goodnight—or good morning now. It's already tomorrow."

"Sharon? Meet me for lunch?"
"I'd like that."
"El Paraíso about noon?"
"I'll be there."

CHAPTER 10

Ryan had always been protective of me. I was seven years old again, back on the Montoyas' patio at a barbacoa for friends and neighbors. I'd been shipped to Aunt Amanda's less than three days ago and was already homesick.

"Se parece 'Little Orphan Annie,'" said one of Erica's uncles. Some of the grownups chuckled.

"She does not look like Little Orfalling Annie," Ryan chimed in, hands clenched in sturdy fists. "She just looks like Sharon."

The uncle started to laugh till something in Ryan's face caused him to reconsider. He placed a gentle hand on Ryan's shoulder. "No one meant to be unkind, mijo. And you are very gallant, to defend the honor of your little friend."

But the uncle was probably right. Except for having large scared eyes instead of blank circles, I must have indeed resembled Little Orphan Annie, with my teddy bear clutched in one hand and my hair in a halo of blond ringlets.

Mrs. Montoya knelt down and took me immediately into her arms and into her heart. I'm sure she couldn't imagine sending her own children away. Especially not to a relative who, though well meaning, knew nothing about children. Nor could she imagine getting a divorce, as my parents were doing.

"Now, now, mijita," she crooned. "Everything will be all right. You'll see." She motioned to Erica, Leo, and Ryan.

"Come here, all of you." She encircled us all in a group hug till we began squirming and giggling and finally broke away.

From then on the four of us—Erica, Leo, Ryan, and I— spent most of our summer days together. Erica's brothers called us "The Four Musketeers" and helped us build a clubhouse. There were other kids around too, and we'd go swimming or catch minnows or play kick-the-can on lazy afternoons.

Whenever Bernice showed up, everyone else trickled away. She'd finally get tired of needling me and go home, and our friends would trickle back again.

The summer between sixth and seventh grade, my mother and stepfather were heading for divorce—my mother's second. I hadn't wanted to talk about it, believing I was the only 12-yearold alive to have such a dysfunctional family. "In my best interests," they'd decided I should stay on with Aunt Amanda and start school in Zapata.

I'm not sure Aunt Amanda was too elated with this arrangement. But as usual Erica and her family took me under their wing, so I spent more time with them anyway, which seemed to pacify my great-aunt.

Since I already had friends in town, the transition to a new school went smoothly. Erica, Laura, and I joined the girls' chorus together, and the three of us walked home from school every day arm in arm.

In seventh grade most of us—boys and girls alike— started wearing braces. That was also the year most of the girls hit puberty while waiting for the boys to catch up. To her dismay, Erica grew a head taller than the boys our age, but that didn't last long.

By the following summer, the boys were well into puberty too, and the dynamics changed. Laura paired up with Yvette somebody. Erica and I were still best friends, but now we saw our old buddies Leo and Ryan with new eyes. The four of us were nearly always together again, but this time it was with a difference.

Sometimes we were two and two. Now it was Ryan who held my hand and walked me home from school every day. Erica had cheerleading practice after school, and Leo was always involved in one sport or another, and later they'd come home together hand in hand.

We discovered the joys of kissing, which we put into practice whenever we could outsmart Erica's ever-watchful brothers. We wondered sometimes if they worked in shifts guarding us.

One day when the four of us were walking home from the park, doing nothing more risqué than holding hands, two of Erica's brothers caught up with us, each grabbing one of the twins by the collar. "You'd better not mess with my sisters," one of them hissed, "or we'll cut off your *cajones*."

Erica hadn't appreciated the brotherly assistance. "I'm telling Papi about the way you're acting!"

Her brothers released Leo and Ryan and shrugged. "Then I guess he'll have to know about you and Brace Face," one of them said.

Leo was every bit as big as Erica's brothers and could probably have squashed them with one blow. But, peacemaker that he was, he refused the bait.

Ryan was small but feisty. His reaction was to turn and kiss me squarely on the lips, right in front of them. For some reason, instead of getting angry, they just laughed and walked away, making those weird wolf-call sounds boys like to make.

I was the one who was miffed. "That wasn't a nice kiss," I told Ryan. "You just did it to show off." I stalked off toward home by myself.

He caught up with me and we continued walking together but didn't say anything to each other till we reached my house, where we saw Aunt Amanda in the side yard puttering in her garden.

"Are you still mad?" Ryan asked.

I looked into those steady brown eyes and softened. "Probably not."

He sat down on the porch swing and pulled me down beside him. He gave the swing a push with his foot and it began moving in a slow zigzag motion. "I didn't mean to make you mad."

"I know. It's okay."

Aunt Amanda appeared on the porch then, and she inspired more fear in us than all four of Erica's brothers put together. Ryan stood up politely to greet my great-aunt, leaving the swing to lurch in a drunken fashion, with me still in it. He stopped the swing, and I got out too.

Aunt Amanda liked Ryan more than she would admit. She scowled at us, then asked us in for lemonade. She asked us questions about school, Ryan answering more than I did. After a while she went back to her gardening.

"I'd better go now," Ryan said. He looked at me, the question in his eyes. A few kisses later, he was on his way home.

* * *

The messages Erica and I got from the grownups about sex were vague and contradictory. We were told the changes we were undergoing were wonderful but we shouldn't think about them. In fact, our overall "education" could be summed up in three words:

"Don't do it."

Bernice had become friends with a girl named Hortencia the year before, and it was rumored that they were doing "it" not only with high-school boys but with Hortencia's cousins. This was a deliciously shocking topic of conversation at eighth-grade slumber parties.

It was also at slumber parties that Erica explained "the rules" to the rest of us. "You shouldn't do it till you're married, or at least till you're 17. If your boyfriend touches you above the waist, that's okay. Anything below the waist, you have to go to confession."

It was reassuring to have a best friend so versed in theology.

Two weeks before we were to enter high school, my mother decided to be a mother again and called Aunt Amanda that she was coming down to pick me up. Her plan was to move us back to Minnesota where she could be with "her people" again.

I was devastated at the thought of being wrenched from everyone I loved. Aunt Amanda, instead of being relieved, was angry and grim-faced. It was a surprise to us both to discover that we'd grown fond of each other over the years.

Erica, her mother—my *nina*—and I all cried profusely when we heard the news. Mr. Montoya's eyes got red as he said, "I'll miss you, mijita," an endearment he'd never used with me before.

Erica's brothers were solemn and subdued, and I heard one of them mumble, "It isn't fair!" Leo didn't say anything, but kissed me on the cheek right in front of Erica's brothers. They even went so far as to leave Ryan and me alone on our last day together, but all we could do was hold each other and cry.

My mother and I made the move. After the first month when our respective parents got their phone bills, the long-distance calls between Ryan and me, and between Erica and me, came to a screeching halt. My mother intercepted and read all my mail, so that gradually ended too.

I ran away once, with a change of clothes and all of $30.00 in my backpack. I walked as far as the nearest truck stop, about seven miles from town. My plan was to hitch-hike the remaining 1600 miles to Zapata. At the lunch counter, I struck up a conversation with a truck driver who told me I'd have to be careful, because there were a lot of men out there who would take advantage of me. Some primal instinct told me that he was one of those men he was warning me about.

I lost my nerve and made a collect call to my soon-to-be stepfather. He came for me and brought me home without lecturing or asking questions. He told my mother to cut me some slack, and things eased up after that. I eventually got on with my life, but I'm not sure I ever recovered completely.

CHAPTER 11

February was just around the corner, which meant summer would arrive in the next few days. Till then, warm clothes still felt good. I hadn't brought a large selection with me, figuring I wouldn't be here long, and I'd worn my favorite outfit yesterday. So now the burning question was, which sweatsuit to wear to the Laundromat?

I decided on the bird-watching outfit instead, showered and dressed quickly, then went to the office to pay another day's rent. With that, free of charge, came my daily dose of Mrs. Pirtle. I wouldn't have admitted it to her, but after the events of yesterday, I found her vigilance with the binoculars vaguely comforting.

I was greeted with her usual glare. "Your girlfriend musta stayed very late last night. I had to go to bed before she left."

"Oh, that's too bad."

"I thought you said you wasn't one of *those*."

I assumed she was referring to the Libyans. "Mrs. Pirtle, if I can't have boyfriends, and I can't have girlfriends, what am I supposed to do?"

"You're supposed to be takin' pitchers, or did you forget?"

Oops. "I'm going out this morning, as a matter of fact. I was just waiting for my next assignment. And I don't want you to worry. I'm a practicing *celibata*."

"If that's Spanish for 'photographer,' you needn't be so hoity-toity, Missy. Just talk plain English from now on."

* * *

55

I'd brought a book to read while waiting for my clothes to go through their cycles, but couldn't concentrate. Catty-cornered from the Laundromat was the library, where I headed after I'd folded my clothes and put them in the back seat of my Honda.

The *Zapata County News* came out weekly, and I wanted to look at all the January issues. Nothing the first few weeks. The most serious disturbance was a report that somebody's cows had wandered into somebody else's yard. No mention of drug busts or other ominous happenings.

A brief obituary appeared in the fourth week's issue.

"Laura Salazar, a primary teacher in the
Zapata Independent School District, died
unexpectedly in her home January 17...."

I hadn't known Laura taught school. I closed my eyes, engulfed in a wave of sadness for her little students. How could such a thing ever be explained to them?

After a few moments, I returned to the article.

"Mrs. Salazar is survived by her husband,
Leo Salazar...."

I skimmed over the list of various relatives, noting only that Ryan was single, and that Alana had married Roberto Meléndez. Times for the Rosary and the Resurrection Mass were listed. Nothing unusual caught my attention.

Nothing, nothing, nothing.

I looked through the news for the following week and again drew a blank. I had mixed feelings. I appreciated the lack of sensationalism in the newspaper. And of course the medical report, according to Erica, was brief and matter-of-fact. But, thanks to my visit to the Super S, I already knew there was quite a buzz along the grapevine. I wondered if anything useful could be sifted from it.

On the way back to my "home-away-from-home"—as I was beginning to think of Los Mareados—I stopped at Linda's Boutique, pretending this stop had nothing to do with Ryan. Ordinarily I detested shopping, but after trying on an attractive burgundy jumpsuit, I couldn't help feeling pleased with the way it flattered me. Unfortunately the mirror revealed once again how unpleased I was with my hair. Maybe I should ask Bernice where she got hers done.

Too late to do anything about it now. I'd barely have time to get to El Paraíso before noon. One consolation: They had the best chicken-fried steak in the state of Texas.

* * *

Ryan was waiting at the restaurant when I arrived. He met me halfway across the parking lot as I was heading toward the door. He looked very professional in white shirt with dark slacks and tie. I was glad I'd changed from my bird-watching uniform.

He kissed me on the cheek and gave me a quick hug. "Change in plans, if that's okay with you."

"Of course." I didn't know if I was disappointed more at the prospect of canceling our date, or of missing out on the chicken-fried steak.

He took me by the hand and led me to his car, a white Saturn. "I thought we could drive down to Miguel Alemán for lunch. I know a good restaurant there. Plus, we'd have a chance to talk on the way down."

"I'd like that." A lot better than chicken-fried, come to think of it.

Zapata had no border crossing, and it was 40 miles to Roma, where we'd cross the international bridge to Miguel Alemán. We left El Paraíso, turning south on 83, drove through town, and were soon on our way. Spring was starting to spring, and I looked with pleasure at the creamy-yellow display of honey mesquite bursting into bloom along the highway.

I turned sideways as much as the seatbelt would allow and looked with pleasure too at Ryan's handsome profile. He was the Ryan I'd always known and, at the same time, a stranger. A fascinating paradox.

He glanced over at me and grinned. "I feel like I'm playing hooky."

"No more teacher's conferences?"

"Not till tomorrow."

"Been a long time since we played hooky."

He reached over and took my hand. "Too long."

I laced my fingers through his, clearing my mind of everything but the warmth of his touch.

After we'd gone a few miles Ryan said, "I thought you were going to tell me your long story."

I'd planned what I was going to say, but now the words deserted me. I turned back in my seat and looked straight ahead. "Erica called me. Out of the blue, really."

Ryan made no comment.

"She'd come down here to coordinate with the Head Start people."

He nodded. Apparently this wasn't news.

"Then some upsetting things began happening. That's when she asked me to come down." I swallowed hard before continuing. "She got some obscene phone calls—threatening calls—and she was pretty frightened."

The car swerved slightly as Ryan turned toward me in disbelief. "Any idea why?"

I shook my head. "That's what's so scary. There's no logical reason."

He turned his attention back to the road. "What kind of threats?"

"Just that she'd better leave town." *Or she'd wind up like Laura.* Somehow the words stuck in my throat.

"Could someone at Head Start be jealous? Think she's going to take over their job?"

"I don't think so. Everyone knows she's just here temporarily."

Ryan frowned as if trying to come up with some other explanation. "Doesn't make sense."

My heart was pounding as I opened my mouth to finish repeating the threat. Before I could say anything, Ryan changed the subject. "How come you're staying at Los Mareados?"

That was easy. "Erica was pretty panicky. She was afraid I might be targeted too, though I don't think that's likely. Anyway, she thought Los Mareados would be safe and out of the way."

Ryan nodded. "Probably a good idea."

"Can you tell me something?" I asked tentatively. "When you were arguing with Bernice last night, before you sort of followed me home, can you tell me what the argument was about?"

He didn't answer right away. "I wish I could. But it involves too many people."

I wondered who the "too many people" could be and if I'd ever find out.

CHAPTER 12

Ryan and I reached Roma, turned onto a narrow side street, and crossed the bridge into Mexico. I liked Miguel Alemán because it was small and untouristy. Even the Norteamericanos seemed unhurried, as if the slower pace of the town had a calming effect.

It was quiet this time of day. The shopkeepers, having swept their sidewalks, had either gone back inside their *tiendas* or were leaning against the doorways, depending on the number of customers.

We drove as far as the plaza, then walked a couple of blocks to Hector's Restaurante. Numerous plants and banners that depicted bright tropical birds hung from the walls, while slender vases of melon-colored bougainvillea graced the tables. We ordered compuestas, and Ryan asked for Tecate for himself and a Dr. Pepper for me.

While we were waiting for our order, I remembered I'd wanted to give him the number to my cell phone.

"You carry one of those?"

"Yes. You make it sound like I'm carrying germs."

"I just want to know if you're planning to take it out and attach it to your ear throughout lunch."

"I only do that when I want to look important. Or if my date is very boring."

"Great. I've got my work cut out for me."

"Don't worry." I touched my fingers to his lips. "Just for you I turned the ringer off."

* * *

After our meal we strolled around the plaza, and it was late afternoon before we started home. It crossed my mind that neither of us had mentioned Leo since yesterday. Even though Erica sensed that Leo and Laura weren't "that much in love," Laura's death still must have come as quite a shock to him. I felt guilty that I hadn't asked sooner.

"How is Leo doing?"

"He's managing." The remote look I'd seen on Ryan's face yesterday returned.

"I'd like to see him—or at least call him."

Ryan raised one eyebrow and stared at me as if I'd suggested boarding a flying saucer. "Suit yourself," he said, returning his attention to the road.

"Ryan, what is wrong? If I'm intruding on something, just tell me."

He shrugged, then replied in a flat tone, "You're right. He'd probably appreciate your concern. Tell you what. I'm going over there tonight, if you want to come with me. Up to you. No matter when you go, it'll be stressful."

Well, I hadn't expected it to be fun. But I cared too much for Leo not to make the effort. I had some misgivings about accepting Ryan's half-hearted invitation, but tonight seemed as good a night as any. I had no other plans. Erica had gone to Laredo for the day to meet with some Head Start people and didn't expect to be back till late. I should be home again before she called.

"Okay. But before we go over there, is there something I should know?"

"Like what?"

"I don't know, Ryan. I just have the feeling something's wrong, and I don't want to make it worse."

"I doubt that's possible. Don't worry. Just be yourself. No, don't be yourself. Don't ask a lot of questions."

"Oh god, Ryan, am I that bad? What on earth would I ask anyway?"

Ryan grinned. "Two in a row. You just can't help it, can you?"

"Look who's talking."

The tension had eased, but we spent the rest of the ride home tiptoeing around any mention of the evening ahead, and I wondered what was in store for me.

Ryan dropped me off at my car and offered to pick me up again about 7:00. As soon as he was out of sight, I checked my cell phone to make sure there were no messages, then drove to Los Mareados. My grocery supply was as meager as my wardrobe, and I decided on soup and salad again, which I picked at again.

I showered, snuggled up in my oversized terry robe, and sipped a cup of chamomile tea. I set the cup on the end table, thinking how nice it would be to take a cat-nap. I hadn't had a decent night's sleep since Erica had first called. Just 10 minutes, that's all I needed. The next thing I knew, Ryan, wearing Levis and a denim shirt, was knocking at the door.

I let him in and apologized for keeping him waiting.

"No hurry. That's sure a sexy outfit, but don't you think you should wear something more casual?"

I made a face at him. "Just give me a minute." I hurried into the bedroom, changed into sweater and slacks, downed a couple of breath mints, and made a last-minute appraisal in the mirror. My hair had dried into something resembling a pinwheel, so I dampened it, smoothed it down as best I could, and pretended it looked nice. It should have been a warning.

CHAPTER 13

The Salazar parents still lived in the house where they'd always lived on Hummingbird Avenue. Alana lived next door, and Leo a couple of houses away. Before they'd moved to California, the Montoyas had lived a few streets over. Ryan told me he'd moved across town, away from the rest of his family—"something my mother still thinks amounts to heresy."

When Ryan and I arrived at Leo's, I had the strange sensation of walking onto a movie set. Seated on the couch and staring straight ahead were Leo and a couple whom Ryan introduced as Leo's friends Tina and Johnny Quemado.

Leo stood and walked toward me, the misery in his eyes so evident it tore at my heart. "Leo, I'm so sorry...."

He gave me a hug and motioned for me to sit in a stuffed armchair angled toward the couch. As I moved closer, I could see the distress on Tina's face, the dazed look on Johnny's. I was at a loss for anything else to say, and Ryan had disappeared into the kitchen. I realized I'd have been smarter to come in my own car so I could say goodbye and leave.

The silence was broken by Ryan muttering, "Christ, Leo, don't you keep anything but beer in the fridge?"

Tina, whose tiny wide-eyed face reminded me of a scared mouse, skittered into the kitchen. "There's lots of food. People keep bringing things. Tamales, sopa...."

"I meant something to drink. Never mind. Tecate, Sharon?"

"Sure." I hated beer, but wanted to end this discussion. I've learned that once you have drink in hand, people don't usually pay attention to whether you actually drink it or not.

Tina fluttered back and took her place on the couch between Leo and Johnny. She looked very tiny seated between them. Wearing sandals, cutoffs, and a white peasant blouse, she seemed much younger than she probably was. Johnny and Leo, wearing Levis and western shirts, hadn't blinked an eye while she was gone, far as I could tell.

I noticed that Leo had become even huskier over the years. Johnny was rather nondescript, except for having thick eyebrows that converged in one straight line across his forehead and seemed at odds with his pencil-thin mustache.

Ryan poured my Tecate into a glass, which he handed me. Then he leaned against the kitchen doorway with his own beer can, effectively keeping detached from the rest of us.

"Oh." Tina stood up again and took a few tentative steps toward the kitchen. "Would you like something to eat with that, Sharon?"

"Thanks."

I wasn't hungry, but the idea of moving into the kitchen was more appealing than sitting in our frozen little tableau. Ryan repositioned himself by another doorway.

I went over to the sink, poured out my beer, and rinsed the glass. "Don't tell," I whispered to Tina.

She looked at me as if I'd done something very brave. "There's bottled water on the counter. I guess Ryan didn't see it."

She rustled around pulling a variety of containers out of the refrigerator and setting them alongside a relish tray and cold cuts already on the counter. She opened one drawer

64

after another looking for forks. "You'll have to excuse me. I just can't think. You know how it is in someone else's kitchen." She looked on the brink of tears.

"Don't apologize. This is a very difficult time for everyone. And I really don't want much to eat."

She nodded. "I haven't been hungry either, and Mrs. Salazar keeps trying to stuff us. Why don't you pick out what you'd like?"

"Thanks." I put a tamale and some frijoles on a paper plate, which Tina took from me and put into the microwave. She then fussed around the kitchen, rearranging food and some cookware.

I surveyed the kitchen, looking for something that would have conveyed Laura's touch, but it seemed oddly bare. I wondered if her mother had removed all Laura's things.

Another possibility came to mind. Laura had always been very religious. Maybe she'd joined one of those cults that persuade people to get rid of all their worldly goods in preparation for the end of the world. No, she'd died a Catholic.

Or maybe not. Maybe her mother had merely conned the newly arrived Fr. Lucero into thinking Laura was an active communicant.

The microwave bell went off, causing us both to jump and my mind to quit whirling. Tina hustled over to take out my plate, as if it would disintegrate if not removed immediately. Her hands shook as she brought it over to me and made a stab at conversation. "Leo tells me you were all good friends when you were growing up."

Tears stung my eyes as long-suppressed memories began to surface. "Laura was one of the sweetest people I knew. Leo was like a brother to me, and Ryan was...Ryan was...gosh, it was so long ago."

She smiled shyly. "I know."

I wanted to get off the subject of my exasperating knight in shining armor. "I take it you and Johnny haven't lived here very long."

"No. We came here to teach a couple of years ago. That's how we met Laura and Leo."

"Is Leo a teacher too?"

"No, he's a loan officer at the Upper Valley Bank."

"Really! I would have pictured him coaching football."

"He says you can't play football forever, but people always need money."

For some odd reason, the statement sounded rehearsed. I began to feel we'd stayed too long in the kitchen.

Evidently Tina had the same thought. "Why don't you bring your plate, and let's go back in the living room."

I returned to the armchair while Tina scurried off to find a TV tray, which she set up beside me. Everyone else was still in place, and Tina scooted back to her assigned spot.

I moved my food from one side of the plate to another, hoping it looked like I was eating, hoping it gave me an excuse not to make conversation. I shot Ryan a dirty look, which he didn't see since he was engrossed in studying the label on his beer can.

There was a knock on the door, and Alana, Beto, and their three sons came in. I judged the oldest boys to be in their mid-teens, and the youngest one about seven or eight. After a rather subdued exchange of greetings, the boys escaped to the back patio where they could shoot basketballs against an improvised hoopstand.

The men pulled up some chairs from the dining room, and Ryan left his post in the doorway and sat next to Beto, Alana's husband. Beto looked much as I remembered him—

short and stocky, with mild gray eyes behind rimless glasses, and closely cut light-brown hair.

Once again Tina assumed the role of hostess, jumping up and asking in a squeaky voice if anyone would like something to eat or drink. No one would, so she sat down again. The conversation consisted mostly of one-syllable words.

Beto was the only one who didn't seem ill at ease. He smiled at me and said, "Alana tells me you're a lawyer. What kind of law do you practice?"

Tina's round eyes got rounder, and everyone seemed to listen intently for my answer. "Well, as my boss likes to remind me, I don't do Perry Mason stuff." I waited in vain for the ha-ha-ha. "What I do, I'm an advocate for migrant workers. It keeps me busy, but I never get tired of talking with people, listening to their stories...." I realized I could get carried away with a subject so dear to my heart, and this didn't seem like the time or place to continue.

Ryan was now looking at me instead of his beer can, and I caught a glimmer of the bond between us.

Beto nodded. "It's your *pasión*. Is that what brings you to Zapata?"

The question caught me off guard. I didn't want to drop Erica's name into this tinderbox, so I put on what I hoped was an innocent expression. "Mm. Más o menos."

"You never were a good liar, Sharon," Alana said without rancor.

"The truth is," Ryan said evenly, "she came down to see Erica." The tension in the room jumped to peak levels. "Erica's been getting obscene phone calls, and she called the one friend she knew she could count on."

Tina began sobbing. "This is so terrible. So terrible!"

Johnny put his arm across her shoulders and patted her awkwardly.

Into this mix came footsteps and voices on the porch. I wished that Ryan had either warned me there'd be a crowd or suggested I wait till another time. The next thing I knew, there was a flurry of activity as Mr. and Mrs. Salazar burst into the room, each carrying a platter of food.

As soon as I saw him, I remembered Mr. Salazar's quiet humor, the way his calm nature complemented his wife's whirlwind exuberance. His hair was still thick, now peppered with gray. I suddenly realized he looked the way Ryan would probably look in years to come. Tonight, however, the lines in his face betrayed a strain beyond the normal toll the years had taken.

Apparently Mrs. Salazar chose to overlook the dreary atmosphere. "I brought you something Mrs. Ortega sent over," she sang out. "You should be eating. You need to keep up your strength."

I thought Tina was going to shrivel into nothing, so I gave her a wink. Despite Mrs. Salazar's bossiness, I recalled her motherly nature and how I'd always liked her. Short and rather plump, her gray hair swept into a French bun, she was still attractive.

Alana offered to help her mother find room for the platters, but Mrs. Salazar waved her away and bustled into the kitchen. "I know this place better than my own."

I smiled to myself. *I bet.*

Alana called her boys in to greet their grandparents. Smiling warmly, Mrs. Salazar came into the living room to exchange effusive hugs and kisses with her grandsons. After the boys had been duly fussed over, they went outside again.

Mrs. Salazar returned to the kitchen. "Mijo, this is no place for the Tupperware," she called out. "What was that girl thinking? Qué el buen señor ten piedad." I could picture Mrs. Salazar crossing herself as she remembered "that girl" would no longer be able to arrange the Tupperware to suit herself.

Leo scowled, as if the same thought occurred to him. Tina seemed to have shrunk as far as possible into the cushions on the sofa. Johnny had quit patting her and simply looked comatose. I wondered why they didn't go home.

I wondered why *I* didn't leave. Because I had no wheels, that's why. And I preferred not to walk along the highway after dark. I stood up and tried to catch Ryan's eye, mentally begging him to take me home, but he was busy studying a spot on the ceiling.

"Well, that's that. Come eat now before everything gets cold." Mrs. Salazar returned to the living room, brushing her hands together, and noticed me for the first time.

"Amá, you remember Sharon," Ryan said, momentarily looking toward me.

She studied me a moment, then, "I certainly do. You're the one who made so much trouble for my son."

The words stung. But if she had calculated a way to bridge the gap between Ryan and me, she couldn't have done a better job. Ryan was by my side in an instant, his arm firmly around my waist.

"You know that's not true, Amá."

"If she hadn't called that boy names, you wouldn't have gotten in a fight with him."

"He'd been bullying Sharon for weeks. I should have beaten him up sooner. And harder."

"You got kicked out of school."

Ryan's eyes narrowed in disbelief. "For five days. Why are you bringing this up? You always liked Sharon."

With that, Mrs. Salazar burst into tears. Alana gave me an apologetic look and put her arm around her mother, speaking soothingly to her in Spanish. "There, there, Amá, don't cry. You're upset about things that have nothing to do with Sharon. Don't be mad at her."

To my dismay, my cell phone picked that moment to ring. Why had I forgotten to turn it off again? "I'm sorry. I'll make this short," I said as I fumbled in my purse for the phone.

The call was from Erica.

"Let me call you back in a little while," I told her.

"Wait till tomorrow and give me a call at Head Start, 'K?"

I turned off the ringer and put the phone away, apologizing to the group again. "That was Erica. I know it seems silly, but I asked her to let me know when she got home safely."

Mrs. Salazar had stopped crying and nodded in appreciation. "I've been trying to get Ryan to get one of those phones for months now."

Ryan nearly choked on his beer, and I guessed it was my turn to come to the rescue. "That might not be such a good idea, Mrs. Salazar. I think he should wait until, uh, the technology improves."

"Listen to Sharon, Amá. She knows all about technology," Ryan said, poker-faced.

"We really need to go," I said, tired of waiting for Ryan to say it. "Leo, you look exhausted. I didn't mean to overstay our welcome." I hoped Alana wouldn't point out I was lying again by using the word "welcome."

Instead she came over, kissed me on the cheek and whispered, "We're the ones who owe you an apology."

Leo's eyes had glazed over and he gave me a perfunctory hug. Johnny stood like a statue, and Tina looked at me as if imploring me to stay. Their tension added to my own was almost tangible. I felt like a toy top someone had wound too tightly and forgotten to turn loose. I still hadn't a clue what was going on here, but something was dreadfully wrong.

CHAPTER 14

When we got to the car, I fastened my seatbelt, and turned slightly away. Ryan turned toward me and reached for my hand. "Sharon, look at me."

I faced him and looked at his eyebrows. If I looked into those deep brown eyes I'd melt, and I wasn't ready to forgive him yet.

"I'm really sorry. I don't know what got into my mother."

"It wasn't just her, Ryan. Don't lay all the blame on her."

"I'm not. But let me ask you something. If I'd told you that's the way it would be over there—if I'd even known how to describe it—would you have believed me?"

I thought that over. "I see what you mean."

He closed his eyes and leaned back in his seat, still holding my hand. For the first time, I realized what a strain this had been on him as well. My own nerves were stretched to the breaking point.

"Ryan, if you can't tell me what's wrong, that's okay."

He squeezed my hand, but didn't answer. After a few minutes he opened his eyes and sat up straight. "I'd better take you home. I have a long day ahead of me." But he made no move to leave. "What did you and Tina talk about?"

"Nothing, really. She's a sweet little thing—seems awfully anxious to please."

"That's Tina."

"I think she and Johnny want to be helpful, they just don't know what to say. Come to think of it, I just described myself."

Ryan looked out the window for several moments, drumming his fingers against the steering wheel. The drumming stopped, but he still didn't look at me. "Sharon, there's something I should tell you."

"What is it?"

He hesitated again, then took a deep breath. "Laura was being blackmailed."

I was too stunned to answer.

"And there are still repercussions." His words sounded fuzzy and far away, as if they had to sift through fog to get to my ears.

"Blackmail! I can't imagine Laura doing anything to be blackmailed for!"

"Believe it. Things—and people—aren't always what they seem."

I didn't care what shameful thing Laura might have done. All I could think of was the evil that had been done to her.

"Who would want to hurt Laura?"

"Guess."

There was only one person it could be. "Bernice?" I whispered.

His silence was my answer.

I'd already suspected that Bernice was somehow involved in everyone's strange behavior, but suddenly I was faced with facts and not just speculation. It jolted me to the core to learn the truth was even uglier than I'd imagined. I began to wonder if Bernice could have gone beyond blackmail to murder. Blackmail. Murder.

Up till now I hadn't allowed myself to think about the details of Laura's death. Death I could handle; the process of dying was entirely different. Suddenly, vivid images of Laura's last agonizing minutes came crashing in on me. The full horror of what she must have experienced. Not only the pain, but the realization that her very life was seeping away.

The weight of the last few days was too much. The stress, the lack of sleep, the erratic eating habits. And now my own imagination. The earth started rotating backwards, and I couldn't make it stop. "I think I'm going to be sick."

"Take a deep breath and don't think about anything but breathing." Ryan came around to my side of the car and helped me out. "Keep deep-breathing."

I sank to the ground and sucked in the cool night air as hard as I could. Ryan sat beside me and held me, stroking my hair and telling me over and over to breathe. The cool air plus the hypnotic effect of his words took hold, and the nausea passed. But then I started shaking.

Ryan helped me back into the car. "Wait here." As if I could move.

A few moments later he and Alana came over and wrapped me in a blanket. "Bring her to my house," Alana said.

"No, I'm taking her home with me."

They argued for a while about whether he could or couldn't do that. I got out of the car, pulling the blanket around me. "I'm okay now. I'm really okay."

"No, you're not. Look at her, Ryan. She looks like a ghost."

Ryan made a sudden decision. "Come on, Sharon. We're staying with Alana. Her house is right here."

"We?" I felt I must be floating between Ryan and Alana as they led me inside. "I don't know what's wrong. I can take care of myself. I practice karate."

Alana was a born manager. "Ryan, go boil some water. There's yerba buena in the cabinet over the sink. You know where the sugar is. I'll take care of Sharon. Ándale."

"I don't want to make extra work for you. I should go home."

"Home?" She put her arm around my waist and led me down the hall. "Back to San Antonio?"

"No, but...."

"No buts."

Alana took me to the guest room and helped me into a flower-sprigged flannel nightgown. "Do you need to go to the bathroom?"

I shook my head, no.

"Then get in bed." She pulled the covers over me and turned the electric blanket up to "high."

"This isn't like me. I know karate."

"So you've said. Hush now."

Ryan came in with some minty-smelling tea and sat down in a chair beside me. I raised myself against the pillows and wrapped my hands around the cup. My hands were still trembling, and the warmth from the cup felt good.

"Ryan, I'll be okay. Don't worry about me. You have to get up early."

"And you don't worry about Ryan," Alana said. "I'll see that he gets some sleep."

"What about you?"

"Tomorrow's my day off. Don't worry about me either. And don't go away. I'm going to get you something to help you relax."

Why did people keep telling me not to go away? There didn't seem to be much connection between my brain and my feet.

Alana came back in with a couple of green pills. "Take these," she ordered.

"Wait a minute," Ryan said. "What are they? You don't even know if she's allergic to anything."

Alana rolled her eyes. "They're just muscle relaxants. They work as a sedative. Are you allergic to anything?"

I frowned, trying to remember. "I'm very healthy."

"Yes, and you do karate. Now take these."

Yes Ma'am. I swallowed the pills with the rest of my tea and handed Alana my cup, which she took back to the kitchen. I slid down under the electric blanket again.

Ryan leaned over and whispered in my ear. "Alana thinks we need a chaperone. What she doesn't know is, between the two of them, her and Amá, they're like a big dose of— what's the opposite of aphrodisiac?"

"I don't believe you."

"But I got you to laugh."

I put my arms around his neck, but didn't have the energy to hold on. He tucked my arms under the blanket again, kissed me on the forehead, and told me to go to sleep. I drifted off obediently but was awake enough to be aware that Alana had re-entered the room. Ryan moved over to the door and they talked in low voices.

"Is she asleep yet?" Alana asked.

"I think so."

"What happened out there? What brought this on?"

"An accumulation of things. I guess the final straw was when I told her about Bernice's hold on Laura."

"You didn't tell her everything!" Even in my woozy state, I could hear the alarm in Alana's voice.

"No. Of course not."

As Alana left the room, her last instructions were for Ryan to get some sleep himself. "There're blankets on the couch. Or you can double up with the boys."

Ryan came back and sat beside me, and I finally fell into a deep sleep.

* * *

Toward morning I began having nightmares. In the latest, Erica, Laura, and I were chained to the couch in Leo's living room while Tina hovered in the corner crying. Mrs. Salazar came bearing down on us with a huge platter of green pills. "You'll never hurt my sons again!" she screamed. Tina jumped up and knocked the tray away. Mrs. Salazar got down on her hands and knees, trying to scoop up all the pills, and screaming, screaming, screaming.

I woke up in a sweat, my heart pounding. It took a few minutes to get my bearings. Why was I so hot? Because the electric blanket was still on "high." I turned it off, threw the covers back, and got out of bed to cool off. I went to the bathroom, then found my way down to the kitchen for a drink of water.

I peeked into the living room and saw Ryan sprawled out on the couch. I walked over and pulled the blanket over him, then leaned down and kissed him on the cheek. He stirred, but didn't wake up.

By now I was starting to feel cold and sleepy again. I wondered if it was the green pills that gave me the nightmares, or just the emotional upheaval I'd been going through. It was really stupid to take a prescription meant for someone else.

I went back into the bathroom, this time to look in the medicine cabinet. There was the normal array of things, plus aspirin, Ipecac, and cough syrup, but not many prescription drugs. Of course the pills might be in another bathroom— probably one off of Alana and Beto's bedroom. No, wait. I moved an economy-sized bottle of Alka-Seltzer and found a smaller bottle behind it. I opened the lid and saw that it contained the green pills I'd taken.

I looked at the label and felt the blood rush from my face. The name of the medicine didn't mean anything to me, but the name of the patient was Laura Salazar. What was this drug, and what was it doing in Alana's house? I slipped a pill out of the bottle and wrapped it in a square of toilet paper, then put the bottle back where I'd found it.

Hearing footsteps in the hall, I flushed the toilet, then let the tap water run for a few seconds. I almost bumped into Alana when I came out. "Oh, you startled me!"

"Are you okay?" she asked.

Alana looked tired, and I suddenly felt ashamed.

"I'm feeling much better."

"Lies, lies, all lies."

"Well, a little better. I had some bad dreams and they woke me up. And I am sorry for waking you up too. I'm sorry I've made so much trouble for you."

She surprised me by giving me a hug. "You're no trouble." She started back to her room. "See you in the morning."

I stuck the confiscated pill into a zippered compartment of my purse, climbed into bed, and fell into a dreamless sleep.

CHAPTER 15

I woke up, if not energetic at least functional. I decided to ask Alana directly about the medication she'd given me, and once that decision was made I felt better. At least my brain hadn't turned completely to oatmeal.

I made up the bed and dressed, then folded the nightgown and laid it at the foot of the bed. I had a comb in my purse, but no toothbrush. I found the toothpaste in the bathroom, put a dab on my finger, and rubbed it across my teeth. That, and a couple of breath mints, would have to do till I got home.

Alana had already set a place for me at the kitchen table and was fixing huevos rancheros for us. She took me up on my offer to help, and let me pour coffee, milk, and juice. Ryan had left earlier, and Beto and the boys were milling around, getting ready for work and school, respectively.

Unlike Laura's kitchen, Alana's was homey, with ruffled curtains and little knickknacks. The atmosphere was as far removed from that of last night as possible, and I was soon caught up in the pleasure of seeing the easy affection between Alana and Beto, and the way it overflowed to their sons. There was the normal teasing and scuffling that goes on between kids, but even that was somehow comforting.

I sat next to the seven-year-old, Carlos, who eyed me curiously. He'd inherited his dad's light coloring—plus a sprinkling of freckles across his nose—and Ryan's slim build.

"Do you really do karate?" he asked.

"Karate?"

"Drink your orange juice, Carlos," Beto said.

Carlos took a couple of swallows. "Well, do you?"

"Would you believe, I'm just one step below brown belt?"

Carlos' eyes widened. "Cool! Jimmy Sosa's just a green belt."

"Well, that's an accomplishment too. Besides, the colors mean different things in different places."

"Do you ever beat anyone up?"

"Not yet."

His shoulders sagged in disappointment.

"But you never know when I might have to."

"Carlos, your breakfast is getting cold," Alana said.

He dutifully took a few mouthfuls. "Will you be my lawyer?"

The older boys snickered, and one of them bopped Carlos on the head. "What do you need a lawyer for, pendejo?"

"Ouch. So I can tell the kids at school I have a lawyer."

Alana had returned to the stove to refill Beto's plate. She turned and waved a spatula at Carlos. "You keep out of trouble, ¿me escuchas?"

I winked at Carlos. "Your mom's right. You need to behave. But I'll still be your lawyer."

"Cool."

Alana placed one hand on Beto's shoulder as she put his plate before him. "Carlitos, you're going to be late for school if you don't finish eating and stop talking."

Beto's gray eyes were twinkling as he reached up and caressed Alana's hand. "Drink your milk, mijo."

"Okay." Two swallows. "Mom, you forgot to tell Sharon to call Uncle Ryan. Remember, he borrowed your cell phone?"

Alana sat down to her own breakfast. "I didn't forget. I thought I'd let her—and you—finish eating first."

"Cell phone? Ryan?" I asked.

"Mom has a cell phone, but she doesn't want Abuela to know."

"Cállete," said one of his brothers, as he bopped Carlos again. "That's nobody else's business."

I was trying hard not to laugh. "I'm very good at keeping secrets. It's part of my job." I made a zipping motion across my lips. "Your grandmother will never hear it from me."

Miguel, the oldest boy, rinsed his plate and put it in the dishwasher. He gave Alana a peck on the cheek, and excused himself to leave for school. Gabe, the middle boy, followed suit, leaving Carlos to dawdle over his breakfast in relative peace. I helped clear the table, while Alana and Beto finished loading the dishwasher.

"I have a quick service call," Beto told Alana. "Mrs. Varela's computer's down again. Be back soon as I can." He smiled at me, hugged Carlos, gave Alana a lingering kiss, and was on his way.

After Carlos had given us both hugs and gotten off to school, Alana gave me her cell-phone number, and I called Ryan. "I hope you're very very busy," I said as soon as he answered.

"You're in luck. I'm in the middle of class. Call you back in a few minutes. No te vayas."

Five minutes later Ryan called. "I wanted everyone to see me looking important, so I'm standing in the hall between classes with this phone stuck in my ear."

"Idiot."

"You sound cheerful. How is everything?"

"Good. Alana's family is like a breath of fresh air."

"I hadn't thought of it that way, but you're right. Did Carlitos talk your ear off?"

I laughed. "Well, he charmed me into being his attorney."

"That's my nephew." Then, "Wait a minute." I could hear muffled voices in the background, followed by a loud buzzing I assumed was the bell for class. "Gotta go. Where will you be all day?"

"Probably with Erica."

"Be careful, both of you."

"I promise."

"Sharon?"

"Yes?"

"Te quiero," he whispered. "Still."

Te quiero. I like you. I love you. I want you. All of the above.

"Te quiero, Ryan," I whispered back. Still.

CHAPTER 16

I gave Erica a call at Head Start, telling her I didn't think there was much point in hiding from each other any more. She agreed, and we made lunch plans.

I got my purse and went to tell Alana goodbye. I'd planned to walk home, thinking the exercise would do me good, but she wouldn't hear of it.

"Don't be silly. It's a couple of miles, and you'll roast in that sweater."

I couldn't argue with that. It was only 9:30, but the temperature was already in the 80s.

"Just give me a few minutes to finish folding these clothes."

I offered to help, and while we folded laundry I told Alana how much I'd enjoyed spending the morning with her family.

"We enjoyed having you. Especially Carlos. You might not realize it, but now that he's talked you into being his lawyer—as if he needs one—I suspect he really considers you his godmother."

"I'm touched—but puzzled."

"His original *nina*—my cousin Gloria—joined the Hare Krishnas and hasn't been heard from since." She made a face. "Poor Carlitos, he's still young enough, he feels left out of the loop sometimes. So, like it or not, he's attached himself to you."

"Well, I feel honored. And the feeling is mutual. He's sure lovable."

Alana smiled. "He reminds me of Ryan in some ways. Funny and inquisitive. And sensitive."

"Is it always this hard to get him off to school?"

"Only on my days off. Most days breakfast is cereal and whatever. That's why I love fussing over them whenever I can—stretching out the morning a little."

The clothes stacked, we started for the door.

"Alana, before we leave, there's something I need to ask you."

"Ask away." Alana's face lost some of its animation.

"What were those pills you gave me last night?"

"Oh. Those. One of Laura's prescriptions. But you know that, don't you."

"Yes. I looked in your medicine cabinet, if that's what you're asking. I was having nightmares, and I thought the pills might have caused them. So I wondered what I'd taken. I still don't know. The label didn't mean anything to me."

"Let's sit down."

Our tension seemed out of place in Alana's cozy living room. She brought us fresh cups of coffee, and I waited while she weighed whatever it was she wanted to tell me. Then, without any preamble, "Laura was addicted to prescription drugs."

I nodded. "I was beginning to wonder if it was something like that."

"She was very clever. She went to God-knows-how-many doctors—in Laredo, McAllen, Harlingen, anyplace but here. They'd each give her a prescription for one thing or another—Valium, Dexedrine—more things than I could name. She'd go to different drugstores in Mexico to get them filled. Some things she'd get without a prescription whenever she could. We didn't know how bad it was till after she died and we went through her things. She had them stashed everywhere—in every cabinet, in every drawer."

"Do you know why she started taking them in the first place?"

"It's complicated."

And that was all the answer I was going to get.

"To get back to what I gave you. That particular prescription was the same as one Miguel had when he was injured playing basketball. So, rather than throw it down the toilet the way we'd done all the others, I brought that one bottle home."

"And you figured since it was safe for your son, it would be safe for me."

"It never occurred to me it might not be. I'd taken them myself a time or two. I feel awful that it caused a bad reaction. Wait here a minute." She went into the room that served as Beto's office to get something from the file cabinet.

She returned and handed me a sheet of paper. "Here. It's one of those pages the drugstore gives you explaining all about it."

"Don't worry. I'm okay now, and I'd just as soon not read about all the horrible reactions that could have happened and didn't. Besides, you probably did the best thing in the long run."

"Hindsight's great, isn't it?"

I hugged her. "Alana, I really do appreciate you. I don't know why I fell apart the way I did, and I'm glad you put me up—or put up with me, however you want to look at it."

She kissed me on the cheek, then started toward the kitchen with our coffee cups.

I stood to leave once again. "Alana, there's one more thing."

She waited, her back to me.

"Why is it that Bernice still has such a grip on everyone?"

She jerked around, her eyes smoldering. I was glad her boys weren't here to thunk me in the head and tell me it was none of my business.

"I'm sorry. I don't mean to pry. I just hate to see everyone so upset."

"I know this all seems strange and new to you, Sharon, but we've been dealing with it for some time now. And we're all managing very well."

I refrained from shouting, "Lies, lies, all lies!" But there was a kernel of truth in what she'd said. "Well, *your* household certainly seems on an even keel."

"Thanks to Beto. I don't know what I'd do without Beto!" Even saying his name softened Alana's whole demeanor.

"He's a dear."

She smiled. "He is that."

* * *

We reached Los Mareados to find Mrs. Pirtle outside watering the oleanders. She watched us pull up to my door and continued glaring at us.

Alana's eyes flashed. "That horrid woman!"

The fierceness in her voice surprised me. "How do you know Mrs. Pirtle?"

"The few times I came with Laura to see Abuelita, Mrs. Pirtle would fly over to complain about our appearance. We were always underdressed and over-made-up to suit her."

I shrugged. "She doesn't approve of *anyone*, best I can tell."

"That's what we thought at first, and we just laughed it off till we found out she was making life miserable for Abuelita."

"What was she doing?" Abuelita must be close to 80 by now, and it was hard to picture her underdressed or over-made-up.

"She accused Abuelita of being a witch and was constantly ranting about how she'd burn the place down with her candles."

"Is that why Abuelita left?"

"Partly. She wasn't here very long. She moved in when Laura's parents moved to Laredo. She wouldn't go with them, and between you and me, I think she was looking for an excuse to go live with her sister in Monterrey."

"That worked out okay?"

"I guess so. I never heard otherwise."

I looked out the side mirror. "Well, Mrs. Pirtle is keeping her distance today."

"Wait till you open the car door."

The prospect of going inside seemed very dreary, especially compared to the cheerfulness of Alana's home, but it was too hot to keep sitting in the car.

"Would you like to come in?"

"Dear god, no. No offense."

I laughed. "I wish you'd quit beating around the bush."

"Look. Go change clothes and come back to my place." She blushed. "But don't come right away."

It was so unlike Alana to be flustered, I couldn't help teasing her. "Beto has the rest of the day off?"

She smiled, and the blush deepened. "One of the advantages of having your own business."

"Maybe I should just make it another day."

"No, no. Today's fine. Just...."

"How many minutes—or hours—or whatever—should I wait?"

"Oh damn. I just remembered." She grimaced. "The kids are off at noon. And I have a conference at 12:30. Let's see. Anytime after 1:00, I guess."

"You know what? It sounds like you're not going to have a lot of time left for lunch. Why don't you join Erica and me at Jacalito's later?"

"Let me think about it."

"Okay." I got out of the car. "One last thing."

"What is it, Ms. Columbo?"

"Where can I get my hair fixed?"

"Diana's." She answered so quickly I suspected she'd been thinking of bringing it up herself. "She's on 1st and Bravo." With that, Alana waved and spun out of the parking lot.

I pretended not to see Mrs. Pirtle's elaborate hand signals, and went inside. Thirty minutes later I came back outside to find her standing by my car. "Excuse me," I said pleasantly. "I'm running late." *Lies, lies, all lies.*

She peered at me over her still-smudged glasses. "I just thought you'd want to know," she huffed, "while you was out gallivantin' with that hussy, your other girlfriend was here lookin' for you."

Erica? She didn't expect to be free till about 12:30. "That's odd."

"I'll say it is. And I think you could do a lot better, even if she does have that fancy car."

A chill ran through me. "What kind of car, exactly?"

"Don't ask me. I don't keep up with those things."

I wanted to shake her. "Do you keep up with things like color? What color was it?"

"Don't be snippy, Miss. It was red. As if you didn't know."

"She's no friend of mine. If you see her around my place again, tell her to leave. If she doesn't leave, don't call Mr. López—call the sheriff. Trespassing is illegal, and I'll have her thrown in jail!"

For once Mrs. Pirtle was speechless. She stalked away, and I peeled off. I was upset that Bernice had found me, upset that she'd been snooping around. I turned around and went back for my laptop. I'd just carry it with me wherever I went. That and my cell phone. Then I'd look *really* important.

I went straight to Diana's. If she couldn't take me, at least I could make an appointment. Or maybe jump off a bridge.

I was in luck. She had an opening if I could wait 15 minutes. The first thing I noticed when I looked in the mirror was that my eyes looked as wild as my hair. If Diana wondered what asylum I'd fled, she was tactful enough not to mention it. By the time she'd finished, I couldn't believe the transformation, and for less than $10.00.

"You're magic. I look normal."

She laughed. "You look very pretty."

I thanked her again and left.

CHAPTER 17

I wished Diana could have fixed the inside of my head as expertly as the outside. Despite my bravado with Mrs. Pirtle, the thought of facing Bernice one on one made my skin crawl. I'd always considered myself a rational person, but around her I could sense of something evil that was beyond analysis. Something all the karate in the world couldn't conquer.

It was all I could do to keep from calling Ryan. I wanted desperately to hear his voice. I wanted to be with him. I wanted...to quit acting like a love-struck teenager. What I *needed* was a good dose of reality.

I picked up my cell phone and forced myself to call Mac MacDougal, half-hoping he would tell me everything at the law firm was chaos without me and I should return home "imedeATily."

Although seeing Erica again was worth the trip—*forget Ryan*—I couldn't think of anything else I could do here. After all, Erica had called me as a friend, not because of my "detecting skills."

And Mac was right. A fine detective I'd turned out to be! I didn't want anything to do with Bernice, the one person I ought to be questioning, and the questions I'd asked other people only served to annoy them.

"Hey, Mac, it's Sharon," I said when he answered.

"Hi, darlin'. Glad to hear from you. We've been wondering how you're doing down there."

Hearing Mac's hearty voice I could almost see him—thick-set, with thick black-rimmed glasses, and thick salt-and-pepper hair. The only thing about Mac that wasn't thick was his mind. He was the most brilliant person I knew.

"Everything under control?" he boomed.

"Mm—más o menos. How 'bout there? Mrs. Lovato's case going okay?"

"We're working on it. Now don't you worry about a thing. Everything's going to work out just fine."

"Oh. Sounds like I'm not even needed."

"Now I didn't say that. Of course we miss you. By the way, Jeff called."

Jeff, I thought guiltily. I should call him. "Well, keep missing me. I don't want to hear you're doing *too* well without me."

"You know better. You'll find plenty enough to do when you get back. But Sharon, do you realize it's been two years since you've taken a real vacation—anything more than a few days here and there?"

"That long?"

"That long. And that's not a good thing. You're a damn good attorney, Sharon, but even you can get burned out, and I don't want that to happen. You hear me?"

"I hear you."

"You take some days off, and don't come back for another week or two anyway. Go down to South Padre or someplace."

"But Mrs. Lovato...."

"Sharon, get off the damn phone and go have some fun."

* * *

Well now, Mac, it's hard to know where to start. I decided going to the library would be a good way to kill time. Besides, it seemed an unlikely place to run into Bernice. On second thought, I'd go directly to the Head Start classrooms. Erica had invited me to visit, and I was curious to see her in action.

Action was the defining word. An hour later I felt both energized and a little exhausted. "I don't see how you do it!"

"How *they* do it. These teachers are the greatest."

I left my car at Head Start, and we drove to Jacalito's in Erica's car. I called Alana on the way to see if she'd decided whether or not to meet us. She sounded glad to hear from me and said she'd be there shortly. Erica and I went inside, got a table, and ordered iced tea while waiting.

"What on earth has been going on?" Erica asked. "Tell me everything."

"I don't have time to go into all of it now, but I do need to tell you this much. I'm afraid our impression was right about Laura being on drugs. Alana says it was only prescription meds, but it has to be more serious than that. Too many things don't add up, and everyone is so tight-lipped."

"I didn't want to believe it, but I wish I could say I was surprised."

"Anyway, I think that—plus a lot of other stuff—is what's behind all their weird behavior."

"I need to tell you something too," Erica said, changing the subject. "Something came up unexpectedly. I'm flying back to L.A. for the weekend."

Before she had a chance to explain, Alana arrived. We all exchanged the usual pleasantries, and I realized somewhat belatedly that asking Alana to join us might be awkward for Erica after her cool reception at Laura's funeral.

Alana broke the ice with an apology. "Please forgive us our bad manners, Erica. The whole family has been on edge."

Bad manners? I let it go. I just wanted to relax and spend a pleasant afternoon together, and I sensed the others felt the same. By the time we'd finished our meal, we were enjoying ourselves too much to call it a day. Erica suggested going out for a drink, so we piled into Alana's van and went to the Purple Sage Lounge.

The atmosphere at the Purple Sage was inviting, the booths upholstered in soothing tones of mauve and gray to match its name. We found a quiet corner where we could let our hair down undisturbed. By the time we'd finished our first round of margaritas, everything seemed very funny to us.

"This is great," Alana said. "I can't remember the last time I had a drink in the middle of the afternoon."

"Beto doesn't mind you boozing it up with us?" Erica asked.

We all giggled as if this were the most humorous remark since the invention of comedy.

"Beto's the best thing that ever happened to me. He keeps me grounded."

"That's not all he does for you," I said.

"Like I said, he's the best." Alana's eyes were shining again.

"That reminds me." Erica turned to me. "I never got around to telling you about Richard."

"Erica, you have a bad habit of withholding information."

She laughed and stretched sensuously, clasping her hands above her head. "Richard and I have been seeing each other for about a year—whenever out schedules mesh. He's a pilot for TWA, and he's in and out of town a lot.

Anyway, his schedule got changed on him, and he's home all next week. So...I'm taking the first flight out of Harlingen tomorrow morning."

"Tell me. Do these long-distance relationships really work?"

"For us they do. He travels, I travel. Sometimes we even travel together. And when we're together—well, what do you think causes all those earthquakes out there?"

"Sin vergüenza. You're shameless!" Alana said in a prudish tone before she burst out laughing. "Next time I hear about earthquakes on the news, I'll know what you and Richard are doing."

"I'll toast to that," I said, raising my glass as the others joined in. "But I'm envious. Alana and Beto are happily married. You and Richard are happily causing earthquakes. For me, there's just Jeff."

"Who's Jeff?" Erica demanded. "If he turns out to be your pet terrier I'm really going to be mad."

"Oh no. He's a real person. He's very nice, and he's very good-looking. And I've been going out with him for about two years."

This announcement was met by rousing silence.

"So you're just leading Ryan on." I'd forgotten how icy Alana's voice could be. "He'd walk on water for you, and you—you just waltz into town and...."

"Alana, no! That's not fair. You know how I feel about Ryan!"

"And how would I know that?"

"Because you're a human polygraph machine, or mind-reader, or something, and you have to know I'm...I'm crazy about him, and I'm not having any more margaritas."

"Then what's with this Jeff person?"

"It was dumb of me to bring him up. Everything I said is true except...Jeff 's not interested in me as a woman, or in any other woman."

Erica took me by the hand. "Then why are you going out with him?"

Why did I bring up things I didn't want to talk about? "A few years ago I was in a relationship that ended badly. I didn't want to go out with anyone, and my friends kept wanting to fix me up. Yuck. Anyway, Jeff and I met for coffee one afternoon, and he said something to the effect that maybe we could get the matchmakers off our backs if we'd go out together."

"Did you know he was gay?" Erica asked.

"Not until he told me. It's not something he goes around shouting from the rooftops and he doesn't fit the stereotype. Most weekends you'll find him barreling around on his Harley."

"And during the week?"

"He's with another law firm."

"Three-piece suits and a heart of stone?" Erica teased.

I laughed. "He doesn't fit that stereotype either. The thing is, and I want you to know this because I don't want you to think I'm just using Jeff. I really like him, as in 'like.' We discovered we enjoyed going places together on our no-pressure dates. So we go out every other Saturday, and he sends flowers to the office in between to keep the busybodies happy. I'm sure Mac knows what's going on— Mac's head of our firm—but he's never said anything."

Alana stared at me wordlessly.

Erica blinked. "And all this time you haven't...?"

"Nope. Not for over two years."

"Well, on that note I think we should have another round of margaritas."

95

Before we could discuss this any further, Bernice's slurred voice broke into our conversation as she staggered to our table, her orange hair jutting out from her head like a stiff pyramid. "Why didn't you ask me to join your little party?" She pulled up a chair and sat at the end of the table.

Alana was rigid.

"Is that why you came by this morning, Bernice?" I asked her. "To invite me out for a drink?"

"I don't know what you're talking about."

I realized at this point that arguing with her was not only pointless, but would also provide her with an excuse to stay at our table longer. And the sensation of wanting to get as far away from her as possible was creeping up my spine like fingernails screeching across a windowpane.

Suddenly Ryan's ploy came to mind. "We're getting tired of this place," I said, standing up, hoping my knees wouldn't buckle under me. "We were just on our way over to Hugo's. The drinks are so much better over there. You can meet us there if you'd like."

Alana stood up with me, but I had to urge Erica from the booth.

Bernice studied us through slitted lids. "I don't think so."

"Suit yourself. It's hot and we're thirsty, so we're not going to stand around talking about it. See you there. Or not. Whatever you decide."

Outside the sun seemed too bright for our mood. I hurried into Alana's van, all but dragging Erica in behind me. The van had bench seats, and the three of us were seated in front, with Erica sitting shotgun. My hands were shaking so, I could hardly buckle my seatbelt. Alana spun out of the parking lot, kicking up rocks behind us, and we headed south toward the Veleño bridge.

"I hope this works," I said nervously.

Alana checked the rearview mirror. "I don't see her." She made a quick left turn down a side street and made a U-turn in someone's driveway. We parked in front of their house and waited till we saw Bernice's red Porsche go past the intersection toward Hugo's. Then Alana pulled back onto 83 and headed north till she reached Jacalito's where she parked under the shade of a mesquite tree. We sat immobilized, still rattled by the whole incident.

"I don't feel right about this," Erica said. "Don't you feel sorry for Bernice sometimes? She has no friends. It must be hard to see us having such a good time together and know she's never included."

"If you're looking for sympathy for that bitch, you've come to the wrong place," Alana said.

Erica looked taken aback, but had more to say. "I think it's cruel to send someone who drinks too much to a bar."

"Erica, we didn't send her anywhere she wouldn't have gone to on her own," Alana said. "That's probably where she spends most of her time anyway. Except when she's in a cave somewhere with the bats."

"She must take some time off for her sugar daddy," I muttered. "Or whoever pays for the Porsche."

Erica frowned. "That's really low. I can't believe you all are being this way."

Alana gave me a sharp look. "You haven't told her yet!"

I realized I'd been putting this off. I only hoped Erica would handle it better than I had.

"Erica, Bernice knew. About Laura. And she was blackmailing her. You can imagine, with Laura being a teacher, how that could destroy her." I paused to let that sink in. "So no, you won't find us having any nice thoughts about Bernice."

Erica's face paled as she turned to stare out her window. "I'm not that shocked to know what Bernice is really like. I think I've known all along and just didn't want to admit it. But I am shocked that she would hurt Laura."

Erica faced the front again, but was still staring fixedly into space. "You know, this is going to sound odd, and I hope you'll take it the right way. But I feel a big weight's been lifted off my shoulders."

I could feel Alana stiffen beside me, and put my hand on her arm. "Let her finish."

Erica continued in a voice that sounded flat and faraway. "I've always felt sorry for Bernice because nobody liked her. Even my mom didn't like her, and you know how she bent over backwards to be fair to everyone."

Erica slipped her hand into mine. "Mami was always so happy when summer came and you were here and I didn't see so much of Bernice. And I was relieved when we started running with different crowds in junior high. Then I felt guilty for feeling relieved, so I kept on defending her. But the guilt trip is over. I've overlooked a lot of things, but I can't forgive her for this."

Erica reached across me to touch Alana's hand. "Alana, I'm so sorry."

"How can I give you a hug when we're buckled up in this damn van?"

The three of us got out of the van and stood there in front of Jacalito's with our arms around each other and shed our tears for Laura.

CHAPTER 18

"I wanted to talk to you, just the two of us," Erica said after Alana had driven away. "I could also use a cup of coffee."

We went to Dairy Queen, then sat outside in the shade with our coffee.

Erica stirred hers absently before speaking. "Sharon, tell me what's been going on."

"Do you have the rest of the day to hear it all?"

"If that's what it takes."

I condensed it as best I could, and filled her in on the highlights. "I feel like an emotional yo-yo. Right now I'm hanging at the halfway point."

"Numb?"

"Yeah."

"I've been thinking," Erica said. "About Laura and Leo. Even though we were right about Laura's drug problem, I think you were off track about the other."

"What other?"

"Leo being involved with Bernice."

I nodded. "You're right. I found that hard to believe myself."

"More likely it's just the opposite—that nothing was going on between them. Bernice has always been so jealous, always wanted what she couldn't have. She couldn't have Leo, and she's never gotten over it."

"So you think—what?"

"She hurt him through Laura. And she'll keep hurting him any way she can." Tears filled Erica's eyes. "Dear sweet Leo."

"I wonder." I could barely voice the thought. "I wonder who else she'll hurt. There must be a lot of people who can't stand her. Ryan for one. Their whole family."

Erica laid her hand on mine. "They do need to be careful. Even though Leo's her real target."

"Why Leo?"

The pain was still in her eyes. "Something that happened back in high school."

"Can you tell me?"

Erica looked away, hesitant. "Oh, one of those things. I don't know exactly—it was long after Leo and I broke up. I just heard talk. The long and the short of it is, Bernice threw herself at Leo. Something...went wrong and he started avoiding her. So she retaliated by saying things to humiliate him."

I was quiet a minute, making a mental note to pursue this later, but for some reason I couldn't fathom, the subject seemed to distress Erica.

I remembered Bernice—with her usual style and sensitivity—saying things to put Leo down at Erica's quinceañera. But I wasn't ready to go there either. Whenever I thought about Erica's quinceañera—her coming-of-age celebration when she turned 15—I tried to focus on how happy she was. Otherwise, I tried not to think about it at all.

I'd been in Minnesota about a year and a half when Erica invited me down. I'd started dating, had even met someone special. So when Erica told me Ryan was seeing someone else too, I thought I was okay with that—till I actually saw them together.

I had wondered, at the age of 15, if I would ever get over loving Ryan, and decided then and there never to come back to Zapata to find out.

"Well," I said, getting back to the subject of Bernice, "I'm glad you finally saw through her. To tell you the truth, I never understood how you became friends in the first place."

"I'm not sure if 'friends' is the exact word. But we did have something in common. We were in school plays together, starting 'way back in third grade. Bernice had quite a flair for drama even then, and I admired her talent."

"Hmm. Makes you wonder how her life would have turned out if she'd used that talent constructively."

"I know. I haven't thought about it in such a long time. But—well, you know Bernice—she was fine as long as she had the starring role. Then in sixth grade something happened that should have clued me in."

Erica became quiet, remembering. "Bernice didn't get the lead in the class play, and the girl who did, fell down some stairs and had to drop out."

I could feel goose bumps prickle my arms. "I suppose it was considered an accident."

Erica nodded. "No accusations were ever made, but that girl became very withdrawn and told our drama coach she thought Bernice should have the part since Bernice knew all the lines anyway."

"Nobody suspected anything?"

A shadow crossed Erica's face. "In the back of my mind, I think I knew. At the same time, it was hard to believe anyone could be so deliberately cruel. You know how your mind makes excuses for things that don't make sense."

"I know." I also knew how Erica's heart made excuses for *people* who don't make sense.

"Then summer came, and she went off to visit an aunt in New Mexico. At least, that was the story. I'm wondering now if she might have been in some kind of psychiatric treatment place. All I know, she came back just as we were starting junior high, and I was thankful she'd discovered boys and decided my company was too boring."

I smiled. "Well, my 'boring' friend, why don't we get another cup of coffee and spend what's left of the afternoon on a happier note."

"Good idea."

We went back in the Dairy Queen for refills, then came back outside. I noticed dark circles under Erica's eyes again, and I knew she was having a hard time trying to strike that happier note.

"I'm glad you're getting away for the weekend," I said. "I just wish things hadn't turned so sour for you."

Erica closed her eyes and pressed her fingers to her temples. "What I feel bad about is dragging you into this mess."

"Erica, you didn't drag me."

"Well, you dropped everything and came running, and I know how busy you were."

"You'd have done the same for me."

"I do appreciate you, Sharon, more than you know. Once you got here everything seemed brighter—until today anyway. But I really didn't have any reason for keeping you here, except I just enjoyed being with you again. I've been very selfish. I wouldn't have even planned to see Richard except I figured you needed to get back home. Your firm must be wondering if you'll ever come back to work."

"Well, there's another guilt trip you don't have to take. Mac all but shoved me out the door at gunpoint, telling me to take a vacation."

"Some vacation!"

"Look at it this way. I feel bad that you went through so much hell. And I'm sorry that's what brought me here. But I'm glad I came. More than *you'll* ever know. For one thing, I'm glad to be with you again too. I can't believe it had gotten so we only wrote each other at Christmas."

"I know. But we've both been so busy."

"*Too* busy."

She gave me a sidelong glance. "And then there's Ryan."

"And then there's Ryan." I took a deep breath. "Maybe I'm in over my head, Erica. Everything seems to be happening so fast. I've only been here a few days, and already...."

"Sharon." She leaned forward. "After all this time, how could everything be happening too fast? It's not like you just met him. And," she added impishly, "it's not like you never slept with him."

"You goofball." I started laughing. "Slept, period. And as I recall, there were four of us."

"Now that sounds pretty racy!"

"And we were seven years old."

On hot July nights we would set up cots or sleeping bags in the Montoyas' back yard—Erica's four brothers and we "four musketeers." Whenever the coyotes began howling, her brothers would tell us that coyotes always ate little kids first. We brave musketeers would make a beeline inside where we'd climb into Erica's bed, snuggle together like little puppies, and finally fall asleep.

"Don't get technical," Erica said. "Listen to me, my dearest bestest friend. I'm being serious now. I don't believe in 'fate' and all that. But I do know you two have always had something special."

"When we were kids. Then I moved away. And he found somebody else."

"Yeah. After he moped around for months and months."

"I moped my whole freshman year."

"And remember what happened your sophomore year?"

I smiled. "Dennis Erickson."

"That's what you're supposed to do at that age, for heaven sake. Wouldn't it be awful if you'd spent twenty years in a vacuum?"

"Erica, I think you're the one who's good medicine for me."

"Good. Because I'm about to give some more advice. It's been long enough for you two—too long. And long-distance relationships can work, if you have your heart in it."

I wasn't sure if I was listening to my heart or to my friend Erica, who liked making up rules, but they both seemed to be heading me in the same direction.

CHAPTER 19

There were three messages on my cell phone—one from Jeff and two from Ryan. I called Jeff and reached his answering machine. I told the machine to tell Jeff I was sorry I'd missed him and would have to cancel out of Saturday's date. It seemed I spent a lot of time lately telling people "I'll explain later."

I called Ryan on Alana's cell phone, hoping he hadn't returned it yet. As tired as I was, it still gave me a lift to hear his voice.

"Hey, Sharon, how was your day?"

"Different. How 'bout yours?"

"Good. Better now that you've called. I'm still tied up till about 7:00, but maybe we could get together then."

"I'd like that, Ryan, except I'm afraid I wouldn't be very good company."

"So?"

"So if you feel like seeing a boring exhausted person, I'm available."

"That's what I was hoping to hear. Listen Sharon, I'm a little tired myself. What say I pick up some pizza, and we just kick back at my place. Watch TV. If you're still a basketball fan, there's a game on tonight."

"Sounds good to me."

Winter darkness was already creeping in, but I still had a couple of hours to kill before meeting Ryan. If I were smart, I'd go home, take a nap, and not be the boring exhausted person I'd promised him I'd be.

Well, it wouldn't hurt if I sidetracked just a tad, I rationalized. Maybe I should gather my courage and stalk Bernice for a change—see if I could locate her bat cave. I headed toward Hugo's, saw Bernice's red Porsche parked there, then wondered what the hell I thought I was doing.

It wasn't the kind of bar women went to alone, unless they had a pick-up in mind. Bernice would probably have already staked out her prey, and they'd be sitting together. I could walk up to their table and say, "May I join you, just long enough to scratch your eyes out?" Or I could sit here in the parking lot waiting for her to leave, but who knows when that would happen.

It seemed a shame to waste the trip, so I got out and went inside. The smoke was so thick I wondered if I could locate Bernice at all. Maybe it would keep anyone from noticing me.

No such luck. Someone stopped me before I'd barely gotten inside the door. "I'm looking for my husband," I told him. "I'm sick of him coming here every night, and I'm going to drag him away bodily." My wannabe one-night-stand looked duly alarmed and vanished.

Hugo's wasn't a large place, and once my eyes got adjusted, there weren't many tables to scan. I didn't see Bernice at any of them. I made my way to the bar, thinking she might be there.

I was surprised to find Leo and Johnny Quemado instead. I hadn't thought of the Quemados since that strange evening at Leo's when Johnny had sat like a statue while Tina skittered around playing hostess.

Leo was just as surprised to see me, and didn't look terribly pleased. "Hey, Sharon, what are you doing here?"

Oh, just looking up old enemies. Tracking down Laura's blackmailer. Looking for my imaginary husband. Stuff like that. Bottom line: I was embarrassed beyond words for anyone I knew to see me in a place like Hugo's.

"Well, it's kind of awkward," I said truthfully. "I forgot I was allergic to smoke."

If Leo noticed that my remarks didn't jibe, he didn't comment. He stubbed out his cigarette, but Johnny continued smoking. Not that it mattered. Their small contribution to the pollution would hardly make a difference.

"The thing is," I said, settling for half-truths, "I heard Bernice was looking for me, and I saw her come in here, so I thought I'd see what she wanted."

Leo's head jerked up, and he gripped my arm. "Stay away from her, Sharon. You're out of your league." The haunted look I'd seen on his face the other night returned, and I felt ashamed for saying anything.

"You're right. It was a stupid idea."

I wanted to reach out to him, this friend I seemed to have lost, but I didn't know how. On impulse I kissed his cheek, then peered around him at Johnny. "Tell Tina hi for me."

"Sure." Through the smoky haze, I could barely see his face, but his voice sounded indifferent. Maybe I should drag Tina's husband home to her.

As I started away, another slobbery drunk jostled me. Leo appeared quietly by my side. "I'll walk you out."

I told him I needed to stop at the restroom. What I really wanted was to make sure Bernice wasn't there. Someone had been sick, and the smell nauseated me, so I didn't linger. Leo was still waiting for me, and we walked to my car together. After I got in, he pushed the lock down and closed my door.

I started the engine and rolled my window down. "Good night, my buddy. And thanks."

"Good night, Sharon. Be careful."

Leo waited till I rolled my window up again, then walked back toward the bar. I noticed Bernice's car still in the parking lot, so I could only assume she'd left with someone else. Another dead end.

As I exited, I heard the sound of an engine starting up somewhere behind me. It was probably just a coincidence, but I hadn't seen anyone else leaving when Leo and I came outside. The reflection in the rearview mirror revealed a surge of headlights, like two disembodied moons that obscured the vehicle they belonged to.

I swung onto the highway, looked over my shoulder, and caught a brief glimpse of a dark truck before it made its turn. I crossed the Veleño bridge, then alternately sped and crept, the truck behind me keeping pace. Seeing several cars parked at the parish hall, I took a quick right and pulled up there, grateful for whatever Friday-night activities were happening.

The truck drove on then, and in the streetlight I could see it was maroon with some kind of jagged gold design painted across the side. The only impression I had of the driver was that he—or she—was thin and wore a cowboy hat. I sat there a few minutes till I felt sure he wouldn't return.

The adrenaline had ebbed, leaving me limp and shaky. I felt I was driving through cobwebs as I headed for home, but at least I didn't see either the red Porsche or the maroon truck on the way. I put my paranoia to rest by telling myself it was probably someone in hopes a patron of Hugo's might have something pornographic in mind. Seeing me at church must have put a damper on that notion.

Everything at Los Mareados looked drearily the same, right down to Mrs. Pirtle's vigilance with the binoculars. It occurred to me she might have been able to tell me something more about Bernice if I'd given her the chance. I knocked on her door, hoping she wouldn't tell me she wasn't home.

I don't know if it's possible to slam a door *open*, but that was certainly the impression Mrs. Pirtle gave. "Your girlfriend has not been back."

"Well, I do appreciate your keeping an eye on things for me."

Mrs. Pirtle appeared somewhat mollified. "She ain't never been too nice."

So this hadn't been Mrs. Pirtle's first encounter with Bernice.

"You wouldn't happen to know where she lives, would you? I could tell her myself not to bother you, and you wouldn't have to deal with her again."

Mrs. Pirtle sniffed. "All I know is she lives over to that trailer park down the road."

Somehow I couldn't picture Bernice and her Porsche in a trailer park.

"She use to come here when that witch lived here," Mrs. Pirtle continued.

Remembering what Alana had told me, I supposed she meant Laura's grandmother. Why would Bernice come to see Laura's grandmother?

"Did she come often?"

"Only when that other girl was here."

"Your tenant's granddaughter?"

Mrs. Pirtle sniffed again. "That one with cat-eyes."

"Blue eyes?"

"Could be."

"Do you remember anything else about their visits?"

"What do you think I am? I mind my own business. I don't know what went on except they tried to burn the place down."

Well, I'd probably had more than my share of Mrs. Pirtle for one day, so I told her good night, and went to my room to shower away the smoky stench of Hugo's before going to Ryan's.

CHAPTER 20

I had told Ryan I'd pick up some stuff to make salad and meet him shortly after 7:00. By the time I got to his house, he'd changed into Levis and a dark blue polo shirt, and was re-warming the pizza.

"Am I that late?"

"No, I had a last minute cancellation. Figures. The parents I needed to see most."

Ryan took the groceries from me and set them on the counter, then got out some bowls and utensils for making salad. As I rinsed the lettuce, Ryan came up behind me, put his arms around my waist and kissed me softly on the cheek. I leaned against him and closed my eyes for a few seconds, wondering if my heart was beating as loudly as it seemed.

A crazy thought flashed through my mind: The passionate scene from the movie *Fatal Attraction* with the main characters in a sexual frenzy in the kitchen sink. It had struck me as terribly uncomfortable. Besides, with knives, scissors, and such on the counter, the concept of unsafe sex soared to whole new levels.

"What's on your mind?" Ryan whispered.

"Naughty thoughts. Now go away and let me finish the salad."

An enormous tiger-striped cat wandered into the kitchen and curled in and out around my ankles, trying to sound pitiful and underfed. Ryan opened a can of Friskies, and dished it out for him.

"What a pretty cat! What's his name?"

"Spot. Spot, this is Sharon."

Spot acknowledged the introduction with a flick of his furry tail.

"Spot! That was the dog's name! The cat was Puff." Though "Puff " wouldn't fit this hulky cat any better. "And neither of them had stripes."

Ryan reached down and scratched Spot behind the ears. "Spot doesn't like to be stereotyped."

We sat down to our supper in Ryan's kitchen, and I thought what a pleasant room it was, furnished very simply. I wondered briefly if Mrs. Salazar approved of the Tupperware arrangement.

"So you did come back," Ryan said, almost inaudibly. He grinned at me, then said in a high little-boy voice, "When is Sharon coming back?"

I laughed with him. "You make me think of the first letter you ever sent me—back in second grade. Written all in crayon."

"You remember that?"

"I still have it somewhere—in my jewelry box, I think. It wasn't hard to memorize: 'Dear Sharon, when are you comming back? Love, Ryan Miguel Salazar.'"

"Alana helped me with the spelling. More likely, 'mis-spelling.' I think I was driving her crazy."

"You must have done the address yourself. Whenever I hear someone badmouth the post office, I think of that letter. You used a Christmas seal for a stamp. But some kind-hearted postal worker saw that I got it."

"You still have that letter," he mused.

"Along with the ring you gave me when we were 14."

"I hope you had that ring insured—it was worth a lot of money."

"Must have been. With all those 'diamonds.'"

"I found it down in Mexico at one of those sidewalk stands. The guy selling it told me it was worth $5000.00. I believed him—it was the prettiest ring I'd ever seen. I told him all I had was seven dollars and fifty-eight cents. He hemmed and hawed and finally said since it was for *mi novia*, and since it was my lucky day, he'd let me have it for $7.58."

"Maybe I'll put it in my safe deposit box."

After we'd eaten, we went into the living room and I noticed once again how comfortable it felt. In one corner were an upright piano and a set of drums.

"Do you still play?"

"Sure do. With some of the same guys too. We get together whenever."

I thought of all those evenings on the Montoyas' patio, when a couple of Erica's brothers had also been in their rock band. Memories came flooding in. The music pulsating up and down the neighborhood. The intoxicating fragrance of the huisache in bloom. Mrs. Montoya bringing us lemonade at the end of the evening when the band broke up. Ryan stealing a kiss before going home....

With an effort, I turned my attention to the rest of the room. On the walls were several paintings, mostly seascapes, and one of a lighthouse that I felt especially drawn to.

"That's Port Isabel. Alana painted it. She painted all of these."

"Really? She's very talented."

"Yes she is. She has a knack for interior decorating too. You can thank her we're not sitting on apple crates."

I thought of the contrast between Alana's cheerful home and Laura's barren one, but couldn't think of a tactful way to broach the subject.

Ryan turned on the TV. "I promised you we'd watch the game. The Spurs are playing tonight—you're a fan of theirs?"

"You bet."

"Well, just to make it interesting, I'll root for the Suns. You need another Dr. Pepper?"

"Maybe later."

He sat beside me with a Tecate in one hand, his other arm around my shoulders. We kicked off our shoes and put our feet up on a large ottoman. Spot strolled in from the kitchen, jumped up on the sofa, and wedged himself between us.

I scratched Spot under the chin. "You'll root for the Spurs, won't you?"

He meowed and began purring contentedly.

At half-time, the Spurs were well ahead. Ryan muted the commercials, then stood and stretched. "Spot, you'll have to go," he said, picking up the cat and setting him on the floor. "We have to keep this game evenly matched—give the Suns a chance." Spot laid one ear back and blinked once or twice, then with an indignant lash of his tail marched off to his own digs in the laundry room.

Ryan sat down again, pulling me closer to him, and kissed me gently. "I'm glad you're back."

"Me too." I moved even closer and returned his kiss with an intensity that surprised us both.

It felt so natural to be in Ryan's arms again, as if there had never been anything to separate us. It also seemed inevitable that we would soon go beyond kissing, our adolescent longings replaced by an even deeper need for fulfillment. Before long, with one mind and without having to say a word, we had moved into the bedroom.

CHAPTER 21

I woke curled up in Ryan's arms, a tangle of sheets all around us. I lay quietly for several minutes, feeling his heart beat, soaking in the sheer delight of being with him. Then I slipped out of bed as gingerly as possible, wrapped a sheet around me, and went to the bathroom. I was getting pretty good at brushing my teeth without a toothbrush.

When I went back into the bedroom, Ryan was awake. He propped himself up on one elbow, laughter touching his eyes. "What's with the toga?"

"I was afraid it would take awhile to collect all my clothes, and besides I'd like to shower first."

"Alone?"

I sashayed out of the room, looking at him over my shoulder. "Unless you have something else in mind." That's when I bumped into the wall.

Ryan came over and put his arms around me, laughing softly. "You nut. Loca mía."

After we'd showered and dressed, I suggested we go back to Los Mareados so I could change clothes. Ryan was staring into the fridge as if it might sprout vocal cords and offer some suggestions for breakfast.

"I have an idea," I told him. "We can have breakfast at my place. I have this enormous box of Cinnamon Toast Crunch that will feed a family of twelve for six months. I'll share."

"Bueno." He closed the fridge. "I have a better idea. Let's get you moved out of that place."

"And then what?"

My question caught him up short. His face became serious. "I don't mean to take you for granted."

"I don't want to take anything for granted."

He looked at me steadily. "Stay with me, Sharon."

Despite what Erica said, I hadn't expected things to move this quickly. But I didn't want to play games and act coy when I already knew the answer. I moved into his arms. "I can't seem to stay away."

His arms tightened around me. "How long would it take you to pack up?"

"Not long. All I have there is a few clothes, a few groceries, my toothbrush and stuff." And if we don't leave soon, we might as well forget about breakfast.

Spot-the-Striped-Cat strolled into the kitchen meowing at top volume as if to say, "Well, you damn sure better not forget *my* breakfast."

"Okay, okay," Ryan said. "Tyrant."

We filled Spot's food and water bowls, then left for Los Mareados.

* * *

Ryan offered to collect the things in the kitchen while I emptied the bathroom cabinets. "There's not much left in the fridge," he called out. "A tomato, couple of cans of Dr. Pepper, half a quart of milk...."

"Don't forget the cabinets."

"You weren't kidding about the size of that cereal box! What else? Tea, peanut butter, Ritz crackers...."

I'd been only half-listening to Ryan's inventory plus the opening and shutting of drawers when I suddenly became aware of the total silence coming from the kitchen. I came in to find Ryan standing dead still holding a small object in his hand.

"What's that?"

Somewhat reluctantly, he handed me a bottle of pills partially wrapped in masking tape that was deteriorating. One of Laura's prescriptions.

"Where did this come from?"

"Not any place you'd think to look. I couldn't get one of the drawers to shut, and I thought it had gotten off the runners. But it was still jammed after I'd adjusted it. So I reached back and found this. It looked like it had been taped underneath the counter over the drawer. I must have jarred it loose."

I read the information on the label—a prescription for Zoloft in Laura's name, dated March of last year. "Alana told me Laura stashed these everywhere. She must have hidden this while her grandmother was living here."

Ryan shook his head. "I should be used to it by now."

I decided against telling Ryan I had searched the place when I moved in. Obviously I hadn't searched well enough. The bottle was still sealed, so I couldn't see any point in keeping it. "I'll just peel off the label and flush that and the rest of the pills down the toilet." I tried to sound matter-of-fact, as if this were something I was accustomed to doing every day. After disposing of the pills and label, I clunked the empty bottle into the trash.

Ryan looked so dejected, I didn't know what else to say. I went over and hugged him. He put his arms around me and buried his face in my hair. "I don't want you to get dragged into this." Almost exactly what Erica had told me.

"I'm not being dragged. Come on. Let's go. I got everything out of the bedroom and bathroom, and if there's anything left in the kitchen, they can have it." I gave the living room and kitchen a quick once-over and we took my things to the car. "I need to check out."

"I'll come with you. I'm curious to meet Mrs. What's-Her-Name."

I wasn't sure this was a good idea, but could tell Ryan was trying to shake off his gloomy mood. "It might really confuse her. She thinks I'm a Libyan."

"A what?"

"She's a little homophobic. A little heterophobic too, I think."

As it turned out, Mrs. López was in the office instead. She greeted us pleasantly. "You must be Erica's friend." She explained that she filled in for Mrs. Pirtle on Saturday and Sunday mornings while her husband did odd maintenance jobs.

Mrs. Pirtle's living quarters were attached to the office, and I caught a sugar-and-spicy aroma coming from her kitchen. Somehow it had never occurred to me to picture her doing something as domestic as baking cookies. Perhaps I'd misjudged her.

Then again, maybe not. She poked her head out the door when she heard my voice and began her usual harangue. "Is that your boyfriend? You ain't supposed to have boyfriends."

"I know. Since I stumbled across this one, I thought I'd better check out. In keeping with your policy."

Mrs. López looked puzzled, but before she could say anything Mrs. Pirtle did an abrupt about-face.

"Now dearie," she said, coming into the office, "there's no need to get hasty. You can stay as long as you want." It was hard for her to get her smile muscles activated after such a long period of disuse, but I gave her credit for trying.

"That's nice of you, but it's better this way."

"Well, at least let us know where we can reach you in case any of your girlfriends call." Hard to tell through her blurred glasses, but she appeared to be giving me a wink.

Leery of her newfound interest in me and my whereabouts, I made an evasive reply that Mrs. López would be able to find me if necessary, and said goodbye.

As we were leaving, we saw Mr. Bigelow emerge from his apartment. I decided his face must be set in a permanent stare.

"Let's go," I urged Ryan. I didn't want any more reminiscences with Mr. Bigelow about where he might or might not have seen someone who might or might not look like me.

"I didn't know he lived here," Ryan said as we got in the car.

"Who is he? He looks familiar, but I can't place him."

"He used to be in politics."

"Oh, I remember now. He'd run for some office every now and then, figuring once he took charge, he could whip the whole town into shape."

"I'm surprised you remember that."

"I'd hear the Montoyas talking about it. They couldn't believe someone so out of touch with the community would even think of running. He didn't like anyone except Anglo-Saxon Protestants."

Ryan laughed. "Yeah. He had his work cut out for him."

"And he seemed to think just because we're on the border...."

"The whole town was crawling with drug lords. You wonder why people like that don't move somewhere else."

Instead of hanging around magnifying their resentment.

In my brief stay at Los Mareados, I'd met only two residents—Mrs. Pirtle and Mr. Bigelow—both disagreeable

119

bigots best I could tell. Probably a good thing I was moving out, in case it was something catching.

* * *

After we returned to Ryan's, he set my suitcase in the bedroom and went to put away the food while I changed into denim shorts and shirt. He had started fixing breakfast when I joined him.

I set the table, and poured coffee. We'd just sat down when the phone rang. "It's Amá," Ryan said. "Let the machine get it." The answering machine was in the bedroom, and we couldn't distinguish the words from where we were sitting.

The phone rang twice more while we were eating. I hid a smile. "You're sure you don't want a cell phone?"

"Come on, let's see what it's all about."

I sat on the edge of the bed while he rewound the tape. Mrs. Salazar spoke in Spanish. "Mijo, I hope you haven't forgotten about coming over for dinner tonight. You can bring that girl if you want to." Click.

Ryan turned red. Before he could say anything, the second message started. This time it was Mr. Salazar, brief and to the point. "Mijo, Sharon is more than welcome." Click.

The third message was from Alana. "Dammit, Ryan, She's doing it otra vez. We didn't forget nada. Beto and I have already made plans. Do whatever you want." Slam.

"Whatever I want.... What do I want? Sharon, let's run away."

"South Padre?"

"Mustang Island."

"You're serious, aren't you!"

"I really need to get away from here. At least for a couple of days." He smiled playfully. "We can spend the whole weekend making love."

"I'm ready. I'm even packed. Why don't you call your mom and take a rain check or something?"

"Will you go there with me if I take a rain check?"

My eyes glazed over.

Ryan put his hand under my chin and kissed me on the forehead. "I'll take that as a 'yes.'"

He dialed his mother. "Sorry, Amá. I'm busy all weekend." He winked at me. I could hear what sounded like chipmunks chattering at the other end of the wire. "Okay, Tuesday."

"What about Spot?" I asked Ryan after he'd hung up.

"I'll call Alana. Carlos thinks Spot is half his anyway, so he'll either take care of him here or bring him to their house."

Carlos answered the phone, so the call took awhile. I smiled watching Ryan's face as he talked to his nephew. It was plain he was enjoying the conversation. "Carlos wants to know if you've had a chance to use your karate yet," Ryan said, his hand covering the mouthpiece.

"Tell him I took down a wall just this morning."

Ryan finished the call and threw a few things together. We left before the phone could ring again.

CHAPTER 22

We took Highway 16 to Hebbronville, where we'd change highways several times before arriving in Port Aransas.

"It's hard to believe I was down this road less than a week ago on my way to Zapata," I said.

Ryan gave me a puzzled look. "You didn't go through Laredo?"

"I like this way better. Not so much traffic."

We were waved through the border patrol checkpoint just outside Hebbronville.

I shivered. "I don't know why those always make me so nervous."

"They usually know what they're looking for."

"Well, I usually seem to be in the tenth car, or whichever one they've picked to check at random."

"That's happened to me a couple of times." He looked at me, then out the window.

I swallowed past a small lump in my throat. "I've seen them stop vans...."

Ryan reached over and took my hand. "I know."

We were both quiet as we drove through Hebbronville, and I had a feeling we were both remembering the same thing. "Ryan, do you ever think about...?"

"About when we worked the onion fields?" he finished my question. "That changed all of us. Look where we are now."

"It's ironic—I used to feel guilty for getting us all in trouble."

"You didn't get us in trouble. We got ourselves in trouble."

"I know. And I finally appreciated what we went through. But at the time...."

* * *

The second semester of eighth grade, I was thrown into classes with a kid who seemed to take a dislike to me for no other reason except that I was blonde. He kept making snide remarks about "la gringa," with a few choice adjectives thrown in. I ignored him till one day he confronted me in the hall between classes, and my reflexes kicked in. I think those few minutes are seared into my brain.

"At least I'm not a scumbag wetback like you, Nestor!" I yelled at him.

Erica was yelling right beside me. "Go back where you come from, wetback!"

A small crowd quickly gathered in the hall. I'm not sure they were necessarily on my side, but they were definitely not on Nestor's. Everyone knew he was a bully, and everyone knew his mother—who worked long hours scrubbing floors—had never gotten her green card.

More words were exchanged. The next thing I knew, Ryan punched Nestor in the nose. Nestor punched back. Things probably would have gotten worse if the principal hadn't stepped in. He called all the parents involved—including Aunt Amanda of course—and we were suspended for five days.

Aunt Amanda turned to Erica's parents in frustration. Mrs. Montoya didn't say anything, but the disappointment in her eyes crushed us. She called Erica's father at his law office, and he came home right away. I can still see the controlled pain and anger in Mr. Montoya's face when he called us into the den to discuss what had happened. I had never seen him angry before.

"You are never *never* to call people names."

"But Papi, Nestor called Sharon names."

"He is not my concern. You girls are. When you call names, you demean yourselves." He paused a moment. "I don't think you even know what you're saying. What is a wetback?"

We both stared at the floor. Finally Erica spoke. "Mr. Bigelow says it's someone who comes over here from across the river, and takes all the good jobs away from hard-working Americans."

Mr. Montoya's eyes blazed. "'Good jobs.' Do you think Nestor's mother has a good job, one she stole from hard-working Americans?"

By then Erica and I were both in tears.

After much discussion and many phone calls, the Montoyas and Aunt Amanda sat us down again. "There's something you will understand only if you experience it," Mr. Montoya said. "Today is Friday. Beginning Monday, you will both work in the onion fields for a week. This time of year, they always need extra workers."

The onion fields! Erica and I were horrified.

"Papi, it's cruel! What will people think?"

"That's enough, Erica," Mrs. Montoya spoke in her gentle way. "We hope this will change the way *you* think. Do you think it's all right for life to be difficult for other people while you have everything?"

Mrs. Montoya turned to me, her dark eyes soft and kind. "Sharon, your mother feels as we do. We are not trying to be cruel. Just the opposite. We are hoping you will learn compassion. Do you understand?"

"Yes, nina."

But I didn't understand. I thought it should be punishment enough that I felt so guilty and miserable.

Sunday morning after Mass, Ryan came up and apologized to Mr. Montoya, saying he was the only one to blame. "Don't punish Sharon and Erica. I'll do the onions."

Stricken, I tugged at Mr. Montoya's hand, trying to pull him away from Ryan, hoping to get him to listen to me instead.

"It wasn't Ryan's fault. And not Erica's either." Tears began sliding down my face and it was all I could do to keep from crying out loud. "It was all my fault. Nobody else's."

Mr. Montoya put his arm around my shoulders and handed me his handkerchief. "We need to talk about this some more."

That afternoon there was another session in the Montoyas' den. This time Ryan, Leo, and their parents were there. We sat in a square. Erica and I were on the loveseat, holding hands as if we were holding each other up. Across from us on one section of a large sofa were the boys. At right angles on the other section were Mr. and Mrs. Salazar. Facing them were the Montoyas and Aunt Amanda, each sitting in an armchair.

Mr. Montoya looked first at Ryan, then at me. "I'm proud of you for accepting the responsibility of what happened. But this isn't about blame. And it's not about punishment."

Erica's mother looked at the Salazars and said in her soft musical voice, "We feel we've sheltered the girls too much. And this was a decision we made concerning only the two of them. We hadn't intended it to go further."

I stole a glance at Ryan and could see that stubborn look come over his face.

"I understand," Mr. Salazar said. "But this is something the boys volunteered to do."

Mrs. Salazar still didn't get it. "Leo wasn't even there. Why is he going too?" Leo, who was joining us out of loyalty to Ryan, or to Erica, or maybe to all of us.

The Montoyas exchanged glances, and Mrs. Montoya tried again. "We are not punishing anyone for anything. And whatever your boys do is your decision."

"And theirs," said Mr. Salazar, ending the discussion.

And so the four of us—"The Four Musketeers"—worked in the onion fields for a week.

None of us had any idea how hard the work would be. The March sun was intense. By midday, the temperature was usually around 100, and the humidity up as well. To keep from getting sunburned we had to keep our skin covered, and our long-sleeved shirts made us feel even hotter and stickier.

We'd been warned not to rub our eyes after handling the onions, so we wrapped large bandanas around our heads to keep the sweat from streaming into our eyes. By the end of each day, we were grimy and sweaty, our backs and knees ached from bending over the rows of onions, our hands felt cramped and raw from pulling and clipping them one by one.

To his credit, Mr. Montoya worked side by side with us. Every day I expected him to go back to his air-conditioned office, but he never did. He saw to it that we took occasional breaks and drank plenty of water. But then we had to use the smelly outhouses, and that was almost worse than being thirsty. I couldn't wait to take long soapy showers as soon as we got home.

Although Mrs. Montoya obviously had second thoughts, she never voiced them. Instead she hovered over us constantly. Before we left each morning, even though we were well covered, she insisted we wear plenty of sunscreen—especially me with my fair skin. Every evening she had hearty meals waiting for us, as Mrs. Salazar did for Ryan and Leo.

Mrs. Montoya always invited Aunt Amanda, who reciprocated by having the Montoyas over for ice-cream afterwards. Sometimes I was too exhausted even to finish dinner, too exhausted to do anything but fall into bed.

I didn't cry though. I saw children younger than I working in the fields, and they never cried.

CHAPTER 23

Ryan pulled into Chente's Nifties Fifties in Alice for lunch, bringing me back to the present. We went into the restaurant, choosing a booth where we could sit side by side. While waiting for our order, Ryan said, "You're so quiet. What are you thinking about?"

"The onion fields. A lot of things. Ryan, I never would have stuck it out without you—if you hadn't been there with me. That first night—well, now that I look back on it, I guess it was pretty funny."

"Funny? Tell me."

"I fell asleep right there at the Montoyas' dinner table. The next thing I knew, my face was in my plate of spaghetti."

"I'm sorry I missed that."

I punched him lightly in the ribs.

"Ouch. Then what?"

"Then Mr. Montoya picked me up and carried me home."

"Did you yell at him to put you down, that you knew karate?"

"If you're not nice, I'm not going to talk to you any more."

"I'm always nice. I want to hear the part about how you can't live without me."

"Don't rush me. Don't you want to hear the part about how Aunt Amanda washed the noodles out of my hair?"

"Another Kodak moment."

I poked him again. "Anyway, if I hadn't set the alarm, Aunt Amanda wouldn't have made me get up because Mr. Montoya told her I could stay home."

Ryan stared at me in surprise. "You could have backed out?"

"That's what he said."

"Well, you probably scared the hell out of him."

"The noodles-in-the-hair look?"

"You know what I mean."

"I know. But there was no way I was going to stay home with the rest of you out there—especially you. It was part guilt and part—I don't know—part stubbornness."

"Determination?"

The waiter brought our cheeseburgers and malts, which we enjoyed as we continued our conversation.

"You're full of surprises, you know that?" Ryan said. "I never knew you had a choice about working the onion fields."

"I think Mr. Montoya was surprised too—surprised to see me come back. What surprised me was when a couple of Erica's brothers showed up."

"I think the only reason they came was so they could spy on us."

I laughed. "Yeah, right."

"And all for nothing. I barely had the energy to prop you up when you fell asleep on the way home."

"I thought it was the other way around."

"Maybe a little of both. Remember riding home in the back of Erica's uncle's pickup?"

By now we were both laughing.

"How could I ever forget?" I said.

"And how could I ever forget you, Sharon? Every time I smell Coppertone, I think of you."

"Looks like this expensive perfume is going to waste."

He put his arm around me and kissed me on the cheek. "Never."

We finished our meal and left the restaurant, my thoughts still on the impact working in the onion fields had made on us. "Those days are never far from my mind," I told Ryan as we fastened our seat-belts and started out again.

"I know. After all this time, it's good to find something to laugh about."

"I've never talked about all this to anyone else."

"Neither have I. How can you explain it? I think that's what Mr. Montoya was trying to tell us."

"The closest I came to telling anyone was my best friend in Minnesota—I did have a friend there, believe it or not. Her name was Katri. We were going to drop out of school the spring of our sophomore year and run away to her uncle's farm in Michigan to pick cherries."

"What changed your mind?"

"Besides the fact that it was the wrong time of year, and her uncle didn't even invite us?"

Ryan chuckled. "You mean there's more?"

I smiled. "I made this passionate—if uninformed—appeal to my stepfather. I told him Mr. Montoya would *want* me to do something like this. My stepfather was a very wise man. Didn't argue, simply said maybe it would be a good idea to call and talk it over with him first."

"This was after they'd moved?"

"Shortly after. First Erica got on the phone. She told me she hated California, that there were no cute boys in the entire state of, and that she'd go to Michigan with Katri and me if I'd tell her how to get there."

Ryan laughed. "Poor Erica."

130

"Then her mom got on the phone and told me she loved me and she always prayed for me. That really got to me. I loved her more than my own mother, and I hadn't realized how much I missed her."

Ryan took my hand and didn't say anything.

"When it was Mr. Montoya's turn, he was very persuasive, telling me I could help people more if I'd quit ditching school and get a good education instead. Then Erica's brothers got on the phone one by one—Larry and Alex were home on spring break—and Larry said since I had such a smart mouth, maybe I should consider being a lawyer."

"Sounds like you were pretty tough."

"I tried. That's what I wanted everyone to think."

And suddenly, remembering how untough and unhappy I'd really been, I was surprised to feel those emotions resurface. I looked out the window, pretending to study the scenery, which was a little blurry.

"You okay?"

I nodded. He linked his fingers through mine, and we drove without saying much till I turned on the radio, found an "oldies" station, and began singing along.

"I can't believe we're hearing 'Journey' on old-folks' radio," Ryan groaned.

"Be quiet and sing."

"Make up your mind."

We sang along with the radio for a while, and soon found ourselves in a lighter mood. It was mid-afternoon when we circled north of Corpus, then crossed the ferry into Port Aransas and arrived at our hotel.

Ryan caught a glimpse of himself in the mirror in the foyer while we waited for the elevator. "Good god, Sharon, why didn't you tell me I forgot to shave?"

"I thought that might be your weekend persona."

"Only when the moon is full."

When we got to our room, he started to kiss me, then said, "I don't want to sandpaper you."

I kissed him anyway. "You're right. Go shave."

"Give me five minutes."

I realized I could put those five minutes to good use myself. I went to the desk and pulled out some hotel stationery. A few nagging thoughts lurked in the back of my mind, and I wanted to pin them down so I could forget about them for the rest of the weekend. I wrote hurriedly, randomly, hoping I'd be able to decipher my handwriting later.

It hurt my feelings more than I wanted to admit that Mrs. Salazar seemed so antagonistic toward me. Although she'd always been rather overbearing, she'd also been friendly to me up till now, and I'd never had any reason not to like her. Besides, I'd never known her to be spiteful, to me or to anyone else.

So when we were at Leo's the other night, why had she brought up Ryan's suspension back in junior high, and my part in it? Alana had told Erica and me over lunch yesterday that Ryan had earned a master's degree in secondary education, graduating with top honors. Missing a few days of school in eighth grade hardly seemed worth getting in a tizzy over.

And Mrs. Salazar's "invitation" for me to join them for dinner was certainly less than gracious. I could only hope her attitude was less personal than it appeared. I jotted down, "What's bothering Mrs. S?"

On the way here Ryan had suggested that working so closely with the migrant workers had led us all to where we are now. Meaning, I suppose, our choice of careers. "All of us," he'd said. With Leo, the effect was certainly less obvious.

I wrote, "Why did Leo go into banking? What access does he have to customers' accounts?" I didn't want to connect the dots—but drugs do cost a lot of money.

I almost x'd that out. Leo had always been my buddy, and I had a deep affection for him. I couldn't bear to think he'd be involved in something corrupt. But it was hard to believe Laura had been caught up in drugs either. They'd both changed, in ways I couldn't grasp.

"Did Laura commit suicide after all?" Much as I wanted to think the worst of Bernice, now that I was thinking more clearly I found it hard to believe she'd poisoned Laura. Blackmailers don't usually get rid of their victims.

"Could someone else have murdered Laura? Who? Why? How?"

And back to Bernice....Despite Alana's denial, there was still some connection between Bernice and all the Salazars. I was more convinced than ever that Laura was only a small part of a much larger puzzle.

Another thought crossed my mind. "Did Laura have something on Bernice?" Interesting speculation.

No time now to speculate. I folded the paper and stuck it in my purse. I suddenly remembered that the green pill I'd taken from Alana's medicine cabinet was still in the zippered compartment. Maybe I should throw it away. Maybe later.

CHAPTER 24

The night air was cool and breezy, so after dinner we changed into warmer clothes and took a long walk on the beach. There was something mystical about walking on the moonlit sand, with no sound around us but the pounding of the waves, the rhythm of the surf. I felt connected not only to Ryan but to the whole universe.

Later, back in our room, I was about to take off my earrings when Ryan came up behind me and put his arms around me. Seeing his face suddenly appear in the dresser mirror made me jump.

"Sorry," he said, stepping back. "I didn't mean to scare you."

"And I didn't mean to scare you away." I smiled at the reflection of the face I loved so well, and felt a sense of calm come over me. "You're good for me," I said. *And someday I'll explain*, I thought as I loosened one earring.

He moved closer again, watching my reflection. "Sharon, I've been wondering, when did you move back to San Antonio?"

My hands stopped in mid-air. I looked down at the dresser and slowly laid down the earring. "My senior year in high school. My stepfather promised if I kept up my grades my junior year, he'd let me board at St. Mary's. That's where I'd gone to grade school."

Ryan turned me toward him without saying anything more until I returned his gaze. "I knew you'd gone to law school in Houston. When I saw the article in the paper, I even tried to call. But you weren't listed. I figured you'd moved—maybe even gone back to Minnesota."

"No, I only went to Houston because of a scholarship. I always knew I'd come back to San Antonio. I feel sad that we missed connections."

I felt like crying. Instead, I closed my mind to "what ifs" and changed the subject. "Strange coincidence. My mother had always told me my father's family didn't want anything to do with me, but that wasn't true. There was a tiny article in the business section of the San Antonio paper when I joined MacDougal and Martínez, and my grandmother found me again."

"You had family there you didn't even know about?"

"Right. I'm so thankful now I had a chance to know her. She was such a dear. She had a heart condition and didn't live much longer. I guess my father really was—well, anyway, he'd fled to greener pastures. My grandmother had one of those old Victorian houses near downtown. She left it to me, and it has a lot of history for me that I'm still getting to know.

"I can understand why it's home, but—close as you are to Zapata—how come you never came back before now?"

Foolish pride. Hard to face up to, even now. "I didn't think I had any reason to. The Montoyas moved to California not long after Erica's quinceañera. Aunt Amanda had moved down to Falfurrias. And you—you'd moved on with your life. Me too, I guess. After that, the only person in Zapata I kept in touch with was Laura, and that fizzled out before long."

Ryan looked away, and I couldn't read his expression. "You still kept up with Erica?" he asked.

"Oh gosh, yes. Up until law school. Then I had my nose to the grindstone, and she was just as busy in her own career. I think we both became workaholics without realizing it.

We'd dash off a note to each other from time to time—mostly at Christmas—but up till now, I hadn't seen her since the family came down to San Antone for my swearing-in."

He thought a minute, then, "How come you lost touch with Laura?"

"We just...you know, it's odd. I'd never really analyzed it. Laura was sweet, but she was also hard to pin down. Her letters never said anything, if you know what I mean. She was fine. Her folks were fine. Abuelita was fine. The weather was fine. School was fine.... We just didn't seem to have anything to talk about anymore."

"Good ole Laura. Everything fine."

There was a trace of bitterness in his voice that I couldn't comprehend. However briefly, she *had* been his sister-in-law, and it seemed he should have some affection for her. Besides, we'd all been friends growing up. I wondered what had happened to cause a rift between them. If that's what it was.

I probably should have shut up while I was ahead, but my curiosity got the better of me. "Erica and I were both surprised to find out Laura had married Leo. When did they get together?"

Like an iron door clanging shut, a mask slid across Ryan's face. I thought of a bumper sticker I'd seen when I was a kid: "Make love, not war." Maybe I should have that tattooed on the inside of my eyelids. We hadn't come to Mustang Island to make war.

"Never mind," I said. I touched his cheek and kissed him softly. "Don't go away. I'm sorry I mentioned it."

Ryan sat on the bed and pulled me onto his lap. "I'm not going anywhere."

I put my arms around his neck and was glad to see the warmth return to his eyes.

"I'm glad Erica got you back here." Ryan brushed my hair from my face, still looking steadily into my eyes. "I didn't think I'd ever see you again."

This time I was the one who looked away. He gently turned my face toward his again.

I tried to keep my voice light. "I was afraid I *would* see you—married to what's-her-face, with a bunch of kids."

A teasing look touched his eyes. "Well, I have a bunch of kids all right—about 150 of them. And that's this year alone."

I smiled. "I think I can handle that. But since we're on the subject, something I've been wondering. How it is I could just 'waltz into town'—as Alana puts it—and find you...unattached."

"I might ask you the same thing. How come, when I was...unattached...you just happened to 'waltz back into my life?'"

"You're not being fair. You ask questions, but you won't answer any."

"Okay, I'll go first. But before this conversation goes any further, I want you to know something."

I traced the line of his face and waited.

He looked at me intently. "Sharon, I'm not going to tell you I've never loved anyone but you. But I've never loved anyone as deeply as you. I feel I've loved you all my life, or as far back as I can remember."

"Maybe that's all I need to know."

"Maybe. But you also have a right to know. I was married once—a long time ago, and for a very short time. We were in college. I thought I was in love. We eloped—went up to Vegas. Disappointed Amá of course. Not that it mattered in the long run."

"What happened?"

"Well, after about six months, I found out she was cheating on me—had been even before our so-called marriage."

I felt such a strange mixture of emotions. How could I be glad Ryan wasn't still married, and at the same time feel so angry that someone had treated him that way? "You didn't deserve that."

"It killed any feeling I'd ever had for her. After that I guess I was leery of getting involved in serious relationships with anyone else. Until you waltzed into town. End of story. No. Beginning of story, I hope."

"Me too."

He moved me off his lap and lay down on his back, his arms behind his head. "Now it's your turn."

I lay on my stomach next to him, propped up on my elbows, my face in my hands. I was quiet for a few moments, then, "I was luckier than you. A few years ago I met 'Mr. Wrong.' We were supposedly engaged, but I found out he was cheating *before* we made it to the altar."

"What a jerk."

I smiled. "Bingo. I think I felt the way you must have felt. He simply wasn't the person I thought he was. So much for him. I'd rather think about you and me."

"Yo también. I still can't believe you lived so close by, and I never knew."

"It hurts me to think I was never planning to come back here."

He turned and put his arms around me. "Sharon," he whispered. "Sharon, the last time you were here—at Erica's quinceañera. Did you think you were the only one who hurt?"

I closed my eyes, shutting away tears. "Now I feel ashamed. You looked happy enough, and I just didn't know what to say—didn't know how to handle my own feelings."

"You looked so beautiful and so sure of yourself."

"If you only knew. I felt so the opposite."

"It looked to me like you were having the time of your life—flirting with all those college guys."

I pulled away, laughing. "Those guys, right. Think about it, Ryan. They were Erica's brother's friends. How safe could I be? But," I added mischievously, "I did have fun with them. I mean I had to have *some* fun there."

He propped himself up on one elbow. "I heard you had fun with Leo."

"Really!" I sat up and hugged my knees to my chest.

"You sure blush easy," Ryan teased, sitting up next to me. "And I was sure jealous when I heard he'd kissed you."

Even though I knew Ryan was teasing, it made me uncomfortable. "It wasn't anything to lose sleep over."

"That's what Leo said. I hope this won't hurt your ego, but he said it was about as exciting as kissing our sister."

I laughed again. "I think he exaggerated—I think it was even less exciting than that. I'm surprised he said anything at all."

Ryan's face hardened. "He wouldn't have, if Bernice hadn't said something first."

"Oh great. What a mess. She misinterpreted something Leo and I wanted her to misinterpret. I guess it backfired on us. Dumb, dumb, dumb. What did she have to say?"

"That you were trying to get back at me by...how shall I put it?"

"Never mind." I turned even redder. "I know her vocabulary. I trust you know me better than that."

139

"I knew she was lying. And I told her so. But I knew *something* had happened, so I asked Leo."

"What did he say?"

"He only had three things—no, four—to tell me. One, you two were trying to make her think something happened, but nothing did—something along those lines. Two, that you still loved me. Three, that if I thought you would hurt me, I was even stupider than he thought I was, and four, that was pretty stupid. He repeated #4 several times."

"Well, that must have made a hit."

"It started a big fight. One of the few times in our life we ever fought. But there was no way I could win against him. So after a few minutes he quit beating up on me. I think he knew I was just mad at myself."

I put my arms around Ryan again. "He was right about a couple of things. I was still in love with you. And I'd never hurt you. As for the rest, I probably wouldn't have even run into Leo if I hadn't gotten tired of trying not to look at you and Mindy."

"I think he was right about me being stupid too. I wanted more than anything to talk to you, but...."

I smiled at him. "I know. You probably felt as awkward as I did. I know you liked Mindy. And it wouldn't have been like you to leave her stranded."

"Leo thought that's exactly what I should have done. I found out later that she'd gone out with me just to make someone else jealous. If I'd known then what I know now."

"And what do you know now?"

He kissed me, then slid his hand under my sweater. "I thought you'd never ask."

CHAPTER 25

After Ryan fell asleep, I lay awake in the comfort of his arms, thinking back on the memories I'd tried so hard to hide from myself. Maybe by now they'd turn out to be only harmless ghosts.

I'd been so excited about coming to Zapata for Erica's quinceañera the January of our sophomore year. My stepfather, who understood how much this meant to me, had even paid for my round-trip ticket from Minneapolis.

In the time since Erica and I had last seen each other, we'd gotten curvier and had also gotten rid of our braces. We both had long hair now. I'd gotten a perm to de-curl mine so that it hung in soft waves just below my shoulders.

"You look so gorgeous!" Erica said, her eyes shining. I knew she meant it even though it wasn't technically accurate. I considered myself average, but her praise made me feel as pretty as she thought I was.

I hugged Erica. "You're the one who's gorgeous. I'm so happy I'm here! I wouldn't have missed this for anything!"

Seeing the open door, Erica's brother Javier came into her room while we were doing our nails. He put his hand on the back of my neck and gave it a quick hard squeeze. "If I'd known you were going to turn out cute, I'd have asked you to the dance."

"Gee, thanks," I said as I considered jabbing him with the emery board. Javier was only a year older than Erica and I were, and it was hard not to think of him as the pest he'd always been. But he'd gotten cuter too, so I had to laugh at our mutual surprise at the changes in us.

"That's a compliment," Erica said. "I'd wanted Javier to invite Laura, but he flatly refused."

"Laura's weird," Javier said, making a sappy face.

Erica twirled the brush in the bottle of nail polish and wrinkled her nose at him. "Like you're such a prize."

Erica had offered to arrange a date for me too, but I didn't want to spend the evening paired up with someone who probably wouldn't even remember me from eighth grade.

"How come Laura isn't making her quinceañera?" I asked.

"Her best friend won't be 15 till June—you remember Yvette. Anyway, Laura wanted to wait so they could have it at the same time. Laura was hoping to see you, but her family decided to go out of town a couple of days ago."

"Yvette's weird too," Javier put in.

Erica blew on her nails and rolled her eyes. "Javier, go play with your Tonka trucks."

They exchanged a few more insults till Javier got tired of bugging us and went off to join his brothers.

For a brief moment I envied Laura and Yvette making their quinceañera together, wishing I could be making mine with Erica. Fifteenth birthdays weren't a big deal up north.

But the moment quickly passed. There was too much excitement in the Montoya household not to get caught up in it. Erica's two oldest brothers had come down from the University of Texas for the occasion, and Larry had brought three of his buddies with him. I think they'd been assigned the job of making sure I didn't get overlooked in the hubbub, which was fine with me.

I'd had a small crush on Larry when he was eighteen and a senior in high school. I was in seventh grade then, waiting for the boys our age to quit acting so squirrely. Now Larry was a junior at the University and, like all the Montoyas, had more than his share of good looks. His buddies weren't bad-looking either.

The Mass was lovely, and everything hummed along beautifully until the dance at the Elks Club that evening. We were wearing dresses with scoop necklines as low as Mrs. Montoya would allow, and feeling pretty full of ourselves. While Erica and the other honorees lined up for more pictures, Larry came over and stood beside me.

I smiled at him, pleased by his attention, then looked across the room and was faced with the sight of Ryan arm in arm with Mindy Torres. Erica had already told me Ryan was going with Mindy, and since I was going with someone in Minnesota, I thought I could handle it. But hearing about it and seeing them together were two totally different things.

The pain must have shown in my face, because Larry took my hand and said gently but firmly, "You'd better act cheerful. Don't spoil this day for Erica."

I looked over at Erica and thought how much I loved her, and I nodded, barely able to talk over the lump in my throat. "Okay," I croaked, smiling a big fake smile.

"Come on, dance with me. They're playing something slow. Even you can keep up."

Larry was a good dancer, and I found myself relaxing.

"Do the boys up north all tell you how pretty you are?" he asked.

I started to glare at him for saying something so corny, until I looked him in the eye and saw that he was teasing me. I laughed with him. "No, never."

He pretended to look shocked. "No! What's the matter with those northern guys? Are they all snow blind?"

"Let me explain. They're all blond like me, and we all look exactly alike. Like clones. I lived up there a whole year before I could tell any of us apart."

"No kidding! You can't even tell the boys from the girls?"

"Nope. Boys, girls, old people, young people, cats, dogs— all alike. It's scary."

"But you found a boyfriend."

"Well, the sun comes out one day a year, and everyone sheds their parkas on that day, and—what can I say?"

"That must be one fun day."

"What about you? How come your girlfriend didn't come with you?"

He looked away. "Oh, she had an exam coming up. Couldn't make it down here."

I stopped dancing and put my hands on my hips. "If she couldn't come with you for your sister's quinceañera, she's not good enough for you!"

"You've really gotten mouthy, haven't you."

I turned red. "I'm sorry. I didn't mean to be rude."

"It's okay. It's nice that someone thinks I'm so deserving," he said in a half-mocking tone.

"Well, you are."

The music stopped, and we walked over to the punch fountain where Larry's friends had gathered. Erica and her boyfriend joined us, both looking starry-eyed. Erica hugged me for the umpteenth time. "I'm so glad you're here. Have you seen Leo yet? He asked about you."

"I'd like to see him." *I don't want to see Ryan. Please don't ask about Ryan.*

Erica continued chattering and beaming. "I don't mean to neglect you...."

"You're not neglecting me, and I'm having fun." Which was partly true. I was happy for Erica, and I also enjoyed dancing and flirting with Larry and his friends. This lasted until I caught another glimpse of Ryan and Mindy slow-dancing together and decided I needed to take a break from being cheerful.

I went out the side door to the courtyard, the immediate area bathed in bright light. Standing nearby and smoking cigarettes were Leo and some of his football buddies. A couple of months ago, they had dyed their hair burgundy, which their irate coach had insisted they shave off. Now they all had burgundy-tinged crew cuts.

They were all husky and broad-shouldered, with necks too thick for their dress shirts. They'd taken off their ties and loosened the collars of their shirts, looking unaccustomed to being out of their jerseys.

Leo turned and smiled at me. "Hey, Sharon."

"Hey, Leo. Can I have one of your cigarettes?"

"No. You can't have one of our cigarettes." He led me to a bench away from where he and his friends had been talking. "When did you start acting so tough?"

"When I moved up north I had to be tough to survive." My voice broke on the last word.

Leo didn't say anything.

"But I'm still a crybaby."

He laughed, a soft gentle laugh. The only things about Ryan and Leo that were identical were their voices and the way they both laughed. Which was a little disconcerting in the dark. He put his arm around me. "You can cry on my shoulder if you want to."

The tears I'd been holding back all night cascaded down my cheeks as I buried my face in his shoulder. "It was a mistake for me to come down here, Leo," I said between sobs. "I'd finally gotten used to living up there, and now that I'm here I wish everything was the way it used to be. I miss Ryan so much. I miss all of us—us four."

"I know. Sometimes I wish we could go back too." He sounded so downhearted, it made me stop crying and look up at him.

"What's going on with you, Leo?"

He took his arm from around my shoulder and leaned forward, his forearms resting on his thighs, and started cracking his knuckles.

"Girl trouble?"

He gave a short laugh. "Not now. We're in training."

"Right. That's why you guys are all smoking."

"You guys! What's this 'you guys' stuff? When did you start talking like a gangster?"

"Excuse me. Y'ALL. Is smoking part of y'all's training program?"

"Yeah. Minimum of two packs a day."

"And you won't even share one with me!"

Without warning I could feel Leo tense. "Can I borrow you a minute?" he asked. "Here comes The Queen Bitch. Act like we're making out."

I followed his line of vision and saw Bernice slithering toward us. Back then she wasn't bad-looking—probably would have been pretty if not for the sneer. "Hey, we can pretend anything you want as long as it irritates her."

He pulled me up and kissed me long and hard on the lips, running one hand through my hair. I didn't particularly like it—his kiss tasted of cigarette. Then to my further surprise, shy quiet Leo cupped his other hand under my breast. I didn't like that either. No one but Ryan had ever touched me—not even my so-called northern boyfriend. My eyes flew open, and Leo dropped his hand to my waist.

"Sorry," he whispered.

The whole thing would have ended right there if Bernice
had only kept her mouth shut. But that wasn't her style.
"Nice try, Sharon, but you're wasting your time," she said.
"Leo can't get it up."

I don't know if it was the remark itself, or the cruelty in
Bernice's voice; but something snapped. After recovering
from the initial shock, I returned Leo's kiss, then gave
Bernice a sidelong glance. "Maybe that's true for you,
Bernice," I said. "Frankly, I don't see how anyone could get
it up with you. But for me, well, all I can say is, Leo
definitely has what it takes."

"You're full of shit, Sharon. When did you figure out the
difference between girls and boys anyway? The fag twins
sure don't get it."

I put my arms around Leo's neck, my face pressed
against his, and whispered in his ear, "Leo, put your arms
around me, and go along with me, okay?"

He hesitated a moment, then held me close. I spoke
softly, but loud enough for Bernice to hear, "Sweetheart, mi
corazón, don't you think three times is enough? Maybe we
should stop for a while and go back inside."

After a few startled moments, shy quiet Leo fell right in
with me. "If you say so, mi vida, but did you remember to
put your panties back on?"

I nearly choked. "But, corazón, I don't know where they
are. Aren't they in your pocket?"

"No, mi vida, I gave them back to you."

By now I was holding onto Leo just to keep from
collapsing in a fit of giggles. I moved his arms away and
turned around with my back to him, then swept my hair up
from my neck in what I hoped resembled a provocative pose
I'd seen in a TV movie. "Corazón, would you see if I got my
bra hooked in the right place?"

Leo still had a few surprises. He suddenly unzipped my dress halfway down my back. "Omigod, mi vida, you lost that too!"

Then he zipped my dress up again and turned me around so we could lean on each other some more. By now we were both shaking with laughter.

And by now Bernice had had enough. "You're sick," she said, and strode away.

Leo and I let go of each other and were laughing so hard we literally doubled over. Leo caught his breath first, and said, "You're nuts."

"Me!"

"Come on. We should go back."

The closer we got to the door, the more my anxiety returned.

"Listen," Leo said, taking my hand, "I'll go in first and see where they are, then I'll take you in the opposite direction. What you can do is look down at the floor and pretend you're looking for all your underwear. Give you something to do."

Something to make me laugh instead of cry.

"Leo." I stopped and brought his hand to my face. "I'm glad you're my bud."

"Me too." He grinned and patted me on the head.

When we reached the lighted area by the door, Leo looked down at me and whispered, "You lost something for reals. Your lipstick is gone."

I looked up at him and said, "I think I found it."

"Your hair's a mess too. We'd better go in the front door by the restrooms."

I began dragging my feet. "I think I'll just go back to Erica's house."

"Don't be dumb. You'll look okay once you get fixed up."

I waited outside the restroom door while Leo retrieved my purse from the table where I'd left it, then went to see if I could do something to measure up to "okay." I dampened a paper towel and wiped my face with it, then splashed cold water into my eyes, mentally thanking some unknown ancestor that I'd never needed to use mascara. I reapplied my lipstick and scrounged around in my purse for some Lifesavers.

Actually, "mess" was probably one of the kinder words Leo could have chosen to describe my hair. The humidity had caused it to curl so that I looked like a blonde version of Shirley Temple gone berserk. I smoothed it down with dubious results.

By the time I emerged, Leo was already surrounded by a bevy of girls. He started toward me, but I smiled and shook my corkscrewed head. I figured he'd done his baby-sitting stint for the night. He winked at me then, and gave a slight nod toward the punch table. I hoped that meant to head in that direction.

Luck was with me—or maybe not. Larry and his friends were there, and Larry gave me a welcoming smile with a question mark in it. "We wondered where you'd disappeared."

"I was talking to Leo."

"Must have been a hilarious conversation. I saw you come in."

I blushed. "Don't worry. We didn't do anything we have to go to confession about."

Larry put his arm around me. "I don't know. Saint Erica keeps rearranging the rules to suit herself."

He changed the subject, and soon we were all talking and laughing again.

It didn't take Bernice long to spot us and invite herself over to join us. "So," she said. "Everybody's in such a good mood. Is she fucking all of you?"

For a few frozen moments, conversation came to a dead halt. I only hoped and prayed her voice hadn't carried any further.

Larry recovered first. "Party's over." He looked around for another of Erica's brothers, and motioned for him to come over. "Bernice must have spiked her own punch. She needs a ride home." The two of them guided Bernice out the door, while I stood glued in mortification. None of us knew what to say.

"Friend of yours?" one of Larry's buddies drawled, breaking the tension. "C'mon, let's dance."

Shake it off, Sharon. I smiled and walked with him to the dance floor. The second I looked over his shoulder I saw Ryan looking at me. It was the only time our eyes met all evening. Mindy might have been by his side, but he didn't look at her the way he looked at me. It was the one bright moment of that seemingly endless night.

CHAPTER 26

Recalling that night and how funny Leo and I thought we were, I wondered how we could have been so naïve. I suspected Erica's brothers had threatened Bernice with mayhem or worse if she said anything else against me, because apparently no stories got around.

Maybe she realized the only person who'd care was Ryan—she couldn't resist twisting the knife in him. But that hadn't worked either; Leo wouldn't let either Ryan or me get hurt. Except, of course, to beat Ryan up. I had to smile. It was hard for me to picture those two ever fighting.

With all the ghosts chased away, I soon fell asleep.

The next morning was overcast, so Ryan and I dressed in warm clothes again, then drove up to the Aransas Wildlife Refuge. I'd never seen a *live* armadillo, and there were whole families of them here. We laughed at one nosy little critter who waddled up to investigate Ryan's camera when he knelt to take its picture.

We had a picnic lunch, then took another walk on the beach before heading back to Zapata. Before going home we stopped at Alana's to pick up Spot. Alana greeted us with hugs. "Turn down the wattage, you two. You're blinding me."

"Can't." Ryan ruffled his sister's hair affectionately.

Beto joined us, smiling warmly. "You should know better, Corazón. 'Diós los crea....'"

Alana smiled back at him. "You and your *dichos*."

At my puzzled look, Beto explained, "It's an old Spanish proverb. 'God creates them; then leaves them to find each other.'"

Ryan pulled me closer, and the way he looked at me made my heart turn over. "I think we're found."

Carlos bounded in and gave us both bear hugs.

"Go look for Spot, mijo, and put him in his carrier," Alana said.

"He won't like that."

"Ándale."

Alana waited till Carlos was out of earshot. "I hate to rain on your parade—"

"Then don't," Ryan said.

I could sense some unnamed tension beneath Alana's lighthearted exterior. Beto put his arm around her and said, "Let's all go sit down." We went into the living room, where Ryan and I sat on the couch, while Alana and Beto drew up chairs facing us.

"I take it we're all going to Amá's for dinner Tuesday," Alana began.

I tried to look pleasant, as if this were something I looked forward to.

"Well, she decided to invite Erica too."

"Why?" Ryan looked about to explode.

Why not? I wondered. I hoped some explanation would emerge.

"I don't know. She's just gotten more and more irrational."

I'm not going to ask questions. I'm not going to ask questions. "What's so irrational about inviting Erica?"

Ryan and Alana exchanged looks, then Alana gave a vague wave of her hand. "Oh, Amá's just going through the change I think."

And I'm Mother Teresa.

Ryan saw the skepticism in my face. "Sharon's not stupid."

Beto agreed. "There are too many secrets. Maybe Sharon should know. She's not exactly an outsider."

Ryan shifted uncomfortably. "No she's not. But let's not throw everything at her at once."

She. Her. I felt like waving my hand. *Here I am, folks.*

Ryan held my hand before I could wave it.

"The whole thing is so awkward," Alana said. "I don't know where to begin. Maybe you already guessed from Amá's remarks the other night, but she didn't like Laura very much."

"Neither did I," Ryan mumbled.

Although their feelings came as no surprise, I still didn't know what lay behind them. Make love, not war, I reminded myself.

"Anyway," Alana continued, "I don't know if it's seeing you two together or what, but here Laura's hardly cold in her grave, and Amá seems to think maybe Leo and Erica...."

"Oh God." Ryan leaned his head against the back of the couch and closed his eyes.

"I agree it's premature, but so what?" I said. "It's not like she's planning a candlelight dinner for two."

"It's not that," Alana said. "It's just, well, she—I don't know—she runs hot and cold with Erica. It's not rational and it makes us all edgy. I know Erica's feelings were hurt at the wake, and I don't want that to happen again."

"Your mom always liked Erica."

"We all like Erica," Ryan interrupted.

"Then what's this 'hot and cold' business?"

This time it was Alana and Beto who exchanged looks. Beto took over. "Like Alana said, it's awkward. You know about Bernice."

I shivered involuntarily. "Only that she was blackmailing Laura."

"Blackmail involves money. Laura and Leo didn't have enough. So my father-in-law had been helping them pay Bernice to keep quiet."

"But that's extortion. That's...."

"Illegal?" Alana's voice was harsh. "I'm sure she liked the money, but what she enjoyed even more was tormenting us—threatening to humiliate us. It's a power thing."

"My mother-in-law doesn't know about any of this," Beto said.

"How could she not know?"

"Partly because she's in denial about a lot of things," Ryan said slowly. "And partly because we try to keep it from her."

Tears hovered on the edge of Alana's eyelashes. "But she started noticing their money disappearing, and that really unhinged her."

"Your poor mother."

Beto gave me a grateful glance. "Amá thinks he's seeing someone else, and it's driving her crazy."

"She's trying to figure out who it can be," Alana said, "and sometimes she suspects—oh, the most unlikely people."

Erica. The unlikeliest of all. I could imagine Erica arriving at the wake, drop-dead gorgeous, innocently hugging Mr. Salazar along with everyone else. But it would have been only her husband Mrs. Salazar would have noticed. And the rest of the family embarrassed, walking on eggs, hoping to avoid a scene.

"I see you get the picture," Alana said, reading my expression. "We've been trying to remind her Erica's the same Erica she's always loved. Mostly she's convinced, but she still vacillates. Problem is, when she's not wavering, she has this notion about getting Erica and Leo together again."

"What about your dad? Is your mom still upset about him?"

"He keeps reassuring her there's no one else, and I think deep down she knows that's true. But she knows *something* was going on, and it still bothers her sometimes."

"Didn't he offer any explanation about the money?"

"Something vague about a land deal he and my uncle wanted to get into," Alana said. "I think she wanted to believe him, but intuitively she knew it wasn't true. So all that did was stir up her doubts again."

"Wouldn't it be better just to tell her the truth?"

"The whole truth, and nothing but? That's asking a lot." Ryan stood up. "Let it go," he said in a tired voice. "I'm beat. Let's get Spot and go home."

"While we're airing our secrets." Alana looked at me as I stood to leave. "Have you told Ryan about Jeff?"

She'd completely blindsided me. I held out my hands in bewilderment. "Why on earth are you bringing this up now?"

"Who's Jeff?" Ryan asked.

"He's a very very good friend."

"Just a friend?"

"I hate it when people say '*just* a friend,' as if friends are somehow not valuable!" I snapped.

Ryan looked puzzled at my vehemence. "What set you off?"

"I don't like labeling people."

Ryan looked at Alana, who raised an eyebrow. Beto gave her a slight warning shake of his head.

This was the damnedest family. And where was Carlos with the cat? As if to answer my question, I saw him standing wide-eyed in the hall. I wondered how long he'd been there. Spot, glowering at us from inside his carrier, looked the way I felt.

I was suddenly ashamed. I didn't want Carlos upset. "Carlitos, come here. I'm sorry I'm so crabby. I'm just very tired." I knelt and held out my arms to him. "¿Abrazo?"

He came over and put his arms around my neck, holding on tight. "It's okay, nina."

We collected Spot and drove home, Spot yowling the whole way, neither Ryan nor I saying anything.

When we got inside, we turned loose an indignant Spot, who huffed off to his quarters without so much as a backward glance.

Ryan turned to me. "I'm sorry for whatever it was I said. I'll sleep on the couch if you want me to."

"I don't want you to sleep on the damn couch. And I don't want to sleep on it either."

He grinned, that slow easy grin of his. "Then you have to quit being mad at me."

"I'm not mad at you. I'm mad at your sister. And I'm not even mad at her. Just annoyed."

"Me too. She can be very annoying. Let's call and tell her so."

For some reason, maybe the complete lack of annoyance in his voice, his remarks made me laugh. "I'm sorry too. I shouldn't have jumped on you. I just felt—cornered. I don't mind telling you about Jeff either."

Ryan looked amused, as if he'd already figured it out. "Tell me."

"Jeff is exactly what I said—a very dear friend. And—it just dawned on me—it's really only myself I'm mad at."

"Don't be mad at you."

"Well I am. Because I feel disloyal 'explaining' Jeff. I never should have mentioned him in the first place, but once I did, Alana thought I was two-timing you or something. So I 'explained' him to her. I didn't think she'd make it sound like I was trying to hide something from you."

"I didn't think that. And I understand, Sharon. I don't like seeing people labeled any more than you do. And neither does Alana. I don't know why she brought it up the way she did. She's usually more direct. Maybe she felt disloyal blabbing our family secrets."

"Maybe so. Maybe she wanted me to see how it felt to be put on the spot."

"Speaking of Spot...."

"He's probably hungry. And so am I."

We had dinner and watched an old Hitchcock movie on TV. Spot, apparently having forgiven us, jumped on the couch between us again, and began purring happily. After a while we left him to watch TV alone, and found something better to do.

CHAPTER 27

I woke in the middle of the night to find Ryan shaking me by the shoulder. "You're talking in your sleep."

I was clutching the sheet to my throat, trying to focus. "I had a bad dream. It was.... Someone was.... What did I say?"

"You were mumbling mostly. Something about a razor and a mirror. And holding on to that sheet for dear life."

I sat up. "No more scary movies for me."

Ryan sat up and placed his hands over mine, gently unclenching them. "Are you sure that's all?"

I looked away. "I don't want to think about it right now."

"I'll get you some water."

"No! Don't leave!"

"I'm right here." He began massaging my shoulders, easing out the tension till I felt sleepy enough to lie down again.

The next thing I knew the alarm was going off.

* * *

We had breakfast together before Ryan left for school. I walked out to the car with him.

"What are you going to do all day?" he asked.

"I either have to do laundry again or go shopping. Or both."

He looked thoughtful. Finally he said, "You didn't pack much, did you."

"I didn't think I'd be in town long."

He was quiet a minute. "When do you have to go back?"

"I'm not sure. A week or so. I have some vacation time coming."

"And what then?"

"I guess that's up to us."

We stood looking at each other without speaking and without touching. The silence between us seemed very loud.

He kissed me gently. "Te quiero, Sharon." Then he got into the car and drove off.

Te quiero, Ryan.

* * *

I dumped some clothes into the washer and called Erica at Head Start. "Is this a bad time to call?"

"No, not at all. What's wrong?"

"You didn't tell me it would be so hard."

"I didn't tell you it would be easy either."

The thought crossed my mind that our verbal shorthand was as strong as ever. "I'm not handling this very well."

"I know. Look, they're doing such a great job here without me, I won't even be missed if I leave a little early. So why don't we go down to Rio Grande City and have lunch at Caro's. Then we can stop at the shrine, or take a walk at the State Park, whatever seems like a good idea. I'll hold your hand for a change. 11:00, 'K?"

The laundry done, I dressed in rust-colored turtleneck shell and slacks, then set up my laptop. Spot thought this was a wonderful new plaything and liked patting the keys. Between him and my erratic handwriting, I somehow managed to type up the notes I'd taken the other day.

I still had time on my hands, so I looked for something to read. Ryan had a lot of books on Texas and Civil War history, but I didn't feel like reading anything I'd have to concentrate on. Spot and I turned on TV instead and settled on a rerun of *Columbo*.

Before leaving, I left a hasty note: "Ryan, if you get back before I do, I'm with Erica. I love you. Sharon." I decided against underlining anything.

* * *

"Here's the plan," Erica said when I picked her up. "We'll stop at the shrine first, then go to Caro's, 'K?" Years ago, someone had built a grotto in Rio Grande City that was supposed to resemble the one at Lourdes. It was a peaceful place to go, easier and cheaper than flying to France, and there were no crowds or souvenir stands. No one else was there when we arrived.

I had thought I wouldn't cry, but I'd thought wrong. Erica put her arms around me without telling me to stop crying or offering any other useless advice.

I finally stopped sniveling and started babbling instead. "Erica, this morning I thought I couldn't bear leaving Ryan. I even turned over the idea of giving up my job, moving here—the whole bit. I'd just hang out all day, do a little laundry, watch some TV, meet Ryan at the door dressed in cellophane, or whatever those magazines suggest. I'd fetch his pipe and slippers and have candlelight dinners waiting. Whatever it took. And I knew I'd be in the nuthouse in a week."

"Damn. Ryan is going to be so disappointed! I'm sure he's been counting on you to be his sex slave!"

"Now I've got the hiccups."

"That's what happens when you laugh and cry at the same time."

I kept hiccupping.

"Or, you could try it the other way around. Have Ryan give up everything and move up to San Antonio. He could do the laundry and TV bit and be *your* sex slave."

"I like that idea better."

"Wonder if you could talk him into the cellophane stuff?"

Some other people had stopped to visit the shrine, and we decided to move on to Caro's so our laughter wouldn't disturb them.

I liked this unpretentious restaurant, tucked away on a side street, with good food and a cozy atmosphere. We ordered their puffy-taco specialty and began chatting again.

"Do you still go to Mass, Erica?"

"More often than not. Do you?"

"Not very often."

"I gave it up totally for a while. Had a problem with the rules, with my 'pick-and-choose' Catholicism. Still do. But then my mom dragged me off to a retreat with her, and I got a different slant on things. I shouldn't say she dragged me. But the only reason I went was to please her."

"What happened?"

"I was impressed with the spiritual director. He was more people-oriented than rule-oriented. In one of his talks, he made the remark that people who never question anything are brain dead. I thought that was a miracle in itself—that he'd even addressed the subject—since I was probably the only heretic there."

"Sounds like my kinda guy."

"You know something? I never question my mother's prayers anymore. I'm sure that priest was an answer to hers." Erica smiled. "She prays for you too, you know."

"I bet she turns to St. Jude whenever she prays for me."

"The patron of hopeless causes? Oh Sharon, you're so funny!"

"No, I'm serious," I said, but I was laughing too. "I bet she asks him to nudge *me* to a retreat. Get me back into the fold. She probably has him working overtime."

"Poor ole Jude. No time for anyone else."

"Erica." My mind skipped back to the notes I'd written up this morning. "I wonder why Leo went into banking. I mean, it's certainly a respectable profession and all that, but...I can't imagine feeling passionate about it."

"Sharon, what do you think he does? Sits behind a desk all day and counts money?"

"And tells people whether or not they can have any of it."

"You'd better watch out with those stereotypes! Who has a reputation for being heartless if not lawyers?"

"Touché. To tell you the truth, I wasn't really thinking about banking as much as about Leo. He just seems so out of sync with the rest of us. Something I can't quite grasp. Something that doesn't have anything to do with Laura."

Erica turned away, but not before I saw the pain in her face. "Things haven't been easy for Leo."

I touched her hand. "Whatever happened with you two?"

She stared off into space, with a trace of a smile. "We had a mutual falling out of love, or out of infatuation, or whatever it was. He broke it off and I was glad. It was time. I guess we're lucky—I think we became even better friends afterwards. Besides, I'd developed a big crush on Danny Maestas, and Leo—well, Leo was a big jock and there were always lots of girls flocking after him."

Despite the show we'd put on for Bernice, I'd always thought of Leo as rather bashful. I was sure being a 'big jock' wouldn't have gone to his head. "Anyone special?"

Erica shrugged. "Mm. Not really. I think he was always more comfortable with the girls who *weren't* chasing him."

"You still have a soft spot for him."

"I do, and that's a good way to describe it."

After lunch, I asked Erica if she'd mind shopping with me. I know some women consider this a form of female bonding, but to me shopping is strictly a necessary evil. Here's my method: Go into the store, find something I like, pay for it, leave. If this can be done in less than 10 minutes, great. If it can be done at Goodwill, where I find bargains on rich people's once-worn castoffs, so much the better.

We went to Beall's where I picked out some shorts sets and a flowered halter-style dress, cut high in front and low in back.

"You have a cute figure," Erica said. "You should pick out something to show it off."

"You don't like this?"

"Sure. It's pretty, and on you it still looks sexy, but...." She cocked her head, her eyes twinkling. "Try on something with a daring neckline. Not quite as revealing as cellophane, but, hmm, inviting."

"Forget it. I've already spent twelve minutes in this store. I'm two minutes over my limit and haven't even checked out."

"Oh Sharon." She shook her head in mock despair. "What am I going to do with you?" She sighed. "Oh well. If it looks good with the pipe and slippers, go ahead."

CHAPTER 28

I got home just before 3:30. Ryan wasn't there, but my note was gone. There was a short note in return: "Love you too." No name. Well, I assumed it was from either Ryan or Spot. I hung up my new dress, and put the other things into my suitcase. No point in feeling too permanent.

Ryan's phone rang, and I heard him say into the answering machine, "Sharon, if you're there, pick up."

"Hi. I'm here."

There was silence on the other end, then, "I'll be home in a minute." His voice sounded hollow, making me uneasy. I wondered why he'd called if he was going to be home so soon anyway.

Ryan arrived a few minutes later, his face drawn. What was wrong? I felt a wave of sympathy for Tina, dithering around trying to fix everything. What can I do? Would you like a drink? Some tamales from Mrs. Ortega? Your pipe and slippers? Oh that's right, you don't smoke.

While Ryan was changing clothes, I went over to look out the sliding glass door at the patio, the bluebonnets popping up randomly along the edge of the grass, the walls bright with deep purple bougainvillea. Spot joined me to watch the green jays.

A few minutes later, Ryan came over and stood beside me, but he seemed distracted. He turned and went into the kitchen, then came back into the living room and sat on the couch. I could hear the pop of the lid on the Tecate.

He was leaning back holding the beer can on one knee, staring straight ahead. He patted the cushion beside him, and I sat next to him. I reached for his hand, and he held on as if I'd offered him a lifeline. Neither of us had spoken since he first came in. I waited.

"One of the girls at school—Teresa Gabaldón," Ryan began at last. "Not long ago I noticed bruises all over her pretty little face. She said she'd fallen down, but I didn't believe her. So I reported it. They checked out her home but didn't find anything."

"One of your students?"

"No, but I knew who she was."

"Did any of her other teachers report it?"

"Yeah. But we were looking in the wrong place. It wasn't her family. It was her slimeball boyfriend."

"What happened?"

"He beat her up. Right now she's in Mercy Hospital in Laredo."

I flinched, and he held my hand even tighter. I covered my chest with my other hand, as if that could somehow shield Teresa from the violence.

"I should have done something—should have talked to her more. Followed through somehow."

I knew that feeling too well, and knew it would take Ryan time to quit blaming himself for things that were beyond his control. I was quiet for a while.

"Ryan, more than once I've wanted to chuck it all. Get a job scrubbing floors so I'd never let anyone down, never overlook anything, never see anyone slip through the cracks. I don't turn in my resignation as often as I used to. It never worked anyway. Mac would come in and stand in front of my desk and make a big production of shredding my letter into little pieces. Then he'd say—and he has this big booming voice—he'd say, 'Goddammit, Sharon, you're not the Messiah!'"

A smile touched Ryan's face briefly, then faded. He brought my hand to his lips, then pressed it against his cheek. "All day I've wanted to hear your voice, Sharon."

"I wish you'd called."

"I came by for a few minutes about noon and got your note, so I figured you'd probably be gone most of the day."

"Oh Ryan, I wish I'd been here!"

"Shhh. Don't. You're with me now."

He closed his eyes and relaxed his grip on my hand. I set his untouched Tecate on the coffee table, and moved closer to him, putting my head on his shoulder and my arm across his waist. He put one arm over mine, more at ease now, or maybe just mentally exhausted.

After a while Spot wandered in, asking about dinner. Ryan fed him while I began fixing an early supper for us. Ryan's edginess had returned, and I suggested he call the hospital. He came back into the kitchen a few minutes later, obviously relieved. "She's doing better than expected. Don't know what'll happen when she comes home again."

"Child Protective Services will be able to step in, now that they know what—who—the problem is." Even if she doesn't want to file charges. Even if it's only a Band-Aid.

* * *

After we'd done the dishes, Ryan started to grade papers, then stopped a few minutes later. "I almost forgot. We're supposed to jam at Tony's tonight. I think I'll just cancel out."

"Maybe it would be a good idea to go."

"Maybe. You want to come?"

"Just the guys?"

"No. No, some of their wives or girlfriends'll be there. They'll be glad to have you too. And so will I. You'll like Patty and Marisa. Patty's a friend of Alana's."

"It sounds like fun. Do you still play rock?"

"That, Tejano, Country."

Ryan packed up all his equipment and we headed over to Tony and Patty Sedillos'. Ryan was right. I liked Patty and Marisa. He hadn't told me about Cici. Cici was a snot.

We hung around the kitchen while the guys set up in the den and Cici gave a boring monologue in Spanish about her shopping trip to Laredo. Ryan came in to get a beer and winked at me. I crossed my eyes at him.

While Patty set out chips and dips, I studied her unobtrusively. Tall and slender, she moved with an easy grace. I gradually connected her with an image from the past—the same heart-shaped face, with dark brown eyes against an ivory complexion. Her ash-blond hair, once worn in a crinkly perm, was now short and smooth.

Patty and I filled our plates with munchies and moved outside to the patio. She smiled at me. "I remember you now. Alana said you were in town. Weren't you a friend of Erica and Laura's?"

"Yes, ever since we were kids."

"That was so sad about Laura. Do you have any idea how Leo's doing? I hate to keep asking Alana."

"Not really. He just seems to keep everything bottled up."

Patty nodded. "You know, he's been that way for a long time—I mean since long before Laura died. In fact, after they got married no one ever saw much of them."

That was news.

"Did you come down for the funeral, Sharon?"

"No, I didn't get here till afterwards."

"It was really strange. Leo just sat like a stone. Laura's friend Tina showed more emotion than anyone in the family—she just bawled and bawled."

"Tina seems easily upset, but she's sweet." Especially after meeting Cici, I was more appreciative of Tina's efforts to be sociable.

Cici and Marisa decided to join us, Cici still babbling in Spanish about her trip to Laredo. She'd gotten up to the part about going to WalMart.

"I remember something else," Patty said softly. "I remember you spoke Tex-Mex with the rest of us."

"Well, don't tell Cici and spoil her fun."

Patty laughed. "I wouldn't dream of it."

"Patty, do you ever run into Bernice Peralta?"

Patty stiffened. "Why?"

Once again I decided on half-truths. "Well, I know this sounds odd, but she's shown up a couple of times unexpectedly—like she's been following me."

Patty shivered. "Creepy. No wonder Ryan doesn't want you out of his sight. Actually, I haven't had the pleasure of seeing her in months. Marisa might have. Her parents are friends of Bernice's parents."

Somehow I'd never thought of Bernice as having parents. I just assumed she'd slithered out full-blown from under a rock.

Tony opened the door and called out, "Hey, Patty, we need you to come sing with us."

Patty turned to me. "Do you like to sing?"

"How'd you guess?"

"Something Ryan said when you first came in. Why don't you harmonize with me? It's always more fun with someone else."

"I'd like that. It sounds like fun."

We came inside and spent the rest of the evening enjoying the music. As we left, Patty said, "Call me." I promised her I would, and wondered if she had something else to tell me about Bernice.

* * *

Ryan was feeling much better by the time we got home. While he graded papers, I took a quick shower, slipped into my Winnie-the-Pooh nightshirt, and curled up in front of the TV with Spot.

Ryan looked up and grinned. "I don't know where you get all those sexy clothes."

"Hey, this isn't even one of my Goodwill specials. I bought it brand new."

He showered, then came in and pulled me off the couch. He kissed me lightly, then unbuttoned the top buttons of my nightshirt and slipped it down around my shoulders. "Tell me."

My hand flew instinctively to my neck.

He moved my hand away gently, exposing a three-inch scar running horizontally below my collarbone. He traced it lightly with his fingertips. "Didn't you think I'd noticed?"

"Of course I knew. It's just—I forget it's there."

"No you don't. Sweetheart, I wouldn't ask, except it still seems to bother you. Still gives you nightmares."

"Not very often. It really wasn't such a big deal. It happened a long time ago, and it happened so fast. I didn't even need stitches—well, not many. It hardly even shows anymore...."

Ryan put one finger to my lips, then placed his hands on my shoulders. "Sharon. It's me you're talking to."

I took a deep breath. "About a year ago, Dave Martínez—Dave and I don't like each other very much, but we work well together because he intimidates people and I don't."

I realized I was still rambling and tried to get back on track. Ryan waited.

"Dave and I had to be in court in this little town outside San Antone. Afterwards I went to the ladies' room, and while I was washing my hands—I mean this was in broad daylight in a nice safe little town in an uncrowded courthouse." After all this time, my voice still echoed my fear and disbelief.

My pain was reflected in Ryan's face. "What happened, Sharon. Tell me. Who hurt you?"

"No one I knew. He was high as a kite. And stupid. I don't know what he thought he could do with a razor blade."

"A lot."

"I think all he wanted was my purse. He came up behind me and put his arm across my neck in a choke-hold." Even now I could see that crazed face next to mine in the restroom mirror.

I shuddered and Ryan pulled me to him, his arms tight around me.

"Are you sure you want to hear all this?" I asked him.

"No. But I think it's something you need to talk about."

I closed my eyes. "After that—I clawed at him, and he slashed. The cut didn't go too deep, but God how it hurt—and bled! I screamed. And screamed. I didn't think I'd ever quit screaming and bleeding."

Ryan stroked my hair and didn't say anything.

"I guess screaming was the best thing I could have done. Dave came running in as he was running out, and Dave

170

knocked him out cold. I don't think he even knew what hit him. After that it was a blur. The paramedics came, and, and...."

I shuddered again. Ryan held me close for a long time. I wasn't sure whose tears I felt on my face.

"Don't let go," I whispered.

"Never."

I wished I could always feel this safe.

CHAPTER 29

After Ryan left for school the next morning, I was faced with the same dilemma. Last night I was ready to send Mac a letter of resignation with no return address. Now, without Ryan here, I felt at loose ends. Everyone I knew had a job to go to. Maybe I could visit Mrs. Pirtle and see if she had any further comments about my sexual orientation.

Thinking of Mrs. Pirtle and how close Los Mareados was to the Rio Grande reminded me of the way I used to enjoy walking by the river. It had been too long since I'd stopped to "smell the roses," or rather, enjoy the bosque in bloom.

On impulse, I jumped into my Honda, drove past Los Mareados, and parked at the end of the road. I walked a few hundred yards to the riverbank. I sat down on the shore cross-legged, elbows propped on my knees, face in my hands, and looked across to Mexico.

Downstream I could see a couple of bass fishermen in a pontoon boat. Gulls circled over their heads while egrets waited patiently onshore, all hoping to share in the catch. A flock of white pelicans glided before me. With huge puffy bodies attached to startled clown faces, they reminded me of inflatable toys children play with in the swimming pool. How could they still be so graceful?

I'd forgotten how relaxing it was simply to sit and watch the unhurried flow of life in this secluded area of the river, to listen to the gentle lapping of the water as it brushed the shoreline. Tiny fuzzy balls of gold were beginning to sprout from the huisache trees on both sides of the shore, and their sweet perfume, more than any other, brought me back to my childhood. Memories filled me, and I realized how much this place, this town, had shaped my life. Maybe I wasn't a trespasser after all.

* * *

I got back before noon, hoping Ryan might come home for lunch again. I stared at the phone, willing it to ring. Then it occurred to me I'd only assumed Patty would be working. Maybe she was home. I looked up her number and gave her a call. She answered on the second ring and invited me over later.

I wondered if I would have called Patty if I hadn't hoped she might have something more to tell me about Bernice. I also felt a little guilty that I was poking my nose in where I'd specifically been asked to keep it out. I salved my conscience on both counts by deciding not to bring the subject up. I liked Patty and knew I'd enjoy seeing her even without ulterior motives.

While I was fixing a sandwich, Ryan called.

"Hi, sweetheart. Guess where I am?"

"I hope you didn't go to Mustang Island without me!"

"Never. I'm at Radio Shack, and I just bought one of those damn phones."

"Really?" I was touched. I knew he'd done it for me, even if he wouldn't come right out and say so.

He gave me the number, then said, "Don't tell anyone else. Call me every five minutes."

"Loco mío."

"I love you too. Gotta go or I'll be late getting back."

* * *

Patty had a pitcher of iced tea waiting when I arrived, and we sat out on her patio under the shade of a palm tree. She told me she enjoyed the luxury of being a stay-at-home mom. Two little girls about four or five that I hadn't seen last night were playing with several naked Barbies while a jillion doll clothes were strewn in disarray around the patio.

"We have Polynesian Barbie, and Doctor Barbie, and I-don't-know-what-else Barbie. Tony calls them all Bimbo Babs, and it really annoys him that with all that wardrobe, Barbie can never seem to stay dressed. He's always stepping on those tiny little shoes, and then the girls cry. We try to pick everything up before he comes home, but...." She gave a placid shrug, and I had a feeling that beneath his grumbling, Tony was a doting father.

"I didn't see the girls last night."

"They usually spend the night at my mom's when the band's over here. She lives next door."

We talked of that and this, and Patty eventually said, "You got me to thinking when you asked about Bernice last night."

"Patty, before you say anything else...." *Damn. Sometimes I wish I didn't have a conscience.* "I shouldn't have said anything. My curiosity just got the best of me."

She looked puzzled. "Well, I should think so, if she's been following you around."

She had a point. No need to bring the Salazars into any of this discussion. "I don't like her, and sometimes I think I suspect her of things for that reason alone."

Patty nodded as if I'd struck a responsive chord. "She made a play for Tony a while back, and I started getting anonymous letters saying they were having an affair. The letters backfired, whoever sent them, because I knew it wasn't true, and the letters didn't make trouble between Tony and me—if that's what they were supposed to do."

"Did you show them to Tony?"

"I did. We both found it upsetting, but we decided to pretend we thought it was a funny joke and tell everyone we knew. It was embarrassing in a way, but it worked. No more letters. We're sure Bernice sent them herself. I don't know anyone else who'd do something like that."

"You know, Erica got some anonymous phone calls not long after—after she got here. Calls telling her to go home or she'd be sorry. Something like that." I didn't feel free to tell Patty the whole message. "I can't think of anyone else who'd make crank calls either. But at the same time, much as I'd like to blame Bernice, I'm not sure she's the one."

"That does seem odd. Erica's the only person who's ever been nice to her. And that's not the kind of threat Bernice usually makes. She likes to dangle some little tidbit over your head that she thinks you wouldn't want anyone to know about. Does this make any sense?"

"Yes, it does."

"Sharon, there's something I probably wouldn't even bring up, except it made me uneasy when you told me about Bernice harassing you. Marisa said she learned something disturbing from her mother just recently. I'm not sure Marisa's mother would have told her this if Bernice hadn't decided to get her hooks into Luis."

I thought of what Erica had said about Bernice only being interested in what she couldn't have. Patty's husband, Tony. Marisa's husband, Luis.

"Bernice's method this time was to tell Luis that Marisa was the one having an affair. With your Ryan, no less."

I blinked.

"One of her many delusions. You see, they—Marisa and Luis—have a son in one of Ryan's classes, and Marisa and Ryan got together over a cup of coffee to talk about some problem he was having in school. I suppose she should have gone to the school to talk about it, but Ryan's a good friend, so they met at McDonald's instead."

I started laughing. "Well, that's sure where I'd go for a clandestine affair."

"Right. I'm glad you can see the humor in it. It was one of those things where nobody knew whether to laugh or cry. Marisa and Luis decided to do what we'd done and treat it as a joke. But it's still unnerving."

"I take it Bernice backed off."

Patty nodded. "Yep. That little scheme died on the vine. But that's not what I started to tell you." She paused. "From what I understand, well, Bernice's parents seem to be normal decent people. It's sad. They don't have much, live over in that trailer park near the river. It's not bad, but you'd think Bernice—with that expensive Porsche and all— would fork out a little for them to have something nicer."

According to Mrs. Pirtle, it was Bernice who lived in the trailer park, but that had always seemed unlikely. "So Bernice doesn't live near them?"

"Heavens no. She has a custom home in Falcon West— something she acquired from one of her ex-husbands."

"Where does she work, or does she?"

"Now there's a novel idea. But why work when she can leech off those discarded husbands?"

I thought of Mrs. Pirtle's comments and paraphrased them in my mind: *You mean a young person like her don't have employment? She just sets around stirrin' up misery for people all day long?*

"You were telling me about her parents," I said.

"Right. Marisa's mother told us they were simply nice middle-class people who were totally unprepared to deal with a child like Bernice. None of us knew any of this when we were kids, of course, and we'd never know now if Bernice hadn't chosen to antagonize Marisa. Anyway, the Peraltas had another child, a little boy, when Bernice was about five or six."

"Really! I never knew she had a brother."

Patty shivered and began rubbing her arms. "He supposedly died in one of those tragic things when infants die in their cribs for no known reason. But some of the circumstances didn't seem to jibe—there were unexplained bruises—and Bernice had been in the room alone with him."

I could feel my skin crawl even as Patty was talking.

"Exactly what happened is all speculation, of course, but...."

The horror of what Patty was implying made me ill. *Keep breathing. Keep breathing. Keep breathing.*

Seeing the look on my face, Patty nodded again, her own face troubled. "Bernice was so young, I don't think anyone was really able to believe—back then—that she might have had anything to do with it. And apparently everyone felt sorry for Mrs. Peralta. Marisa's mother said Mrs. Peralta told her later that although she'd wanted a big family at one time, she'd changed her mind. That's all she ever said."

Patty's children were tired of playing Barbies, and wanted to climb in her lap and hear stories. I stayed for a while and hugged them and read them stories along with Patty. I needed their warmth—I needed something sweet and innocent to take away the bitter taste of the things Patty had told me.

CHAPTER 30

As Patty walked me out to the car, we were both startled by the sound of a truck roaring down her otherwise quiet street. A maroon truck with gold zigzag stripes along the side.

Patty's eyes narrowed. "What's he up to now?"

"Who is he? A neighbor?"

"Elmer Smithers? Not quite. His parents own a mansion that takes up a city block all by itself. More money than they know what to do with. Every time Elmer wrecks a car, they just buy him another one."

"So he doesn't need to work either."

"He's still in school. Supposedly. I think his chief recreation is ditching."

If I told Patty I thought this kid had been following me too, she might start to think I was delusional, imagining stalkers behind every bush. Instead I mentioned seeing him at Hugo's.

"Hugo's!" she snorted. "They should close that place down." She paused. "What were you doing there?"

I laughed. "Slumming. Playing Nancy Drew. I'd thought of following Bernice there, then thought better of it."

"Well, keep thinking better of it!" She hugged me. "Where else will I find someone to harmonize the way we do?"

I hugged her in return. "I'll be careful." How often had I made that promise lately?

* * *

When Ryan came home we sat on the patio and watched Spot watching the grackles. When Ryan asked about my day, I told him about going to the river and to Patty's. I wanted to keep it upbeat, so told him about the Barbies and some other innocuous things Patty and I had talked about.

I decided against mentioning Bernice or the maroon truck, for now at least. I dreaded going over to the Salazars for dinner and didn't need any more stressful things to compound the situation. I wondered where Mrs. Salazar would be on the rationality scale. I also wondered if the atmosphere would be as dismal as it had been at Leo's.

"Will Tina and Johnny be coming too?" I asked.

"Why would they be there?"

"I don't know. I just thought since they're such good friends of Leo's...next-door neighbors...."

Ryan got that stubborn look on his face, and I began feeling stubborn too. "I always seem to say the wrong thing, and then you shut me out, and I could use a little hint about how to avoid another evening like last time."

"I'm sorry. It won't be like last time. For one thing, to answer your question, Tina and Johnny won't be there."

"Are they the problem?"

He was quiet a minute. "I never could see what Laura saw in Tina."

"Johnny's not exactly Mr. Personality either."

"I guess Leo sees him differently. Listen. Let's not talk about this right now." He stood, pulling me up with him, then put his hand under my chin and gave me a quick kiss. "I'll be nice. I promise. And I promise to explain later."

* * *

The Salazar home hadn't changed in 22 years, and I was caught up in an unexpected flow of nostalgia. Everything looked and smelled the same, and I felt a childish urge to touch everything, from the daffodilled wallpaper to the statue of San Pascual, plump and benign, smiling over Mrs. Salazar's cozy kitchen from his perch on the windowsill.

Mrs. Salazar seemed cheerful, but looked as if she'd been crying. I realized I'd never thought of her as vulnerable, and my heart went out to her. I gave her a warm hug, and she looked both pleased and surprised.

"I'm glad you're here, mija. You make my Ryan happy. I'm sorry about the other night."

I kissed her on the cheek. "What other night? Now, tell me what I can do to help get dinner ready."

She seemed more like her old self as she shooed me out of the kitchen. "Everything's ready. I just need to get everyone to the table before dinner gets cold."

The dining room was quite large, and the table laden with a variety of things Mrs. Salazar must have spent all day cooking. The Salazars sat at either end of the table, with Carlos sitting next to his grandmother.

Alana and Beto's teenage boys, Miguel and Gabe, were sitting across from each other, near their grandfather. Sixteen-year-old Miguel, with his dark good looks, resembled the Salazar side of the family. Gabe, fourteen, reminded me of Beto, both in looks and temperament.

Gabe, Alana, Erica, and I lined up along one side of the table. I was sitting across from Beto, Alana across from Ryan. Evidently it suited Mrs. Salazar's matchmaking plans to have Erica and Leo facing each other. Erica appeared not to notice, and Leo still seemed too unhappy to care. At best he faded in and out of whatever conversation was going on. Miguel, on the other hand, was completely captivated by

Erica, which I was pretty sure wasn't what Mrs. Salazar had in mind.

As usual, Beto seemed to be the designated put-everyone-at-ease person. "So we have 'The Four Musketeers' together again."

"One for all. All for one," said Erica. "Cross one of us and you'd have the others to answer to."

"And we had your brothers to answer to," Ryan said.

"And they made us think there was nothing between them and God."

Everyone laughed except Leo, who just looked blank. Suddenly I felt like crying. One for all. All for one. Leo, when did we lose you?

I don't know if Beto sensed my change in mood, but he steered the conversation in a different direction, asking Erica about Head Start, and me about my work. "MacDougal and Martínez," he said with respect in his voice. "They have a very good reputation."

"I'm really lucky. They hired me partly because on my résumé I'd said I spoke Spanish fluently. My interview with Mac MacDougal went fine. I sounded fluent enough to him. So no one questioned me about my language skills till after I was hired.

"And that got me off on the wrong foot with Dave Martínez—he's the nephew of the senior partner, Vince Martínez. I guess Vince trusted Mac's judgment. But Dave said I talked like a pachuco, and some of our clients were very well educated."

Erica laughed. "I've been there."

"I should have known better. When we moved to Minnesota my freshman year, I took Spanish in high school thinking it would be a snap. They taught 'Cathtillian Thpanith.' They might as well have been speaking Swahili,

181

and I flunked big time. I thought, 'What do they know anyway?'"

Miguel and Gabe were listening with interest now, a mischievous glint in their eyes.

"So when I went to college, I took French, s'il vous plait. I figured if my border Spanish was good enough for me, it should be good enough for the whole world."

Everyone was laughing again. Even Leo managed a smile.

"Did that Dave Martínez guy try to fire you?" Gabe asked.

"No. I think he did me a favor in the long run. When he pointed out my shortcomings, I felt very stupid. But it also made me a little mad. So I went to night school and studied my brains out—improved my grammar a lot and my accent a little."

"Did Dave ever forgive you?" Alana asked.

"Oh, get this. One day one of our clients asked if I came from Mexico City! Ooooh! The egg on his face! He began mellowing after that."

Gabe spoke up. "Hey, Uncle Ryan, you should get her to come to your classes. She says what you're always trying to tell us."

"You should do that," Ryan said. "I keep telling my kids I don't care how they talk at home or with their friends, but it'll be different if they go up north. That's why I'm so hard-nosed in class."

"Maybe you could come to my school and teach us karate," Carlos said.

"Karate? You're into karate?" Leo asked.

I was surprised that he'd actually volunteered something to the conversation.

"She's almost a brown belt," Carlos offered, as proud as if he'd earned it himself.

"No kidding," Leo said. "How come?"

I caught Ryan's glance and folded my hands in my lap, willing myself not to reach for my throat. I certainly didn't want to talk about the attack on me at the courthouse that had led me to take karate. I turned to Leo, keeping my tone light. "I got tired of being some wimp who couldn't ever take care of herself."

Our eyes met, and for a brief instant I saw a trace of a smile in Leo's. I realized with a start that we were both thinking of the same incident.

"Okay," said Alana, "What's that look all about."

"Nothing gets past you, does it, sis." Leo said.

Everyone seemed to be waiting. Leo raised one eyebrow and looked at me as if to say, "Your call."

Oh great. With any luck I could get this past Alana's radar. "Well, back in my damsel-in-distress days, back in eighth grade, there was this kid in our class the girls called Erpy."

"Good ole Erpy," Erica murmured. "I remember him well."

Alana nodded. "Oh yes. He had a brother we called Slimy."

"No doubt they had the same obnoxious habits. Anyway, Erpy was pestering me one afternoon when Leo came along and picked him up by the scruff of the neck and dangled him like one of those cartoon characters—legs and arms going in all directions. Then Leo deposited him a few yards away. Good ole Erpy never bothered me—or any of the other girls—again."

"How come I never heard about this?" Ryan asked.

"Because, big brother," Leo said, "it was my job to keep you out of trouble."

Oh God, please please please please let's not get on the subject of Ryan fighting over me.

God answered my prayer via Carlos. "Uncle Leo, why do you call Uncle Ryan 'big brother'? You're bigger than he is."

"Your Uncle Ryan is 10 minutes older than I am, and he's never let me forget it."

I was thankful we were off on another tangent. I'd almost forgotten about "Erpy" Sosa, the boy who'd been "pestering" me, and Leo's gallant rescue. Erpy liked to go around snapping girls' bras. All the eighth-grade girls hated him.

I'd stayed after school one day and was walking home when Erpy came up behind me and pulled the band of my bra like a sling shot. To my utter 13-year-old mortification, it came unhooked. It didn't matter that no one could see through my blouse. I just knew the straps would slip down my arms at any moment and the whole world would know. I crossed my arms over my chest, my hands on opposite shoulders, and wheeled around to face Erpy, yelling and kicking at him. Erpy just giggled and made a game of dodging me.

Leo was coming home from football practice and had already trotted past us when he heard the commotion. He trotted backwards a few steps till he reached us, then grabbed Erpy by the collar, twisting it and pulling hard. When Erpy started choking, Leo let go, and Erpy ran home crying. I had quit yelling and was standing like a marble statue, hoping the ground would open up and let me fall in.

Knowing Erpy's reputation, Leo probably thought he'd ripped the back of my blouse. Leo came over and put his jersey around my shoulders, tying the sleeves in front. We walked to my house side by side without saying a word, my arms still clasped to my chest, Leo's jersey—stained with grass and smelling faintly of salty sweat—wrapped around me like a security blanket.

Leo waited on the porch while I went inside to change. I came back out, handed him his jersey, and said, "Thank you," very formally. I couldn't look him in the eye.

"It's okay, little sister." Leo smiled, patted me on the head, and went home. And never told.

* * *

Mrs. Salazar pulled me back to the present asking everyone to take second helpings. I figured I was well on my way to blimphood, but took another chili relleno. Leo had withdrawn into his shell again, and it occurred to me that mentioning karate was something that seemed to spark his interest.

"Leo, are you involved in karate too?"

"No."

"Oh. I wondered, since you'd asked...." My sentence dribbled into oblivion.

"Well Sharon," Alana said, "I must confess. It's not something I picture you doing either."

"Gotta watch out for those stereotypes!"

"What's a stereothing?" asked Carlos.

"It's when you have ideas of the way you think people should be, even if those ideas are wrong," Ryan answered.

"I don't get it."

Miguel sent Carlos a withering look. "It doesn't take brain surgery, pendejo. It means that just because Sharon's pretty doesn't mean she can't knock the—" Miguel caught his grandfather's frown. "—you-know-what out of somebody."

"Cool," said Carlos, ignoring the insult.

I was hoping we'd get on to another subject, but the one Mrs. Salazar picked next was worse. Maybe she was afraid the evening would slip away before she could play cupid.

"It makes me so happy to have all of you together again—just like the old days."

"It is nice to touch base with old friends," Erica said tactfully. "To spend a few days together before we go our separate ways again."

This went over Mrs. Salazar's head. "I was looking at this picture today, and it gave me such a nice feeling, I wanted to show it to you too. I'll be right back."

She hurried into the den, leaving the rest of us trying to think of what to say next. Even Beto seemed unable to come up with anything. We didn't have long to puzzle before she returned with a large photo album.

Ryan and Miguel tilted their chairs back and gazed at the ceiling, looking more like identical twins than Ryan and Leo had ever looked.

"Sharon," Alana said, "Will you help me clear the plates, and then we can bring in dessert."

Once we were in the kitchen, she whispered, "We've got to divert her."

Mrs. Salazar bustled into the kitchen, telling us she could handle everything. Alana winked at me and began scooping ice cream as if her mother hadn't said anything.

But Mrs. Salazar was not to be sidetracked. After dessert was served, she opened the album and passed around a picture of our eighth-grade graduation. In a way I was glad. It was a sweet picture. Innocent. Erica and Leo were smiling. Ryan and I, clasping hands like there was no tomorrow, were practically glowing. Or maybe that was just the light bouncing off our braces.

"I can't believe I was ever that young," I said, as I passed the photo to Erica.

"I can't believe I wore those stupid shoes."

"My turn," said Alana. "Yeah. I see what you mean."

"I can't believe Uncle Ryan wore his hair that long," Gabe said when the picture reached him. He passed it to his grandfather.

Mr. Salazar adjusted his glasses. "Ay, mijo, that hair!"

He handed it to Miguel, who snickered before giving it to Ryan.

"Hey, I thought I was a pretty sharp dude." Ryan winked at me. "And look at the cool chick I was with."

Leo looked at the photo and smiled without saying anything. Then he passed it to Beto.

"Mm hmm. I'd have to agree about Erica's shoes," he said with a twinkle in his eye.

We all relaxed a little. Hardly any romantic overtones in a conversation about Erica's ugly shoes. We could pretend we hadn't noticed the rest of her was beautiful.

Mrs. Salazar was nothing if not tenacious. "I think el buen señor has a way of bringing people back together."

I didn't think God had anything to do with this gathering that Mrs. Salazar had arranged, but also didn't think it would help to mention it. I concentrated instead on smearing my ice cream around in the bowl.

"That's a nice thought," said Erica, "but I think He likes to see us find our own paths. They're not always the paths other people would choose for us."

I remembered Beto's dicho. "God creates us; then frees us," I murmured.

Erica looked Leo in the eye, and he met her gaze without looking away. "Diós nos crea, Leo. All of us. And he allows us to find our own special person."

"Who's your special person?" Carlos asked.

"His name is Richard," Erica answered.

I glanced at Mrs. Salazar for her reaction, but once again she chose not to hear.

Erica and Leo were still looking intently at each other, and Alana and Ryan exchanged glances that I couldn't decipher. Beto was watching me, his gray eyes kind as always, and I blinked as if I'd gotten a sudden telepathic message. Beto gave me a slight nod as everything fell into place. Leo's unhappiness, all the secrecy....

"This has been a wonderful evening," Erica said graciously, "but I need to be going. I have to get up very early tomorrow."

"I'll walk you out," Leo said.

I sat transfixed. From where I was seated, I could see Erica and Leo by the living room door, their arms wrapped around each other. Tender-hearted Erica and dear sweet Leo. Leo, who was finally pouring out to his lifelong friend things he'd kept bottled up for so long. Leo, who—I realized now—wasn't interested in women, whose "special person" was probably Johnny Quemado. How long had she known?

CHAPTER 31

Alana and I loaded the dishwasher in silence while Mrs. Salazar put away leftovers, chattering happily about what a nice evening it had been.

"It was a nice evening," I said. It had its moments.

Alana's boys had gone home, and everyone else had gone into the living room.

"Amá, why don't you go sit down," Alana said. "You've been on your feet all day. Sharon and I can finish up."

"Well," she hesitated. "I did want to talk to Ryan some more about getting one of those phones."

I stuck my head in the dishwasher and prayed to St. Jude that this nice evening would end soon.

"Sharon," Alana began as soon as her mother had left the room, "about the other night. I'm sorry I put you on the defensive about Jeff."

"So why did you?"

Alana busied herself wiping off the counter. "I don't know. I didn't think it through at the time. I think it was partly so you'd understand—when the time came—about Leo living a lie too."

Too? Ouch. I had to sort this out. "I'd understand because you think I'm living a lie?"

"You said yourself you'd been—misleading—people with Jeff for over two years."

I closed my eyes for a moment. "Interesting, the excuses we make for ourselves."

"I think that's what I meant, Sharon. You're the most honest person I know. But you've been carrying on this charade—or whatever you want to call it—with Jeff, and it doesn't seem to bother you."

"Maybe because it doesn't affect anyone else either—except the busybodies. Maybe that's the difference."

Alana turned to face me, leaning against the counter, her arms folded. "But don't you see? That's how it started with Leo and Laura. Just a way to fool the busybodies. Just a matter of convenience...."

I nodded slowly. "I see what you're saying." I paused, wondering. "Both of them?"

"Both of them. Talk about not thinking things through. I liked Laura even though Ryan didn't, but she was a real ditz. I don't suppose she'd given any thought to acquiring a bunch of nosy in-laws in the deal. Family dinners grew more and more tedious, and less and less frequent. Amá knew something was wrong right from the beginning."

"How much do your parents know?"

"About Leo being gay? He tried to talk to them years ago, and it was like talking to the proverbial brick wall. They didn't mean to be cruel. They just couldn't grasp it."

"That must have hurt Leo a lot."

"In more ways than one. Oddly enough, I don't think he ever got over feeling he was the one who'd disappointed them instead of the other way around."

"At least you and Ryan were there for him."

"And now he knows he can count on you and Erica too. Who knows? Maybe even my parents after all this time. Maybe my mom would even get off her matchmaking kick. Especially after seeing how miserable Leo's been. He's basically an honest person too, and he just hasn't been the same. It's been a disaster."

Alana turned her attention to wiping off the stovetop, her back to me once again. "'Oh, what a tangled web' and all that."

"I think you're right about your parents. About this being the right time. I can't imagine they'd ever love Leo any less."

Alana faced me again, tears coming to her eyes. "It helps to talk to you, Sharon. In a way, I wish we'd done it sooner. Sometimes it's hard to talk to Ryan about our parents—he doesn't want to risk upsetting them any more."

"Maybe it's hard for them to bring it up too."

"I wonder. At least Ryan and I see eye to eye about Leo. Our problem is not with him, but with his choice of partners."

"I can't say I'm too impressed with Johnny Quemado."

"Ryan can't stand him. It's all he can do to stay in the same room with him and be civil."

I thought back to that strained evening at Leo's. "So I noticed."

"Anyway, getting back to what I started to say. I really do feel bad throwing you a curve about Jeff. If it makes you feel any better, it ticked off Beto too. He hardly ever gets mad at me, and when he does, it crushes me. So I got my payback."

"Alana, that doesn't make me feel better. I like you, and I don't want hurt feelings between Beto and you—or between us. Sit down a minute. The other afternoon when we were having drinks together, I didn't really explain what I needed to explain."

We sat at the kitchen table, Alana watching me carefully.

"When I said I envied you, that was the point I was making, and that was the part you didn't hear."

"No, I guess I didn't."

"I thought I had my life in order. I'd been very...
content...with my non-romantic existence. But after seeing
Ryan again, I knew it wasn't enough. We'd just barely
started seeing each other, so maybe I was afraid to get my
hopes up. At the time, I didn't have any reason to assume—
anything."

Alana nodded. "Just because it was obvious to me."

"I'd like to blame the margaritas, but whatever it was,
I'm the one who feels bad about bringing Jeff into this. The
idea going through my mind—I knew I'd be going back to
San Antone soon, and I suddenly saw my future as very
bleak. Maybe the reason I mentioned Jeff is that during
those few bleak moments, I pictured myself at the age of 90
still going out with him on Saturday nights."

Alana smiled. "No wonder." She paused. "About you and
me, could we start again please?"

"I'd like to. I love Ryan with all my heart. You know that.
And I love Leo too. In a different way of course. I'd like to
feel the same toward you. But sometimes I feel we're
dancing around each other deciding whether or not to trust
each other."

"Funny you should bring that up. You should have known
I'd count those pills, honey. What did you do with it?"

That startled me. Then I blushed. "Funny you should
bring that up yourself. I have it with me. Where did your
mother put my purse?"

"Come on." Alana led me to her parents' room and my
purse on the bed.

"Your turn. Follow me." I led Alana into the bathroom off
the master bedroom and took the green pill from my purse.
I held it high over the commode and dropped it in. We both
watched it float in circles.

"Should we say a few words of farewell, or just let it go?" I asked.

"We should probably make a speech, but I can't think of anything offhand. The Gettysburg Address?"

"The world will little note nor long remember what we say here, but you and I will never forget what we did here."

"Very good," Alana said. "We need to pull the handle together."

We flushed and watched it disappear. "Adiós pill," we said in unison.

"What are you two doing?"

We turned to see Ryan watching us quizzically from the bathroom door.

"It's called female bonding," Alana said.

"And you say guys are weird."

"Has Amá talked you into a phone yet?" Alana asked.

Ryan looked at me, and I pressed my lips together.

"No. But Leo's been waiting for you to finish bonding so he can go home."

Alana and I looked at each other guiltily, then sandwiched Ryan, each of us taking him by the hand, and started for the living room.

"Where were you?" Mrs. Salazar asked. "I looked in the kitchen and you were gone."

"We were in the bathroom," Alana said.

"Together?"

"Sharon needed a safety pin."

Ryan shook his head and grinned. "They were flushing safety pins down the toilet."

"Mijo, I don't think that's very funny."

Any minute the Mad Hatter was going to show up. I hugged Mrs. Salazar and whispered, "He was just kidding."

Ryan hugged his mother, then put his arm around me. "Come on, sweetheart, we need to go home."

Mr. Salazar came over to stand by his wife, kissing her fondly on the cheek. Once again I was reminded of his quiet strength. I wondered when she had lost her grip on reality.

We all said our goodbyes, and when we were outside I went over to Leo and hugged him. "Leo," I whispered, "I've missed you."

To my surprise he didn't let go but kept hugging me. "Sharon honey," he whispered, "let me tell you something. Before you run off and get yourself a black belt, just remember a guy likes to be a hero now and then."

I gave him a sisterly kiss on the lips. "You'll always be that to me."

CHAPTER 32

The next morning I sat on the counter in the bathroom, watching Ryan shave. He rinsed off his razor, then eyed me in amusement. "I can see those wheels turning around in your head."

"I'm not going to ask questions, so you'll have to read my mind."

"I'd have better luck reading tea leaves."

There wasn't time to answer everything I wanted to know anyway, so I gave it up for the time being, hopped down from the counter, and headed for the kitchen.

Over breakfast Ryan asked, "So, what evil schemes are you and Erica hatching up today?"

"No schemes. She has to work, remember? I think she's trying to wind things up with her program. I'll just hang out here and paint my toenails."

Ryan was quiet. "I guess we need to talk about you and me."

"Sometime. When we have more time."

"What's wrong with now?"

I suddenly waffled. What exactly did I want?

Ryan took his dishes to the sink, then went to make a phone call. When he came back, he said, "First period's covered. The whole day, if I need it."

We went into the living room and sat sideways on the couch, facing each other. Good for you, Sharon, I told myself. You've made him rearrange his whole schedule, and now you're tongue-tied.

Ryan laughed softly, mischief gleaming in his eyes. "Well, sweetheart, evidently I'm the only one here who's given this any thought."

"That's not true. I just don't know where to start."

"Then I'll start. Sharon, do you remember the first time I asked you to marry me?"

"Of course. I think we were seven years old. Leo was going to marry Erica, and we were all going to live in the clubhouse together and build a spaceship. And your mom was supposed to bring over tamales every day."

"I'd forgotten all about that."

"And you asked if *I* remembered!"

"Moving right along, do you remember the last time?"

"The summer we were 14."

"Do you remember what you told me?"

"I always said yes."

"Have you changed your mind?"

"No, but...."

"Sharon, I love you. I still want to marry you."

"I love you too, honey, but—we're not 14 anymore."

"Well, duh."

"Quit laughing at me. You make it sound so easy. It's not that simple."

"Well, we can make it complicated if you want to."

"It's just—there's a lot of things we need to work out— married or not."

"Then let's start working them out. Sharon, I don't expect to iron everything out in the next half-hour. I'd just like to know if we're heading in the same direction."

"Ryan, it's not that. The problem's not between *you* and me. It's between *me* and me. And I'm sorry I didn't figure this out before I disrupted your whole day."

His eyes were still laughing at me. "Too late now. So tell me about this problem between you and you."

I thought a minute. "What I want is to have it all. I want to stay here with you. *And* I want to keep my job in San Antonio. Logical, no?"

"Sharon, do you think I'd want you to lounge around the house and paint your toenails all day long? I'd never expect you to give up the work you do. It's part of who you are."

"I think what bothers me, I don't know how to... divide... myself. I don't want to have two separate lives—one here with you, and another...disconnected from you. I'm not explaining this very well."

"Honey, the highway runs both ways. Don't you think I want to be part of your life there? I want to know where you live, where you work. I want to meet Mac who likes you and Dave who doesn't." His mouth twitched at the corners. "I want to meet Jeff too. I want to be with you whenever— wherever—we can."

"Mi casa, su casa; su casa, mi casa?"

"Sí. I couldn't have said it better."

"Take turns on that two-way highway every weekend?"

"You bet. And remember, besides weekends I have summers, long breaks. And since you've introduced me to the telephone, you can't ever be that far away in between."

"I could call you at school. Every five minutes."

Ryan laughed. "That's what I was hoping to hear." He leaned over and kissed me. "And now for the rest of the day...."

"I can practice being a good wife and see that you get off to work."

He kissed me again. "There are other ways of practicing."

Before we could practice any further, the phone rang.

"Damn," Ryan said. "I was supposed to call back."

We went into the bedroom, sat on the edge of the bed, and listened to the answering machine. "Ryan, it's Mary Ellen. Sorry, but you're on after all. Joaquín and Celia both called in sick. Is there something going around?"

We fell back on the bed, laughing. "I'll be damned. Joaquín and Celia," Ryan said. He stood up and got ready to leave again. "Save this afternoon for me, okay? And try not to get in trouble."

"And what trouble would that be?" I asked Spot after Ryan drove off. I tidied up a bit, then sat at the piano. Despite having been away from it awhile, I was pleased and surprised at how some of my favorite pieces came back. Spot was pleased too, and accompanied me in several duets.

When the phone rang, I went to listen to the message. "Hey, Sharon, it's Erica. Are you there?"

I picked up the receiver and turned off the machine. "Hey, Erica. ¿Qué pasó?"

"I just have a minute. Emma—Mrs. López—wanted me to give you a message. Mrs. Pirtle told her you'd left something at The Seasick, and she wondered if you'd come by and get it."

"Did she say what it was?"

"No. You know how she is."

"Hmm. I haven't noticed anything missing."

"Whatever. I'm just passing the word along. Are you doing anything for lunch? It would have to be early. I have to be back here around noon."

We made plans to meet at the Pizza Hut since it was a short walk from Head Start, and hung up.

Having nothing else to do, I drove over to Los Mareados to see what it was Mrs. Pirtle thought I'd left behind. Ever since I'd moved out, she'd been trying to be nice, which I found oddly jarring. I preferred her grouchiness to her fake friendliness.

"I thought you mighta needed this," she said as she handed me a bottle of cheap cologne.

Good perfume was one of the few luxuries I afforded myself, and I never would have used this stuff. "You found this in my room?"

"That's what the maid said. She coulda had it mixed up."

"Yes. Definitely. But thanks for checking anyway."

As I turned to leave, Mrs. Pirtle clawed at my arm. She gave me what, in other people, might have passed for a smile. As usual I couldn't see her eyes.

"Here I brought you all the way over here for nothin'," she said. "Let me give you somethin' for your trouble." She disappeared into her quarters and returned with a paper plate filled with raisin cookies topped with powdered-sugar frosting. "I always do my bakin' on Saturdays, so these ain't fresh outta the oven, but they're still good."

I remembered the cinnamon aroma I'd smelled when I was moving out, and was ashamed of myself for not appreciating Mrs. Pirtle's efforts to make amends.

"Thank you. I'm sure we'll enjoy these."

I set the plate on the seat beside me and drove away. I didn't like raisins, but could surely find someone who did.

* * *

"No thanks," Erica said when I met her for lunch. "Don't you remember the time the four of us got into that huge box of raisins, and spent the afternoon in our 'clubhouse' eating the whole damn thing—along with those rotten peaches?"

"And spent the evening and half the night throwing up."

"Maybe Alana's family would like them."

We finished our meal without touching on anything serious, then paid our bill and went outside.

"Erica, you said you were pressed for time."

"Oh, that. Some VIPs are coming in this afternoon to observe us. Why? You look like you have something on your mind."

"Mm. Couple of things. It can wait."

"Hey, nobody's more VIP than you! *They* can wait."

I laughed. "Okay. Good news first. I think Ryan and I are getting married."

"You think?"

"Well, I'm still getting used to the idea. I thought maybe if I said it out loud, it might seem real. But it won't be for a while. We haven't made any definite plans yet. So I'm not ready to tell the whole world yet—just you."

Erica hugged me. "Don't rush into anything," she teased. "What else besides the good news?"

I hesitated. "Erica, how long have you known—about Leo?"

"Not very long. Come on, why don't you leave your car here and walk back with me. We can talk on the way."

The sun was warm but there was a gentle breeze, and the fresh air felt good.

"About Leo," Erica said as we ambled toward Head Start. "I didn't tune in till I started looking back. Even in eighth grade, when I was so in love with him, I knew he didn't feel the same way about me. But I thought he was just shy."

"I can't believe he didn't love you."

"He did—as his best friend. I think we might have kidded ourselves that it was something more. But he never looked at me the way Ryan looked at you. Even then I noticed it. Like I say, I just chalked it up to shyness."

"He wasn't too shy about kissing you."

She smiled. "No, that was fun. For a while. Then it...."
She shrugged. "It just died away. I thought it was me. That
he'd just lost interest in me. And of course, I realize now, he
couldn't explain. I don't know if he even knew himself."

"I wonder when he realized."

"Sometime in high school, I'm guessing. I don't think he
came to grips with it even then. He was just so unhappy.
And there were all these girls who were dying to go out with
him. I think he tried to 'prove' he was straight with some of
them, and that made it worse."

"Is that what happened with Bernice?"

"That's what I heard—overheard—my brothers talking
about. They didn't like Bernice, so they just thought it was
funny, especially since Bernice thought all the guys were
drooling over her. Apparently she was very
'accommodating.' Anyway, one night she invited Leo along
with four or five other jocks over to 'party.'" Erica paused.
"Guys that age are so weird."

I rolled my eyes in agreement. "I take it Leo—couldn't."

"He couldn't, and Ryan wouldn't."

I stopped dead still. "Ryan was there? He wasn't a jock."

"No, but he tagged along."

"Oh God, not Bernice—anyone but her."

"Honey, listen to me. I'm not saying this just to make you
feel better. I'm quoting my brothers. They were friends with
a couple of the guys who were there. They said the only
reason Ryan went was to bail Leo out, and he just sat there
in the living room and glared at everyone. Anyway, he left
when Leo did."

We started walking again.

"How did you feel about the whole thing, Erica?"

"It bothered me, but not because it was Bernice especially. It just seemed so sleazy. And of course there was a lot of booze involved. My brothers seemed to take it all as a big joke."

"It must have been awful for Leo."

"I'm sure it was. He wasn't the only one who didn't follow through, but he was Bernice's real target. She'd been chasing him for some time. If it had been anyone else, she might have let it go. But she took it as a personal insult and was determined to get even."

"Figures."

"She told everyone he and Ryan were 'queers'—one of the nicer terms she used. I don't think anyone paid attention, to tell you the truth. You know Ryan, he just flipped her off and went on his merry way."

"But if Leo was having self-doubts to begin with...."

Erica nodded. "I don't know what went on after that. A few months later we moved, and after a while—you know how it is—I finally adjusted to California, and—life goes on."

"And when you came back a few weeks ago and saw Leo and Laura...."

"I should have picked up on it then—I told you how they acted—but it was the furthest thing from my mind. I should have picked up on it at the wake when I saw Leo give Johnny the kind of look I used to wish he'd give me. I guess it slipped into my subconscious, but it didn't register at the time. There was so much else to think about."

"So when did it click?"

"Hard to say, exactly A couple of things didn't jibe. The blackmail started me thinking. If Laura was the one being blackmailed, why is the family still so uptight about Bernice? It all comes back to Leo, and how she's always wanted to hurt him. I remembered what started it all, and that's when I started putting the pieces together."

"I thought she might have something on Leo too, but I thought maybe something—more serious."

"I know. That day you asked me about Leo and banking. I'm ashamed to say that thought crossed my mind too. As for being gay, he seems relieved not to have to keep it from you and me anymore, especially since it's still such a thorny issue with his parents. You know Leo, he'd never flaunt it, but I don't think he'd let himself be blackmailed over it either."

"But he's still hiding something," I mused.

"It is puzzling. Maybe it has to do with protecting Johnny Jerk. What does Johnny teach? I bet his classes are duller than dirt."

"Wish I'd thought to ask. I can picture Tina teaching little ones. Laura too. But you're right about Jerky."

"Something else occurred to me when you told me about not seeing anything of Laura in 'her' kitchen. When I visited them, I was too unnerved by their robot personalities to even notice the surroundings. This is only a guess, but I've come to think Leo and Johnny must share one house, and Tina and Laura share—used to share—the other."

"It still blows me away. Laura!" I shook my head. "You know what? Poor Tina. She must be going through hell."

"She must be. Maybe we should call her and—I don't know—offer her a little support. Right now I suppose I'd better get back to work after all. Hard to believe I'll be finished the end of this week."

Work. What was that? I was grateful Ryan understood. In the meantime, maybe I'd paint Spot's toenails too.

CHAPTER 33

On the way home, my cell phone rang.

"Hey, sweetheart, where are you?"

"I had lunch with Erica. Did you try to call me at home?"

"I did. Couple of times. Listen, I've been thinking. About what Gabe said. Why don't you come here and talk to my afternoon classes? They're the freshmen, and they're the ones who need to listen to someone else."

"Ryan, I can't just come up with something on the spur of the moment!"

"Why not? Isn't that what you were doing last night?"

"Well, yeah."

"Come on. The less you think about it, the better you'll do. Besides, you're a lawyer—you must be used to thinking on your feet."

"You're the one—what a sweet talker!"

"Is that a 'yes'?"

I laughed. "I didn't bring any of my lawyer suits with me. I'll have to come casual."

"Not that bathrobe! Go borrow something from Alana— she's about your size. See you whenever you get here. Call me when you're on the way, and I'll meet you at the main office."

This is nuts, I thought, as I phoned Alana at El Tigre. She laughed and said she'd call Beto that I was coming over. While I was there, I asked Beto if they'd be interested in the raisin cookies.

He smiled, that gentle spark of humor in his eyes. "No, guess it's something we inherited from all the Salazars. Seems the twins got sick on raisins one time when they were little, and—well, it wasn't a pretty picture."

"It wasn't pretty for Erica and me either."

"You know who likes raisin cookies is Tina. You could leave them at her place. Or I can take them over later if you're in a hurry."

I agreed, and went to change clothes. I felt strange going through Alana's closet, even with her permission, but fifteen minutes later I'd changed into a tailored navy-blue dress and was on my way.

* * *

I was glad Gabe wasn't in the first class of the afternoon. If I made a fool of myself, Ryan would have only himself to blame, but at least Gabe wouldn't have to suffer too.

After Ryan introduced me, I suddenly got stage fright. The way I always did in court. Twelve jurors or twenty-five freshmen—didn't matter. Not my area of expertise. I'd found the key to getting beyond my nervousness was to focus on individuals instead of numbers. Right now I suspected the kids were focused on their own adolescent concerns. I scanned the room for faces that looked other than politely bored, and found one or two that reflected curiosity.

"I'll tell you something about myself before I became a lawyer. And then you can ask questions.

"I grew up in South Texas—went to seventh and eighth grades here in Zapata. When I was a freshman, we moved up north, and I had nothing to say about it. I hated it."

So far, so good. A few quit looking glassy-eyed.

"After I ran away from home a couple of times and dropped out of school one semester, my stepfather—who'd been very patient up till then—finally had it. All he said was, 'You're right, Sharon. It wasn't your fault, and it wasn't fair. Life sucks. Now deal with it.'"

A few more quit looking out the window.

"I wish I could say the light dawned. But he still had to spell it out for me. If I got an education I could still be a bag-lady if that's what I wanted. But at least I'd have a choice."

Where to go from here? I cleaned up my act, kids, and the moral of this story is.... I looked to Ryan for help, but he just winked at me and grinned.

"I think I'll do better answering questions."

I was surprised at the number of hands that went up. I called on first one and then another.

"Didn't they kick you out of school for ditching so much?"

"Yes. But they let me back in on probation. Because I'd goofed off so much, I spent my last three years of high school in summer school, which was a drag."

"If you didn't like school, why did you go to law school?"

"Good question. I guess I thought it would be a good way to help people, but it took some growing up to feel that way."

"Couldn't you help people doing something else?"

"You bet. In fact, most jobs are probably helpful in one way or another, so I had lots of options. But my best friend's father was a lawyer, and he was a big influence on me."

"My dad says all lawyers are crooks."

How often had I heard *that* opinion! "Unfortunately some are, but they're only a small percentage. My friend's father was honest and kind."

"Do you solve murders? Like on TV?"

I knew it was innocent curiosity, but the question made me think of Laura. *No, I fail at that.* "No, I'm involved with helping migrant workers."

"Are they mostly wetbacks?"

My eyes locked with Ryan's. "I don't use that term, but no, most of the people I work with are already U.S. citizens."

"Do you make a lot of money?"

"No. Much of my work is pro bono—that means 'free.'"

"Nah. How can you work for free?"

"The firm I work for makes money doing other kinds of things—divorces, estate planning—things like that. We work as a team, so we all get paid."

Someday Ryan should invite Vince Martínez to tell how his parents had been treated when they came over from Mexico, and how this led Vince to become so involved in immigration law.

Another hand went up. "Why do you do the free stuff?"

Because I'm good at it. "Because—like any team—we each have things we do best. The person I work with most, for example, is razor sharp in court—I mean, if you were ever on trial, you'd want Dave in your corner. But sometimes he scares our clients as well as the people we're up against. So that makes it hard for him to get all the information he needs. And that's where I come in."

"What do you do?"

"Listen to people, to start with. A lot of people find the legal system scary, and they need to know someone is on their side before they can go any further. Then we can sort out the details—decide what's helpful and what isn't."

"Don't you ever scare anyone?"

I laughed. "Not too often."

One solemn girl with short straight hair and oversized glasses raised her hand and said timidly, "I wish you'd talk to my dad. I told him I wanted to be a lawyer, and he said...he said...women lawyers are all...." She turned brick red. The word "ballbusters" or its Spanish equivalent hung unspoken in the air, like an arcing hot-wire.

The sudden silence was palpable. I realized they were all listening intently for my response.

"Pushy?" I said softly.

There was a wave of knowing laughter.

"Well, some women have legitimate battles against discrimination. Others just...have a chip on their shoulders. But most of us are simply dedicated to doing our jobs. And there's quite a wide range of jobs in the legal field."

"The people you talk to, what do they tell you?"

"If they're not being paid a fair wage, or if their children are being kept out of school—things like that. Sometimes more personal things. Often they don't speak English, so it's easy for people to take advantage of them."

"Do you speak Spanish?"

"Qué sí. Desde que era chiquita. I grew up speaking Spanish."

After about 15 or 20 minutes in each class, Ryan would let me off the hook and continue with whatever he'd planned for that period. It gave me an insight into his own dedication to teaching, his own natural talent, the way the kids responded to him.

After the first class, I took aside the girl who wanted to be a lawyer. "The way to win over your father? Practice being persuasive without being pushy. Takes some work, but it's the best job training I can think of."

She smiled shyly. "Thanks."

When she'd gone, Ryan whispered, "Nice touch—making them think you work for free."

"Got their attention, no?"

By the end of the day, I'd revised my spiel here and there and answered all kinds of questions, some about the cost of law school, some about the cost of goofing off. Gabe grinned and gave me a thumbs-up as he left his class, which was encouraging, but I decided I still liked working with people one on one much better than I would ever like teaching—or addressing a jury.

After the last class, Ryan left me alone with the Trujillo girls, who approached me hesitantly. "Mr. Salazar told us we should apologize to you for being rude at the bakery that day," Dora began.

It seemed so long ago I'd almost forgotten about it. And though it wasn't polite, their remark that all *hueras* look the same had simply struck me as funny. Especially since the girls, though they weren't identical, looked remarkably alike. With shiny black hair pulled back into neat French braids, and large appealing eyes, they had a prettiness that would soon blossom into beauty.

"I wasn't mad. But I do appreciate the apology. It's always good to let people know when you're sorry." I motioned for us to sit down at the classroom desks. I turned my desk to face theirs.

"I'll tell you a secret. When I moved up north—and I mean *really* north, not just beyond the Nueces...." I leaned toward them conspiratorially and opened my eyes as wide as I could. "Everyone in my school was pale and blond. And I thought, 'My God, we all look exactly alike! I'll never be able to tell us apart!'"

The girls bubbled over, unable to hold back their giggles.

Viola said, "I'm glad you're Mr. Salazar's novia. I didn't know old people fell in love."

Old people! I had to laugh. I stood to go, but Dora seemed reluctant to leave, as if something else was on her mind, so I sat down again.

Finally Dora asked, "When you moved up north, when you were our age, did you have a boyfriend?"

"Yes. After a while." I wondered where this was leading.

"Did he want you to—you know?"

"Dora!" Viola poked her sister. "That's not nice to ask!"

"But it would help to know, wouldn't it." Even after all these years, I could relate to the anguish Dora felt. "Yes, he did. And no, I didn't."

"Is that why you broke up?"

I nodded. "Yes. It really hurt at the time." But not for long. I guess I hadn't liked my northern boyfriend as much as I'd thought.

Dora looked so miserable, I reached over and held her hand. "Listen to me. Any guy who tries to make you feel guilty about not having sex with him doesn't appreciate you. Sex is too precious to waste on someone who doesn't appreciate you. Do you understand what I'm trying to tell you?"

Dora sniffed and nodded. I found a box of Kleenex on Ryan's desk, handed her a tissue, then held her hand again. I wanted to say more, but didn't want to risk getting preachy. I was touched that Dora would bring this up with me, and also gratified to realize that—surveys notwithstanding—there wasn't such a gap between teenage girls today and those of my generation after all.

"You're so nice," Dora said. "I don't like that other lady."

"What other lady?"

"That one in the red car."

My mouth went dry. "Where—how do you know her? Does she come here to the school?"

The girls looked at each other. "Sometimes she parks outside the gate," Dora said. "But when we see her, we go the other way."

"Have you ever talked to her?"

"One time," Viola answered, twisting a loose strand of hair. "She came in the bakery one day when we were there."

"She came and sat down with us just like we knew her, or she was our friend or something," Dora continued, indignation in her voice.

"When was this?"

"I don't know. Maybe two weeks ago. Three weeks," Viola said.

"What did she want?"

The girls looked at each other again, and squirmed in their seats.

"I'm sorry." I folded my arms on the desk, and leaned toward them again. "I know this makes you uncomfortable, but it might be important."

Dora folded her hands and looked down at them. "She asked if Mr. Salazar was our teacher. And she said he was so nice blah blah blah."

"She didn't sound, you know, sincere," Viola added. "I mean, he is nice, but, I don't know." She looked to Dora, her eyes troubled.

"He's nice, but you thought she didn't like him?" I asked.

"Yeah. That's what I meant," Viola said. She continued twisting her hair, her other hand tapping the desk nervously.

"Then," Dora said, "she asked us if *everybody* liked him, if all the girls liked him, like she was hoping maybe somebody didn't."

"That's very perceptive. I imagine that's exactly what she was hoping."

"It made us mad, but kind of scared too," Viola said.

"I can see why. What did you tell her?"

"We just said everybody liked him, even though Priscilla Moreno doesn't, but we weren't going to tell her anything," Viola continued.

Thank God.

"She was so weird, and we just wanted her to go away," Dora said. "We told her we had to go home and do our homework."

"We didn't even finish our conchas," Viola said, miffed.

"Did you tell Mr. Salazar?"

Dora looked down at her hands again, and I saw the beginning of tears in her eyes. "It was too embarrassing."

I placed my hand over hers and nodded sympathetically. "Believe me, I understand. But I think he needs to know."

Viola's eyes were pleading. "Will you tell him for us?"

"Okay. And if anything like that happens again, will you let him know, or let me know? It's really important," I repeated. "Besides, you don't have to put up with people bothering you like that."

Almost as an afterthought I asked, "Has she been talking to anyone else that you know of?"

Dora wrinkled her nose. "I've seen her with Elmer Smithers sometimes."

Bernice and Elmer? The boy with the maroon pickup? Now there was an odd couple. "Tell me about Elmer."

"He's a senior—kind of wild." Viola pointed a finger toward her mouth and made a gagging sound. "And she's so OLD. It's gross."

Since Bernice was my age, I found this assessment a little disconcerting, but I could remember when I was a teenager and thought anyone over 25 was ancient.

"Are they, um, dating?"

Viola shrugged, tucking the loose strand back into her braid. "All I know is, I've seen them sitting in her fancy car, talking I guess."

Was it possible that Bernice was using Elmer just to rattle me? I couldn't think of any other reason he'd tail me.

"I've heard that he—" Dora began just as the custodian came into the room.

"Can you give us another minute?" I asked.

He glared at us and began running his broom up the last aisle.

"Guess not. Well, I probably shouldn't keep you any longer. Your mom might start to get worried."

They each gave me an unexpected hug, and started for home.

CHAPTER 34

Ryan was talking with another teacher, his eyes lighting up when he saw me come out of the classroom. His expression changed as I came closer and he saw the look on my face.

He introduced me to the other teacher, and I made automatic responses, hoping my smile didn't look too fake. Ryan made excuses for us to leave, and we started for the parking lot.

"What's wrong?" he asked.

"I'll explain as soon as we get home." I wished we weren't in separate cars, but it took only a few minutes to drive back to Ryan's.

We sat at the kitchen table, and I told him about Bernice trying to weasel her way into the Trujillo girls' confidence. "I tried to be calm around them, but inside I was coming unglued."

The steely anger I'd seen only once before—that time Bernice had followed us to the church parking lot—reappeared in his face. "I never thought she'd stalk my kids."

I shivered. "Ryan, please tell me what's going on. Either I'm in this with you, or I'm not."

He looked at me for a long moment, then stood up and began pacing, finally sitting down again. "Sometimes I'm afraid I've told you too much already. Maybe the less you know, the less she can hurt you." He took both my hands in his. "God, Sharon, if she starts harassing you...."

"Ryan, what could she do to me?" I wasn't sure if I was trying to ease Ryan's mind or my own. "And what could she say about me that she hasn't already said? What she thrives on is planting suspicion in people's minds. I think the more we know, the less she can hurt any of us."

"I hope you're right. I know you're right about Bernice playing mind games. She thought...." He shook his head. "She thought she'd driven Laura to suicide, and—I know this sounds insane—instead of feeling guilty, it only egged her on. She just got bolder and more demanding."

"It does sound insane, but in a way it's not that surprising."

Ryan stood up again and walked over to the sliding glass door, staring unseeingly at the patio. I came and stood beside him, putting my arm around his waist, my head on his shoulder. He put his arm around me and drew me closer.

"Sharon, this is hard to talk about. It's ugly."

"I know."

"A few days after Laura died, Bernice approached me in the parking lot after school. Offered to buy me a 'friendly little drink.'" Ryan grimaced. "Said she had something to discuss with me."

He paused, still staring into space. "I didn't want to drink with her, or discuss with her, or anything-else with her. I told her the school had a strict policy about who was and wasn't allowed on campus, and not to show up there again. She turned nasty—said the school probably had a strict policy about teachers fucking their students. It didn't register at first that this was aimed at me."

My stomach lurched. "No, I guess not."

"She said she knew several girls who were willing to tell everyone that I'd been coming on to them. But, for a price, she could talk them out of it. Words to that effect."

"What did you tell her?"

"I told her to go to hell."

"Too bad she didn't follow your advice."

He hugged me to his side again. "Let's sit down. This might take a while."

We moved over to the couch and sat quietly for a few minutes before Ryan spoke again.

"Later," he said, "when I thought it over—what Bernice had said—it really shook me up. I didn't know of anyone who'd want to get even with me, for a bad grade or whatever. But I'm not dumb enough to think every single one of my students likes me."

"Probably not. But I can't believe most of your kids wouldn't rally around you."

"That's what I'd like to think. But even if they did, once ideas are planted...." Ryan's face took on a distant look again. "I've seen people—I've seen my brother—nearly destroyed by rumors. Maybe for that reason, I've been even more careful than I've needed to be."

"How do you mean?"

He gave a short laugh. "Among other things, the way some of these girls dress—sometimes I think I'll get a permanent crick in my neck trying not to look below their chins."

I smiled. "Pobrecito."

"I hardly ever touch anyone—boy or girl—not even to give someone a pat on the back. I never talk to any of my kids alone." Ryan paused, anguish clouding his face. "When I knew poor little bruised up Teresa Gabaldón needed someone to talk to, did I ask her to stop by my room after school?"

"Ryan, don't do this to yourself."

"I'd always been careful anyway, but after Bernice's threat, I felt like a spotlight was on me."

"It bothers me that Bernice has gotten away with this for so long." I paused a minute, then, "Would you be willing to talk to her again? With a tape recorder this time?"

"I'd just as soon swallow ground glass. Sharon, even if we got something on tape, she'd manage to twist it so we still couldn't prove anything."

"She wouldn't know that. In fact, maybe we could make her think you had a tape recorder last time. She probably doesn't remember exactly what she said. Maybe we could turn the tables."

"I'll have to think about it."

"I wonder, if she was hanging out at the school, if Miguel or Gabe ever saw her, or if they heard anything. It wouldn't hurt to ask them."

"I don't want to drag my nephews into this either."

"Well, since nobody's talking to anybody, they might already be dragged in—maybe they've heard things they don't want to tell you."

"You have a devious mind."

"Occupational hazard."

"You're right, though. And I suppose the sooner we get this in the open, the better. Maybe we should go over and talk to the boys after basketball practice. Give 'em another hour or so."

CHAPTER 35

It was too early for supper, so I got us something to drink instead, then sat on the couch, tucking my feet up under me.

"Oh no," Ryan moaned. "I see those damn wheels turning again. Another occupational hazard?"

"I'll try not to be obnoxious."

"I'm waiting."

"You said something about Bernice admitting she'd driven Laura over the brink."

"Only if you read between the lines. Nothing incriminating. Something sarcastic like, 'Look what happened to poor Laura.'"

"I can't help wondering. Bernice seems to enjoy making people miserable just for the sake of it. Like Alana says, it's a power thing. She's tried getting her claws in other people—Patty and Tony, for instance—but she's backed down. With you and Leo she's like a dog with a bone. Why can't you shake her off?"

"From square one?"

"Maybe square two. I know she's always wanted to hurt Leo. From what Erica said, it was because he wouldn't, or couldn't, have sex with her."

Ryan looked at me a minute, as if mulling over how much I knew about square one. Finally he said, "It wasn't just that. It was Bernice herself. Leo found her repulsive, and she sensed it. That was the ultimate rejection. She went around telling everyone we were fags. Oddly enough I don't think she even suspected Leo was gay—hell, Leo couldn't even admit it to himself at the time. It was just her way of saving face."

"Does she know now?"

"Yeah, but she also knows that doesn't have anything to do with the way he feels about her. That's what she can't get over."

Ryan took a deep breath. "It's hard to imagine anyone so vindictive. Just waiting. Hoping to catch Leo in some compromising situation. But he's kept a pretty low profile. Nothing to attract the attention of the gay-bashers or anything like that. There was never anyone here in town—at least not till Johnny Quemado."

"I'm surprised she didn't try to use it against him anyway."

"Oh, she tried all right. Gave him a jolt when she threw it at him. But then he figured he didn't have anything to lose by trying to outbluff her. He said something like, 'So what's new?' and told her if she found anyone who cared to let him know."

"Wouldn't it have upset your parents?"

"She must have assumed they already knew. At any rate, either the bluff worked or she was just trying to bug Leo to begin with."

"So Johnny wasn't Leo's problem."

"Nope. Laura was."

I caught the bitterness in his voice, and didn't say anything.

"Laura was just using Leo. Laura and Tina had gotten...whatever, and Tina confided that she and Johnny were putting on this big front so they wouldn't lose their jobs. Maybe in a big city, it wouldn't have mattered. Hard to say. Anyway, Laura knew—or guessed—about Leo, and she asked him out so she could set him up with Johnny. They hit it off. I still haven't figured out why."

"That is a mystery. Who knows. Maybe the timing was right."

"Next thing I knew, Laura had cooked up this harebrained idea of marrying Leo so she could hide her relationship with Tina. Maybe she'd planned it all along. She and Tina—and Johnny—were the only ones who had anything to gain."

"It's still hard for me to picture Laura being so—scheming."

"Picture it. I tried to talk Leo out of it, but there was only so much I could say. The one thing he balked at was having a church wedding. Guess he felt the hypocrisy could stretch just so far. They told everyone they'd eloped, gotten married in Mexico. Had a big shindig afterwards. You want to know what I think? I don't think any of 'em were ever married. I bet the whole setup was a farce from the get-go."

"Maybe. Either way, somehow Bernice found out."

"Or maybe just took a stab in the dark. It wouldn't have been too hard for someone like Bernice to sniff out. Laura wasn't at all subtle once she thought she'd fooled everyone."

"So then Bernice threatened to expose everyone?"

"Supposedly just Laura. But Bernice knew it would get Leo caught up in a scandal as well. She never really cared what would happen to Johnny and Tina. Laura began unraveling pretty fast. Bernice took great delight in it."

I was quiet, thinking it still didn't jibe that Bernice would have poisoned Laura. Not if she enjoyed torturing her instead. I also realized I'd had it backwards. "Laura wasn't blackmailed because she turned to drugs, was she. She started on drugs because she was being blackmailed. And after a while it was more than just prescriptions, wasn't it."

He nodded. "That's when Bernice hit pay dirt. Spreading rumors about their 'perversion,' as she called it, could have been damaging, but all she had was guesswork. With the cocaine—with something illegal—that was concrete."

"How did she find out?"

"Good question. I've wondered if Bernice was supplying it herself. More likely, she was blackmailing the dealer too."

"That would be more her style."

"Well, as if reveling in Laura's misery wasn't enough, Bernice demanded more money to keep quiet. Laura became more and more desperate. Our dad had about reached his limit. So Leo...took out a loan without going through all the channels."

Seeing the dismay on my face, Ryan hastened to explain, "It's not like it sounds. It was a standard short-term loan, and in Leo's name. Everything in black and white. But he already had a couple of loans out and knew it would raise questions if he kept borrowing more. So he just didn't get all the signatures needed on the paperwork."

"Sounds risky to me. Wouldn't someone notice?"

"Someone did. The same day as it turned out. See, Leo figured he could shuffle the papers around for several days without any problem. By the following week he could pay off the loan from a CD that was coming due, then lose the paperwork forever. Not very smart, but Leo was feeling pretty desperate too."

"And he figured wrong. He didn't have several days."

"That was weird too. Leo began having second thoughts almost right away. That's when he came to me. We scraped together enough for him to repay it the very next day. But someone had already discovered it. Word leaked out—don't ask me how. Bernice pounced on it."

My eyes widened. "Bad enough to have Bernice find out. But I'd think Leo would be in even bigger trouble with the bank!"

"Apparently they let it go. Maybe since the loan was repaid so quickly."

Several red flags began waving in my mind. Although it was a risk, Leo must have had good reason to think the odds were with him. Strange that his "incomplete" paperwork was discovered so quickly, and just as strange that Bernice got wind of it. And why would the bank just shrug it off? I put this on the back burner to think about later.

My thoughts went back to Laura. "I wonder how long Leo could have kept on bailing Laura out. I guess anyone else would have walked out on her."

"No. Leo wouldn't do that. But he finally did give her an ultimatum. Only part of that loan was for Bernice. The rest was for a rehab clinic. He convinced her the drugs were doing her more harm than any rumors could."

Even if Ryan had come to dislike Laura, I couldn't forget the sweet girl I used to know, and I found it unbearably sad that she never had a chance to get her life back in order. And there were still so many unanswered questions.

"Ryan, you said that after Laura died Bernice just got bolder."

"Obsessed is more like it. She hinted to Leo that she could destroy his credibility at the bank by planting rumors that he's tampering with people's accounts. She might be able to pull it off too. Up till now, Laura's drug problem hasn't been general knowledge. But if that came to light, added to the bank rumors, it might appear that he was involved in drug payoffs."

"That's quite a leap, but there's a certain logic to it."

"Bernice has a talent for twisted logic."

"And if Leo doesn't scare, she'll try to get to him through you. Like Erica says, one way or another she wants to hurt anyone he cares about."

"And get to me through my kids—through Dora and Viola, and God-knows-who-else. Not just trying to dig up dirt, but upsetting them in the process." Ryan reached over and pulled me closer to him. "I figure it's only a matter of time before she gets to you. And that scares me."

I put my head on his shoulder. "Well, at least the girls weren't taken in. And Bernice knows I'm hardly a naïve teenager anymore." I didn't want to say it out loud, but maybe Bernice simply hadn't figured a way to strike out at me yet.

"I guess I can be glad—as far as I know, anyway—she hasn't picked on any of the kids who don't like me. If Leo knew Bernice was threatening me, he'd probably keep paying her off. Sometimes Leo is *too* loyal."

"You said Leo'd been hurt by rumors before. Was this Bernice's doing too?"

"No. It was back in college. Strange. Everything started out so great. Leo got a football scholarship to a small school in the Panhandle, so of course I tagged along. It turned grim. We'd never known discrimination—never been called 'spics' before."

My throat closed up, anger wrapping itself around me like an itchy blanket.

"Leo decided the scholarship wasn't worth it. So we lasted about two weeks and went to the University instead. Leo managed to get a walk-on slot on the freshman team. He was going to major in phys ed—be a football coach."

Ryan paused, then continued. "I don't know if it was going someplace where nobody knew us or what, but Leo got involved with another guy for the first time—another player. Word got around. Bottom line—he was told he might as well forget about coaching—or anything to do with kids. We stuck it out till the end of the semester, then went to El Paso and finally finished college."

Tears pricked my eyes. "How cruel! Leo of all people would never hurt kids—or anyone else."

Ryan looked thoughtful. "Maybe that's why he was willing to go along with Laura's marriage scheme. He would have hated to see her lose her chance to teach. One thing I'll say for her, she was a good teacher—great with kids from what I hear. I think my nephews liked her, at first anyway. And then she began avoiding us all."

"Maybe she was more uncomfortable with the pretense than you realized."

"Could be."

I sat down close to Ryan again, wishing I could turn back the clock, thinking how one turning point leads to another. "Why didn't Leo stay in the city after college?"

"You weren't the only one who goofed off in high school," Ryan said wryly, putting his arm around me. "If it hadn't been for the teachers here—the ones who didn't give up on me—I'd probably be a professional dishwasher by now. But I knew all along I wanted to give back. So when I came back here, so did Leo."

"You've always looked out for each other, haven't you."

"Yeah. Whenever one of us was doing something dumb, the other one seemed to be around picking up the pieces."

"Must have kept you busy all these years."

Ryan laughed. "You can say that again. I never told you about the time I ran away to see you, did I? Not long after you'd moved to Minnesota."

"No, I never knew about that!"

"Well, it wasn't one of my finer hours," Ryan said soberly. "Leo went with me, of course. Good thing too. We borrowed Danny Maestas' beat-up old van and away we went. We got picked up by the Border Patrol just north of Laredo. No driver's license. No ID. Nothing but a few dollars for gas and Cokes."

"What did they do?"

"Harassed us mostly. Kept asking us if we'd stolen the van, and if we were sure we weren't wetbacks. They were mean, and I was scared. Leo was the one who kept his cool. He said our dad was a lawyer. I don't know if they believed him, but after a while they let him make a phone call, and he called Erica's dad. It's one of those things that when you look back, parts of it are funny. Like when he called Mr. Montoya—I can hear him now." Ryan mimicked Leo's gruff businesslike tone. "'Hey, Dad, this is your son Leo.'"

I smiled. "Knowing Mr. Montoya, I'm sure he picked up on it pretty quick."

"You bet. After Leo told him where we were, he called our dad, and Alana told him everything."

"Alana knew?"

"Leo told her before we left home. He thought somebody ought to know, even if I didn't think so. So Apá and Mr. Montoya came to get us and Danny's van, and I think a few heads rolled."

"Did Alana come with them?"

"Are you kidding? Someone had to stay home and make sure Amá didn't find out. Tell you what, dingaling though she is, I love my mom, and I was sure glad to see her again. And she sure was pleased that Leo and I kept hugging her the rest of the evening."

"We were some tough kids, weren't we? I'm impressed though. You and Leo got about—hmm, 40-something miles further than I did when I tried running away."

Ryan kissed me on the cheek. "Maybe we're luckier than we thought we were."

He got up and chucked his Tecate can in the trash. "Well, let's go talk to Gabe and Miguel and see if this afternoon can get any worse."

CHAPTER 36

Carlos was watching for us from the window. As soon as we came in, he ran up and hugged us both, then stayed glued to my side without saying anything. Beto greeted us without his customary smile. What was wrong?

"Are the boys home from practice yet?" Ryan asked.

"Should be here any minute."

"Carlitos, why don't you show us the model airplanes you've been building?" I asked, looking for a glimmer of the happy little boy I'd expected to see.

He trudged off to his room with Ryan and me in his wake, then described the models without any enthusiasm. When we heard the door slam telling us his brothers had finally gotten home, Carlos jumped like a scared cat, then turned away from us, rubbing his eyes to keep from crying.

Ryan and I looked at each other and then back at Carlos. "Come on," I said, taking him by the hand. "Let's go see what the boys are up to. Maybe get some lemonade."

Carlos held tight to my hand as we went into the kitchen. After we'd gotten something to drink, Ryan motioned for Miguel and Gabe to go into the living room with him.

Carlos was still clinging to me, and I looked to Beto for clues. He shook his head, puzzled and worried. "Let's go in here," Beto said, leading us into his office.

In his office was a huge stuffed armchair, large enough for Carlos and me both. "We can sit here and talk," I told him as we sat down. Carlos' eyes widened in fear, and tears began rolling down his face, now white beneath his freckles.

"Or not talk. We'll just sit here awhile." I pulled him onto my lap and began rocking him gently. He buried his head in my neck and didn't say anything.

Beto and I looked at each other helplessly. He pulled up a chair near us and waited along with me.

After a while I asked the question that Beto had surely already asked. "Carlos, did somebody hurt you?"

He shook his head, no.

"Something happened that scared you. Can you tell us what it was?"

His body tensed. Finally he said, "I promised not to tell."

Now we were getting somewhere. "There's a rule about promises," I said, thinking of Erica and her creative way with rules. "You should always keep a promise. Almost always. There are some exceptions. Are you listening?"

He sat up straighter, and I quit rocking.

"If a promise makes you scared, it's not a good promise. And the rule then is, you're *supposed* to break it. You *have to* break it. Just as soon as you can. That's the rule. It's—it's in the catechism. You should tell your dad or mom— someone in your family. Your lawyer, your nina."

"It's about you, nina."

"About me?" This was a surprise.

"Tell us, mijo," Beto said quietly.

"That *fea* said she'd hurt you if I told."

I could feel the little hairs rise on my arms, and wondered why any mention of Bernice always caused such a physical reaction in me. And I knew beyond any doubt that he was talking about Bernice.

"The *ugly lady* in the red car?" I asked.

He nodded.

"She likes to scare people. And she likes to do it by making them keep secrets. And once the secrets are out, then 'poof!' she shrivels up." I snapped my fingers. "Just like that."

"Like the witch on the Wizard of Oz? Could we pour water on her and make her melt?" Carlos slid off my lap, and seemed to revive a little at the thought of dissolving Bernice.

"We'll see."

"Come here, mijo," Beto said.

Carlos went and sat on Beto's knee, putting his arm around Beto's neck. Beto, like Leo at times, reminded me of a big teddy bear—kind and comforting. I was glad to let him take over the questioning.

"Tell me, Carlitos, when did you talk to this *fea*?"

"After school. I was walking home with Jimmy and Sara, and she drove up beside us."

"What did she say?"

"She said she needed to talk to me, and Jimmy and Sara ran away."

"Then what?" Beto asked in a mild voice.

"She told me to get in her car, that she was your friend and she had a secret to tell me."

My blood ran cold. Beto and I exchanged uneasy looks.

"I knew she wasn't your friend and I didn't want to hear her secret. I just started walking real fast."

"That's good. That was smart."

"But she kept on driving beside me, and I couldn't walk fast enough."

"That must have been scary."

"It was." Carlos' tears started again, and Beto hugged him. I was glad Beto wasn't one of those pseudo-macho guys who think little boys shouldn't cry.

"She told me...." Carlos' voice was muffled against Beto's chest. "She told me Uncle Ryan was going to get in real trouble if I didn't go with her. Uncle Leo too."

A wave of nausea swept over me. *Breathe, breathe, breathe.*

"What did you tell her?" I whispered.

"I didn't say anything. I didn't want Uncle Ryan and Uncle Leo to get in trouble, and I didn't want to go with her."

Beto nodded, and we waited in chilled silence for Carlos to continue.

"Then she tried acting all nice again and said she liked children, that she had a little brother once. And we could have a lot of fun."

My stomach churned as I tried to push aside thoughts of whatever sadistic things Bernice might have in mind. Then Patty's story about Bernice's brother's mysterious death came screaming up at me, and I knew the breathing wasn't going to work this time. I fled to the bathroom and threw up the lemonade I'd had so recently.

I rinsed my mouth, then found some mouthwash in the medicine cabinet. I can't keep falling apart like this, I told myself. I pulled down the lid on the commode and sat there, my forehead pressed against the coolness of the sink, willing the shakiness to stop.

There was a knock at the door. "Sharon, are you okay?"

"I'll be out in a minute."

I used somebody's washcloth and towel and laid them on the tub, then sprayed air-freshener around the bathroom, and opened the door.

Ryan was waiting outside, looking as sick as I'd felt. He put his arms around me and held me as if he were afraid I'd disappear. We went back into Beto's office, where Miguel and Gabe were waiting. They were staring at me with the same horrified look I'd seen on Ryan's face. Carlos was still crying, Beto rocking him now.

"What happened?" I whispered to Ryan.

"Later."

"Do you mind if I have some yerba buena?" I asked Beto. I needed something to settle the queasiness.

"Of course not. You can find your way around the kitchen?"

I nodded.

"Come on, mijo," Beto said to Carlos. "Let's go wash your face and wait for mom to come home. Sharon's here, and nobody's going to hurt her. I'll go with you to school tomorrow, and nobody will hurt you either."

After Beto and Carlos left the room, the rest of us went into the kitchen. I started the teakettle boiling, then asked Ryan again what had happened.

"I don't know what led up to it, but when we went into Beto's office—after we saw you flying down the hall—he was asking Carlos how he got away from Bernice."

A metallic taste filled my mouth. "How?"

"His friend Jimmy showed up with his brother, thank God. When Bernice saw them coming, she drove away." Ryan's mouth tightened and the sick look reappeared.

I knew there was more, but no one said anything.

"She must have threatened him first," I said, putting the pieces together. "Made him promise not to tell anyone she'd talked to him."

Still, no one said anything.

"Or she'd hurt me." Carlos had told us as much. "I guess she must have gone into detail. Poor Carlos." I was in tears now. "He shouldn't have to hear the awful way she talks. He must have been terrified."

"She said she'd cut your face up," Gabe said, "and...do some other stuff."

"That's enough," Ryan said sharply.

"She should be arrested," I said. "Not for what she said about me—secondhand threats don't mean much." No matter how graphically she'd described whatever mutilation she claimed to have in mind for me. "But for stalking and terrorizing Carlos."

Gabe came over and hugged Ryan and me together, then turned away rubbing his eyes, looking much the way Carlos had looked earlier.

The teakettle whistled, and I turned the heat off. My hands shook as I poured boiling water over the yerba buena. I added an ice cube to mine, and took a long swallow of the soothing tea, hoping it would keep me from getting sick again.

"She overstepped herself this time," I said. "We need to tell the authorities and have her locked up."

"And then what? She'll just get some big-city hotshot lawyer to get her off," Miguel said. "Sorry," he added, "I forgot."

"Don't apologize. I don't like it any better than you do, Miguel."

"I am sorry, Sharon."

"Maybe it's not such a bad idea to think like Bernice's hotshot lawyer. Whatever happens in the long run, the sooner we report this the better. That's one of the first things a good lawyer would look at. As soon as your mom gets home, well, we can talk about it then." I didn't relish the steps that lay ahead.

Carlos came into the kitchen, dressed in his Batman pajamas, and Beto turned to Ryan and me, unable to hide the anxiety in his eyes. "I'm going to get Alana. Will you wait here?"

Gabe's face was chalky, his voice cracked. "She won't hurt Mom, will she?"

"No, mijo."

Miguel looked away, his jaw set.

I wanted to get the ugly pictures out of Carlos' head, but didn't know how. I knelt beside him. "Look at me, Carlitos. This is the face I want you to remember." I crossed my eyes and made a clown face.

He giggled, then hiccupped. I knew it would take more than funny faces to drive away the ugly pictures Bernice had created, but at least I'd gotten a smile.

We went into the living room then and waited. Carlos curled up on my lap, his head on my breast. Ryan sat beside us, his arms around us both. I told Carlos over and over that everything would be all right, hoping Alana would forgive the lie, knowing she would probably have told the same one.

Miguel and Gabe couldn't sit still, and wandered from one room to another. Ten minutes later Beto and Alana drove up and we breathed a collective sigh of relief. All three boys ran to meet their mother at the door and held on to her as if they thought they'd never see her again.

CHAPTER 37

"Well, Sharon, you're the lawyer," Alana said. "If I drive a stake through her heart, would it be justifiable homicide?"

"If I had anything to say about it."

Carlos had fallen asleep in Alana's arms, and was unaware of our discussion. I wondered if the older boys should be in on it, but decided Alana and Beto knew best. Earlier the boys had gone to Church's and brought home fried chicken for dinner, but none of us had much appetite, or much to say. Now we were all in the living room again.

"My best advice right now is to call another lawyer," I said.

"Who would that be? We haven't needed a lawyer since Beto started his business years ago."

"What about Andy Estrada?" Ryan offered.

"Carlos asked you, Sharon," Gabe said in a voice suggesting that Ryan and I were committing treason to recommend anyone else.

"Honey, the problem is, it would seem I had a personal ax to grind because of her threat against me. And believe me, I'd love to grind a few axes." Maybe grind them right into Bernice's skull while Alana did the stake thing, but some things are better left unsaid. "You need someone objective. But I'm sure Andy would tell you the same thing—to call the sheriff as soon as possible."

Alana wrapped her arms more securely around Carlos. "I don't want someone asking Carlos a lot of questions and upsetting him again."

"Alana, I promise, you can stop the questions any time. All Carlos needs to do is make a statement. 'Someone' tried to pick him up against his will. Period." I took a deep breath, knowing she wouldn't like what I had to say next. "Listen, Alana, please bear with me. If Carlos talks to Julio or one of his deputies while he's still upset, so much the better. It's important that it doesn't sound rehearsed."

"Let's call Andy," Beto said wearily.

Gabe was already at his side with the phone.

"Well, we interrupted his dinner, but he'll be right over," Beto said after talking to Andy.

Ryan and I had gone to school with Andy Estrada, and once again I had a hard time picturing a friend I remembered from eighth grade as an adult, let alone as a successful attorney. Apparently the feeling was mutual. As soon as he arrived, Andy and I mentally circled each other for a few minutes, then dropped our guard and began working together.

Andy was tall and thin, with thick black hair that would have curled if it hadn't been cut so short. I remembered he'd worn it in an afro in junior high, along with wild shirts and gold chains. Tonight he was wearing dark slacks and shirt, and the only gold he sported was in his wire-rimmed glasses.

"Sharon's right," he said after Beto explained what had happened. "The sooner we file a report the better. You know Billy Archuleta, don't you? He's good—has boys of his own. Should be easy for Carlos to talk to. I'll see if Julio can send him." Andy didn't waste any time getting calls made, then asked, "Any suggestions, Sharon, before Billy gets here?"

"Nothing you wouldn't remind him about yourself. Well, maybe one. Carlos doesn't know her by name, but I have a feeling Billy's going to figure it out. He'll have to be careful that he doesn't let it slip."

Andy nodded. "I'll warn him."

"Also, she made threats against me. That's all Carlos needs to say. Tell Billy not to ask for details. It doesn't matter at this point."

Andy studied me a minute, then nodded again. "Carlos trusts you. Why don't you tell him what to expect from Billy?"

Beto woke Carlos up, and he came over to sit by me while I explained what was going on. Beto told me that Carlos already knew both Andy and Billy, whose sons played on his Little League team.

"Eddie Archuleta's dad is coming over to ask you some questions about what happened this afternoon," I said.

Carlos tensed, and I put my arm around him.

"It won't take very long, and the questions won't be hard, but it'll help keep something like this from happening again, okay?"

He nodded reluctantly.

"Your dad and mom will be here, Carlitos. And so will Mr. Estrada. But pretend they're not around and just talk to Eddie's dad, okay?"

"Where will you be? You're my lawyer, not Mr. Estrada."

"I'll be nearby. But we lawyers work as a team, and tonight's not my turn. So pretend I'm not here either."

That seemed to satisfy him, and he gave me a hug before going back to sit with Alana and Beto.

Billy showed up shortly afterwards. Short and barrel-chested, with bushy hair and beard, he looked more like a biker than a sheriff 's deputy. After Andy briefed him, Billy talked with Carlos about baseball for a few minutes till Carlos felt at ease with him.

Then Billy spoke to Andy again. "I'd like to get this on videotape, if that's okay with you."

Andy frowned, but waited for Billy to continue.

"Another kid, it might be a little dicey. But if this goes the way I think it will, it'll be more effective on tape. And if I'm wrong, we can always go back to a written report."

After more discussion, Billy set up a small camcorder on the kitchen counter, then sat at the table with Carlos facing him, the camera slightly angled. The rest of us moved to the side, but still within camera range. Andy reminded Carlos again to pretend we weren't there, and the session started.

After answering a few low-key questions, Carlos told Billy that "an ugly lady" had tried to make him go with her in her car.

"Can you describe the lady or her car?" Billy asked.

"Her hair was orange and stuck out, and she was driving a Porsche Carrera."

How could I have forgotten that boy children—even from the womb—know every model of car on the planet?

Billy clamped his jaws together and rubbed his bearded chin. Obviously the description rang a bell. "Are you sure it wasn't a Porsche Boxster?"

Carlos frowned at Billy for asking such a stupid question. "'Course not. A Carrera looks like a Carrera, and a Boxster looks like a Boxster."

"What happened then?"

"I just walked faster and faster." Carlos began squirming, his eyes troubled as the memories came hurtling back. "But she kept on following me." By now, tears were rolling down his face.

Good, I thought, even as I wanted to wipe away the tears. Carlos' reaction was genuine and spontaneous under Billy's gentle questioning.

"And then what?"

"She said if I didn't go with her, my uncles would be in big trouble."

"Anything else?"

Carlos began crying in earnest, and I could see Alana's agitation mounting. I pleaded with her mentally to wait just a few more seconds.

"She made me promise not to tell anyone or she'd hurt my nina."

Andy made a cutting motion with his hand. Billy made some concluding remarks for the tape, then told Carlos he'd been very helpful. Alana scooped Carlos up in her arms and sailed out of the room.

The rest of us moved back into the living room. Beto and the boys sat stone-faced, and the strain showed in Ryan's face as well. I felt like crying myself, but knew I had a perspective they didn't.

"Poor kid," Billy said.

"What now?" Miguel asked, not bothering to hide the sarcasm. "Round up all the ugly ladies in town and have my little brother pick one from the lineup?"

"No, son," Andy answered him evenly. "With any luck, that's one ugly lady he'll never have to face again. I know this isn't easy for any of you, but you did the right thing."

"What do you think, Counselor?" Billy directed his remark at me. "To tell you the truth, I haven't had a lot of experience with something like this."

"I'm glad you thought to videotape it. And throwing in that part about the Boxster was perfect. I wish we had a close-up of the disgust on Carlos' face—no way could that have been faked!"

I slipped my hand into Ryan's, then turned to Beto. "Some psychologists might consider it therapeutic for Carlos

238

to talk about this again and again. Personally, I'm not sure about that. But I do know too much repetition could work against him in a police report. After a while, kids either tend to embellish or say what they think you want to hear. The worst thing would be if it looked like he'd been coached."

Ryan squeezed my hand.

Beto took off his glasses and rubbed his eyes. "I hope you're right."

"I couldn't have explained it better," Andy said. "Look, we'll have Billy talk to the other kids first thing tomorrow. See if they remember something Carlos didn't."

Billy grinned at me. "I got three boys—I can talk about cars and baseball. Maybe you should talk to Sara."

I shook my head. "I'd like to, but I've got to stay out of this. Maybe I can hide under the window and pop up with cue cards."

Andy laughed. "What would those cue cards say?"

"I'd talk to Sara before Jimmy, for one thing. This sounds terribly sexist, and I can think of some people who'd string me up by the toes for saying it. But I suspect Sara might not know the first thing about cars, and it's better if she doesn't get any ideas from the boys. However—if she was there long enough to see her—she might come up with some kind of description for Bernice. Sara might know what color nail polish 'the lady in the red car' was wearing; what kind of jewelry, make-up, clothes, things like that."

Miguel folded his arms across his chest. "Let me know when the mutual-admiration society is adjourned."

"Back off, Miguel," I said. "We're not the enemy here."

Miguel dropped the sarcasm, but the pain beneath it showed through. "Even if you get her arrested, she'll be out on bail in a heartbeat, and then what'll she do to my brother for snitching?"

Andy and I looked at each other for a moment. "One thing at a time, son," Andy said, turning his attention to Miguel. "We're not going to do anything to jeopardize your brother. This isn't TV. Nobody's going to rush in and arrest Bernice without something to make it stick. Right now we really don't have a lot to go on. But while Billy's talking to Jimmy and Sara tomorrow, I'm going to see if anyone else has filed a complaint against *la fea*."

Andy was kind enough not to add that the word of one little boy against someone as manipulative as Bernice could be a legal minefield. Andy and Billy left soon after that, leaving me to be the designated bad guy. Miguel is right, I thought. How could I have risked putting Carlos in danger again?

CHAPTER 38

Alana rejoined us in the living room. "Well, I finally got him settled down again. I hope you're happy, Sharon."

"Not especially."

"Come on, Mom," Gabe said. "She's not the enemy."

"No she's not," Ryan said. "From what Sharon told me this afternoon—and the boys confirmed it—Bernice has been harassing a lot of people."

Startled, Alana looked toward Miguel and Gabe, who looked away. I realized I'd been so caught up in Carlos' ordeal, this was the first I'd heard of their talk with Ryan.

"And since no one calls her on it," Ryan continued, "she just keeps on harassing."

It's amazing what a little vote of confidence will do. "Well," I said slowly, thinking out loud, "Miguel had a good point earlier. And maybe I'm beginning to see the light."

"Damn wheels spinning again," Ryan murmured.

"I wish Leo were here."

Alana's eyes met mine. "Call him."

Ryan stood up. "I'll go get him. Fill him in."

Before long they were back, Leo looking as tense and angry as everyone else. He sat on the couch with Ryan and me and waited.

"Miguel got me thinking," I began carefully. "There's somebody out there who'd be willing to pay Bernice's bail. Somebody who'd see to it she has a 'hotshot' attorney. Somebody with a guilty conscience and lots of bucks.

Someone—I suspect—who's a 'hotshot' at the bank. It's just a guess, but how does it add up to you, Leo?"

Leo looked at me intently, as if the wheels could be seen turning in his head too. "Percy Smithers."

"Who is Percy Smithers?" *And why did that name sound familiar?*

"One of the vice presidents. There've been rumors about Bernice and Percy, but I never paid much attention. Bernice and rumors go hand in hand."

"Leo." I paused, wondering how to word this, wondering how much the boys knew. "I think Percy saw a chance to take advantage of you for something—something he himself might have done."

"I don't follow you."

"You don't need to beat around the bush, Sharon," Miguel mumbled.

Gabe looked down at the floor. "That *fea* wanted us to think Uncle Leo stole money from the bank. When we told Uncle Ryan about it, he told us what really happened."

Anger blanketed me. "Why was she telling you this? In exchange for what?"

Miguel scowled. "We didn't stay around to find out. We knew she was lying."

Leo rubbed the back of his neck. "I didn't know she was bothering you kids too."

The anguish in Beto's face deepened. "You should have told us."

Gabe looked up, distress in his own eyes. "We didn't want you to worry."

"Sharon's right about something else too," Ryan said. "We've all been bending over backwards not to worry each other. And Bernice has really worked that to her advantage."

Alana blinked back tears. "Hindsight again."

Gabe went over and sat beside her, giving her a hug. Miguel stared at his hands, clenched tightly together, and looked as if he were fighting back tears himself.

"Well, I think we're back on track now," Ryan said.

But still sorting things out. I turned to Leo again. "Getting back to Percy, how did that paperwork get from your desk to his?"

"Interesting. He said the bank was due an audit, and he was making some preliminary 'assessments,' I think he called it. The loan came up on his computer, and he came in my office saying he needed to see the application. Really caught me off guard."

"I can see why."

"I didn't even bother to make excuses. Just handed it to him and waited to see what he had to say. He surprised me—said I shouldn't have 'cut corners,' but since I'd always had a good record, he was willing to overlook it."

"That's what rings false to me, Leo. Overlooking it, I mean. It's not something he'd just blow off—*especially* when it's someone with a good record."

"I was just glad to be off the hook."

I touched Leo's hand. "You got yourself off the hook. Percy's the one who got you back on. Doesn't it seem a little too coincidental that he picked that particular day to make his preliminary whatever-he-called-it? And made sure Bernice knew. How else could she have found out?"

Leo frowned. "I thought through Laura. I'd made the mistake of telling Laura I'd take care of everything, and I figured she got the picture and Bernice wormed it out of her."

My wheels were going full circle. "Or maybe I have this backwards too."

Ryan shook his head and squeezed my hand again. "Are we supposed to get out the tea leaves?"

"Well, I could use a few. It's just an idea, but I wonder if it was Bernice who alerted Percy, instead of the other way around. Maybe he made preliminary doodads every time Bernice told him Laura gave her a payment. They knew sooner or later, Leo, you'd be crunched."

Leo's eyebrows went up. "It makes sense either way."

"I wonder how Percy's books would stand up in an audit."

"Be hard to prove anything."

"Proof doesn't seem to be an issue with Bernice. Is Percy married?"

"Yes. Has a kid too. Kind of a problem kid, so I hear."

Of course. Elmer Smithers. The boy Bernice had been talking to in the school parking lot, according to the Trujillo girls. The boy who'd followed me out of Hugo's.

"So Percy's married," I mused. "Muy good."

"Sharon," Alana interrupted. "Just exactly what do you have in mind?"

"I don't know. Exactly. I don't know how the legal wheels will turn. But I'd sure like a chance at Bernice off the record. Face to face. I'd like to arrange to meet her someplace—"

"No!" Ryan and Leo said at the same time.

"Listen a minute. I'm not into phony heroics. We could all be there—Eloy's or wherever. A parking lot—she seems to like parking lots."

"A lynch mob?" Alana asked.

"Close. We'll give her hell but skip the execution."

"Go on."

"I think I could fake her out. If you wouldn't point out when I was lying. And I could get by with it, because I'd be mad enough not to care."

Ryan patted my hand as if I were demented. "Sharon, I think that's a really stupid idea."

Leo grinned. "Ditto." He reached behind me and punched Ryan in the shoulder, gave me a hug, then got up and went into the kitchen. "Hey, sis, don't you keep anything but healthy stuff in your fridge?"

Alana rolled her eyes and ignored him. "Sharon, I like your idea."

CHAPTER 39

The phone rang, and Beto got up to answer it, then, grimfaced, came in to tell us Tina was sick and needed someone to take her to the emergency room.

"Damn," Alana said. "There should be a rule. Only one crisis per day. Tina always overreacts to everything anyway. If she wants to dash off to the clinic, why can't the creep take her?"

"Johnny doesn't like to be around people who vomit," Beto said without expression.

Alana didn't bother to hide her disgust. "What a prince!"

"That's my favorite thing," I said. "I'll go check on her."

Leo had returned from the kitchen with a glass of apple juice, catching the end of our conversation. He set the juice on the coffee table. "I'll go with you."

Ryan joined us as we started out. I was heading for Tina's when Leo steered me toward his house, explaining briefly that Tina had moved in with them soon after Laura's death. Timid Tina, afraid of being alone.

We found her on her knees in the bathroom, hunched over the commode, her face the ashiest I'd ever seen. Leo lifted her gently in his arms without saying a word and carried her to his car. I almost had to run to keep up with him; Ryan was there before me, opening the door.

I slipped into the back seat. "Put her back here with me."

Leo leaned Tina against me; then he and Ryan jumped in front and took off. I had grabbed a towel from the bathroom on the way out, but it didn't seem to matter. By now, Tina was racked with dry heaves.

"Honey, do you know what made you so sick?" I asked her.

"Cookies," she managed between gasps. "Bitter."

"Bitter cookies?"

"Icing."

"Oh god." The light dawned. "She put something in them!"

Ryan looked back at me. "What are you talking about?"

"Those raisin cookies Mrs. Pirtle gave me. She put something in them—in the icing. Beto took them over for Tina. I'll never forgive myself...."

"Mrs. Pirtle gave you cookies to take to Tina?"

Now wasn't the time to tell him the cookies were meant for me.

Ryan was still trying to piece it together. "Sweetheart, how could you know there was something wrong with the cookies? Don't blame yourself."

However irrational, I did blame myself, and prayed we weren't too late. It seemed to take forever to reach the clinic, but in reality we were there in little more than five minutes. The doctor on call, Dr. Aguirre, was another family friend. Thank God for small-town ties. He didn't waste time wading through red tape, but began emergency procedures as soon as we told him Tina had been poisoned.

Leo went outside to smoke while Ryan and I sat numbly in the waiting room. I got up to call Alana, asking her to remove the cookies before anyone else—who else but Johnny?—ate them. Much as I disliked Johnny, I didn't want him on my conscience too.

"Put everything in a Ziplock bag—paper plate and all," I said. "Mark it 'poison' in big letters, and tell the kids not to touch it till we have a chance to turn it over to Julio."

"What is going on?"

"It's a long bizarre story, and none of it makes sense. Ask Beto about the cookies—he can fill in some of the blanks for you. I'll tell you more when I find out more."

"Okay. Sharon? I'm glad you called. I needed to tell you— I'm sorry I was so rough on you." There was a catch in her voice.

My voice was a little unsteady as well. "Well, I don't blame you. I need to tell you—I don't like being the wicked witch."

"You're never that, honey."

I promised I'd call her as soon as we had word on Tina, then hung up and sat next to Ryan again. Leo came back and joined us in our glum vigil. We had lots of time to wait and too much time to think.

"Sharon," Ryan said, "something doesn't add up. Why would Mrs. Pirtle ask you to take cookies to Tina?"

"She didn't." I told them about Mrs. Pirtle's ploy to get me to come over. "Lucky for me I don't like raisins."

The color left Ryan's face. "How can you be so flip?"

"I'm not really. I just don't know how to deal with it."

He put his arm around me. When he felt my trembling, he was the one who lightened his tone. "I just can't turn you loose, can I. No telling what you'll get into."

Leo slumped down in his chair and shook his head. "Why would she want to hurt you, Sharon?"

"I wish I knew. It's scary. But I'm through being Perry Mason. Julio can handle this from here on out."

"I'm taking off school tomorrow anyway," Ryan said. "Joaquín and Celia owe me one."

"I think I'll take off too," Leo said. "I need to take care of some things."

Ryan made some calls, then the three of us alternated between sitting and pacing.

Dr. Aguirre finally came in and told us Tina was stabilized. "Close call. Good thing you brought her in when you did."

I began breathing freely again. "When can she leave?"

"We'll keep her here tonight. See how she feels tomorrow. She's sleeping now."

* * *

There was a message from Alana when we got home asking us to call NO MATTER HOW LATE. Her voice underlined the words.

I felt my worry return. "I don't think I can take any more bad news."

"Don't jump to conclusions."

Despite his words, I could hear the worry in Ryan's voice. We stood by the night table, too keyed up even to sit down, while Ryan dialed Alana's number, holding the receiver so we both could hear.

Alana asked about Tina, then said, "I have good news too. Carlos is doing much better. You wouldn't believe the change."

On hearing this, we could feel the tension drain from us like air from a dizzy balloon. We sank to the edge of the bed, still holding the phone together.

"Before I explain," she continued, "why don't you put Sharon on speakerphone."

"I don't have speakerphone."

"The extension?"

249

"No extension either."

"God, Ryan, why don't you join the 21st century like a normal person?"

"I think you answered your own question."

"Let me talk to Sharon then. It's your own fault you'll have to hear everything second-hand."

"Suit yourself." Ryan handed me the phone, then began unbuttoning my blouse and whispering erotic suggestions in my other ear.

"What's so funny?" Alana demanded.

"Ryan's distracting me. I think we're both a little unhinged right now." I put my hand over the receiver. "Go away."

"Never mind," she said. "It's late. Call me tomorrow after Ryan's left."

"Mm, he's taking the day off."

"Call me early then. On second thought, let me talk to Ryan again."

I handed him the phone. "Turnabout's fair play," I whispered.

"But I won't tell you to go away," he whispered back.

"RYAN," Alana yelled.

I quit distracting and let him finish the conversation.

"She wants us to come over for breakfast tomorrow," Ryan said after hanging up. "Early. Beto's walking Carlos and his friends to school. Otherwise, they decided to make the day as normal as possible."

"Good idea."

"Better idea. Where were we?"

"You don't remember?"

He remembered.

CHAPTER 40

Carlos was watching for us again, this time minus the worry. He ran up and hugged us both, then led us into the kitchen. It was a work day for Alana, so breakfast was, as she put it, "cinnamon toast and whatever." As usual there was the quiet hum of togetherness that defined their family.

"Sara's mother called the school," Carlos reported, "so that ugly lady won't bother us any more."

Both Ryan and I raised our eyebrows as we looked to Alana for explanations.

"Eat your toast, Carlitos," Beto reminded him.

Carlos took two bites. "But Dad's going to walk us to school anyway. And I heard Mom tell Dad that Uncle Ryan's not going to let you out of his sight, nina. So you'll be safe too. That *fea* can't find you and cut off your chi-chis."

"Wow. I'm glad everything's all worked out."

Miguel reddened and thunked Carlos in the head. "Blabbermouth."

Yes indeed, things were looking back to normal.

Once Beto and the boys left for school, we helped Alana clear away the breakfast dishes, then sat in the living room while she explained everything. She told us that shortly after I'd called from the hospital, she'd gotten a call from Ella Romero, Sara's mother. Ella was disturbed because Sara told her someone had tried to pick up Carlos.

"Of course the Romeros have never dealt with Bernice, so Ella didn't hesitate to call the kids' teacher, the principal, the sheriff, Jimmy's mother, me, all her sisters and brothers, and anyone else she could think of."

Alana went on to say that Billy Archuleta was turning in his report when Ella's call came in, so he asked if he could come talk to them right then instead of waiting till the next day.

"Billy asked all the right questions, and Sara was very talkative. You were right about the car, Sharon. Sara knew it was red and it wasn't a pickup. You were right about what she did notice too. And what do you know!" Alana's eyes gleamed in triumph. "When Bernice rolled down the window, she rested her arm on the door frame. And Sara noticed she had large rings on each and every finger, and a small tattoo on the back of her wrist."

"A tattoo?"

"A gecko, I think. Sara called it a little lizard shaped like the letter C."

"That's very helpful." I hesitated. "Did Sara hear anything Bernice said to Carlos?"

Alana frowned slightly. "Not really. She heard Bernice say, 'Hi, Carlos, remember me?' and then she and Jimmy ran away. I guess something in Bernice's manner scared them, but at least they weren't terrified the way Carlos was. I think that's why it was so easy for Sara to talk to Billy."

Alana brightened again. "Anyway, Carlos woke up when the phone rang, and after I'd finished talking with Ella, I told him 'everyone in town' was watching out for him. Slight exaggeration, but I was amazed at how it reassured him."

"He sure seems to have bounced back," Ryan said.

Alana nodded. "Getting his appetite back was the first good sign. After I told everyone about Ella's call, we all came in the kitchen and polished off the chicken. Carlos still had a few qualms though. He didn't want to sleep alone, so he climbed in bed with Miguel, and Miguel didn't even gripe about it for once. Later, when I went to check on them, all three boys were sound asleep."

Alana stood up, telling us she hated to hustle us out but needed to get ready for work. She walked us to the door and we exchanged hugs. We were halfway to the car when she called me back.

"There's not enough to charge her with anything, is there." Alana made it a statement, not a question.

"No. I guess you figured it out. Sara's description is everything you could hope for, but...." I shook my head. "It's unfair, but without a witness to back up Carlos' story, there are too many loopholes. That's why you needed a cooler head than mine. I'm glad we have Andy on our side."

"What about a restraining order?"

"That might slow her down for a few days—till she gets a hearing anyway. After that, who knows? It's all so iffy. But to tell you the truth, I think Ella's 'guardian-angel brigade' will work even better. With everyone on the lookout, it'll be hard for Bernice to approach *any* of the children."

Alana thought this over. "You know what, Sharon. I still like your idea about confronting Bernice ourselves. Call me whenever Ryan lets you out of his sight. Maybe you can call from the bathroom on your cell phone."

I laughed. "Good. We'll think of something."

* * *

It was still early in the morning when Ryan and I picked up Leo and went to check on Tina at the clinic.

"Are you Sharon?" the receptionist asked.

I nodded.

"She's been asking for you."

253

"We'll wait out here," Ryan said. He and Leo settled in the waiting room while I went to see Tina.

Tina looked even tinier and more fragile than usual, her eyes wide and scared.

I held her hand. "What's wrong, honey? Something else is bothering you, isn't it?"

Tears slipped down her face. "I feel so ashamed." She looked away. "I'm the one who made those calls to Erica."

"You?" I wondered if the poison had caused brain damage.

Tina sobbed for a while, but was finally able to speak. "I thought it was Mrs. Salazar who'd done something to Laura. She never did like Laura. And after the Salazars were so mean to Erica, I was afraid Mrs. Salazar would hurt Erica too. But I couldn't just come right out and tell her."

I found myself wanting to defend Mrs. Salazar. I was fond of her, "dingaling though she might be," as Ryan would say.

"I don't think this needs to go any further than you, me, and Erica. But I'd like to know why you misjudged Mrs. Salazar."

Tina looked down at her hands, still holding mine. Her account was a little disjointed, but I tracked it as best I could.

"That morning Mrs. Salazar stopped Laura on the way to school to bring us some sopa she'd made. I thought that's what had killed Laura."

"You thought Mrs. Salazar had put something in it?"
Tina nodded.

"But she wouldn't have sent something that could have...poisoned...Leo too!"

"Laura's was in a separate container. Mrs. Salazar knew Laura liked her sopa but didn't like cilantro, so she always fixed hers separately. Laura had it for lunch."

I felt a wave of sympathy for Mrs. Salazar, making an effort to overcome her personal feelings, for Leo's sake if nothing else. "When did you realize you were wrong?"

"It wasn't till last night when you told me that crazy woman had sent the cookies that I remembered."

"Mrs. Pirtle? What was it you remembered?"

"Laura went to see her right after lunch. She called Laura to tell her she had some candles or something that belonged to Laura's grandmother, and Laura went to get them. While she was there, she ate some cookies. She didn't think anything about it either, except to tell me Mrs. Pirtle was a terrible cook."

"The cookies didn't make her sick right away?"

"Probably, but they worked slower on Laura, because she was used to the barbiturates in them."

"Hmm. Sounds like she must have been feeling bad already, but just chalked it up to 'Mrs. Pirtle's bad cooking.'"

"It seems so clear now. But at the time—at the time—I went back to school right after Laura got back home, and I never thought about the cookies again. I was so sure it was the sopa."

"You and Laura didn't go back to school together?"

Tina shook her head, a fresh flow of tears streaming down her face. "We both had errands to do. If only we hadn't come in separate cars. If only I hadn't gone back to school so soon."

I heard myself echoing Ryan's words. "It wasn't your fault. You couldn't have known."

But Tina was still blaming herself. "If only I hadn't stayed to work on my bulletin board. But I didn't get home till nearly dinnertime."

"And then?"

"Laura was already in a coma. By the time the paramedics arrived it was too late. I knew Laura would never OD. After they said it was barbiturates, all I could think was, they must have been in the sopa." Tina reached for more tissues and wiped her eyes. "I really loved Laura."

"I know. I'm so sorry. It never should have happened." My own eyes filled with tears.

Neither of us spoke for a while. Finally I said, "Tina, we need to tell the sheriff all this. Not about the calls or about the sopa—or anything else. Just about the cookies—both times. Do you want me to call him now, or wait till you get home?"

Tina looked away again. "I'll probably leave as soon as Dr. Aguirre comes by. We might as well wait till after I get...back. It's hard to think of it as home." For once Tina didn't seem terrified, just depressed. "Will you be there when I talk to Julio?"

"Might as well. That way he can kill two birds with one stone." Bad choice of clichés, but I was too numb to care. I patted her hand and got up to leave. "I'm going to run along. Give us a call when you're ready to go, and we'll come by for you."

* * *

I rejoined Ryan and Leo in the waiting room, and we walked to the car.

"I'll sit in back," I said. "That way, Leo won't have to be all scrunched up."

Ryan winked at Leo. "Sharon's practicing being a wife."

Leo winked back. I wondered what they'd discussed while I was with Tina. I leaned forward between the two bucket seats and told them Tina believed Mrs. Pirtle was responsible for poisoning Laura too.

Leo looked back at me and shook his head. "Laura wasn't poisoned. She OD'd on her own drugs—some kind of barbiturate."

"It seems odd they didn't find cocaine in her system too."

"No. She told me she'd gotten off that. I wasn't sure I believed her, but I guess she was telling the truth. After...afterwards, I thought she must have gone back to relying on the prescription stuff again."

"Well, it was the prescription stuff that Mrs. Pirtle used to poison both of them."

"How could she do that?" Leo asked.

"Easy," Ryan said. "Sharon, remember when you were moving out of that place, and we found that prescription of Laura's?" He explained our discovery to Leo. "No telling how much stuff Mrs. Pirtle found in there after Abuelita left."

"Or maybe even before," I added. "I wouldn't put it past her to go snooping in all her tenants' rooms."

Leo looked out the window so I couldn't see his face, but his voice sounded husky. "Poor Laura."

I heard a quiver in my own voice as I laid my hand on Leo's shoulder. "I don't know which is worse—thinking she'd take her own life, or thinking someone would take it from her."

Leo reached for my hand, but kept looking out the window. "It still doesn't make sense, honey. Why would that woman want to hurt either of you?"

"Because she's wacko."

Leo squeezed my hand, then let go. "Well, that explains everything."

I veered away from the subject of Mrs. Pirtle's homophobia. "At least it explains that Laura didn't kill herself. Everyone seems to have a hard time believing that anyway."

"No. That didn't make sense to me either. She'd told me just the day before she'd learned something that would make Bernice leave us alone. She didn't say what, but she seemed more together than I'd seen her in a long time."

If only I knew what Laura meant. I wondered if she'd said anything to Alana.

Instead of driving to Leo's, Ryan pulled up in front of his own house. "Come on in, bro."

"Okay. Can't stay long. Got lots to do."

Once again Leo mentioned things he needed to do; at the same time he didn't seem anxious to go home. As we sauntered toward the house, I couldn't help being curious.

"No questions, sweetheart," Ryan whispered, giving me a hug after we came inside.

"And you said you couldn't read my mind."

"More than you know." He grinned. "Just to remind me it's not one of your wifely duties, you're going to force me to make the coffee, aren't you?"

I laughed, hugging him back. "I don't mind. Just so you don't expect me to dress in cellophane."

Leo came into the kitchen. "Cellophane!"

"You weren't supposed to hear that," I said.

"I don't know what she's talking about either," Ryan said, "but I'm trying to figure out if I have a choice."

"Too late. No choices."

Ryan and Leo sat at the kitchen table, discussing the appropriate dress code for making coffee, while I busied myself getting it ready. Spot wandered into the kitchen and jumped onto the chair beside Ryan, apparently so he could voice his opinion as well.

No questions indeed! We'd see about that.

CHAPTER 41

"Why don't we go home with you?" Ryan said to Leo after we'd finished our coffee and cleared away the cups. "That way we can help you finish sooner."

"Sure. Let's go."

"We?" I asked. "What is it 'we're' finishing?"

They looked at each other. Leo shrugged.

"Leo's planning a little surprise for Johnny," Ryan said in a voice that suggested he was trying not to do handsprings.

"I'm moving him out," Leo said noncommittally.

"I see." Somehow I'd guessed they weren't planning a party. "You can probably do just as well without me."

Ryan grinned. "Probably. But I'd feel better if you were with us."

"Ryan, we can't—I think you're overreacting to everything."

"No we're not," Leo said.

"Yes you are. And see what's happening? Already we're arguing, and soon we'll be snarling."

They both started laughing instead.

"And now you're making me mad. I should just stay here and wait for Tina's call."

"I suppose Spot could stand guard," Leo offered.

On hearing his name, Spot began purring loudly.

"That's a comfort," Ryan said, as he scratched Spot under the chin.

"I'm serious, you two."

"And we're serious, Sharon." Ryan had quit laughing, the anxiety reappearing in his face. "Until we know what's going on, you're safer if we stay together."

"How about a compromise? I'll go with you all till Tina calls. Then I'll pick her up, we'll go to the sheriff 's, then—what?"

"God, I think Spot's more help than Tina."

"C'mon," Leo said. "We can decide once we get to my place. Today's Amá's shopping day, and she should be on her way to Rio Grande City by now. I'd like to get finished before she gets back. If she sees Ryan's car out front, she'll call to find out why we're not both at work."

* * *

None of the furniture was Johnny's, which simplified the move next door. Walls banked with deep fuchsia bougainvillea surrounded their adjoining back yards, making it easy to go unobserved between the two houses. At last I got a look at "Laura and Tina's" home. It was pink and busy—too overdone for my taste. Ryan mumbled that he couldn't breathe, and I wondered how Johnny would fare.

Ryan carried over dresser drawers one by one, and dumped the contents on one of the ruffled beds. I filled an empty closet till I ran out of room, then placed everything else on top of Ryan's stacks. Leo boxed up books and personal items. With the three of us working together, we made good time.

I was helping Leo divvy up canned goods when Tina called. Ryan went to get her, leaping at the chance to get away from the house of suffocation and leaving Leo to be the designated jailer.

After we'd finished a couple of boxes, Leo suggested we take a break too. "Coke okay?" he asked. "I don't have any other soft drinks. It's that or Tecate."

"Coke'll be fine."

He got us each something to drink, and we sat on the patio. Since Ryan wasn't here to remind me not to ask questions, I plunged right in.

"Leo, does Tina have any idea—about Johnny moving out?"

He shifted positions, rolling his shoulders, then slouched down in his lawnchair and looked across the patio at the row of lemon trees between the two yards. "Nope. I didn't decide for sure myself till last night."

"Sounds like you'd been thinking about it before then."

"Yeah. Ever since Tina moved in, I guess. I didn't like the way he treated her. It made me see a side of him—well, never mind."

"It hurts, doesn't it." I said softly.

He looked at me then. "Yeah, it does." He was quiet a minute.

"Sharon—thanks."

"Hey, you're still my best friend—'of a boy.'"

He laughed. "And you're still going to love me forever?"

"Oh gosh. Did I say that too?" Of course I did. I'd told him one afternoon when he'd stopped Erica's brother Javier from putting spiders down my dress.

"I remember everything," Leo teased. "You must have had the makings of a lawyer even then, splitting hairs over semantics."

I laughed with him. "Well, everything was so clear when I was seven years old."

That long-ago afternoon I'd gone on to explain to Leo, "You're my best friend of a boy, but Ryan's my best *boyfriend*. That's not the same. I'm going to marry Ryan."

"Tell you what, Leo," I said, looking at him across the patio table. "From now on, I'm keeping all my promises."

"About time."

* * *

Leo and I finished packing up the last few items, and still Ryan and Tina hadn't returned. I wished I didn't feel so uneasy.

I looked out the window, willing Ryan's car to appear. "What's taking them so long? They should be here by now."

"Now you know how we feel when you're running loose."

"Running loose! You make me sound like an untrained puppy."

Leo hid a smile. "Don't worry, honey. We didn't have to go through a lot of red tape when we brought Tina in, so they're probably making up for it before they let her check out."

He was right. Ryan called a few minutes later, frazzled, telling us he'd called the sheriff from the clinic. "He's waiting for us, so why don't you and Leo meet us there?"

We all arrived about the same time. As Tina and I talked to Julio, I became aware of how unbelievable our stories sounded even to my own ears. Julio listened courteously and recorded everything we told him. I couldn't help wondering if he'd file the report under "crackpot," and only hoped he didn't think we were the only ones.

CHAPTER 42

Ryan and I went to El Paraíso for lunch after Ryan assured himself that Leo and Tina weren't coming with us.

"No wonder Leo smokes. Another 15 minutes with Tina, and I'd take it up too," Ryan said. "She's probably the real reason Laura went on Valium."

"You're awful. Is she going to stay at Leo's or what?"

"God, I hope not. Leo needs to get his own life squared away."

We finished lunch and went home to find a slew of messages on the answering machine.

"I don't care what Joaquín and Celia are up to," Ryan muttered. "I'm not going back in."

We were in luck. No messages from school.

First was from Erica. "Sharon, are you there...? Hello...? Sharon, where are you? It's Erica. Call me!"

Next was Alana. "Sharon, haven't you gone to the bathroom yet?"

"I'm not even going to ask," Ryan said.

Erica again. "Sharon, it's me. Tina called. What on earth is going on? WHERE ARE YOU? Isn't your cell phone working?"

"Interesting," Ryan said. "I only live here, and nobody calls me."

Leo was next. "Call me."

"I suppose that's for you too."

"Of course!"

Mrs. Salazar was last, her message in Spanish. "Mijo, I just got back from Rio Grande City, and Lola Ulibarrí called to tell me that silly girl who lives next door was in the hospital overnight. Did her husband poison her? I always knew there was something wrong with him. I called your sister at the store, but she couldn't come to the phone. I called the bank. Leo's not there, and his car's not in the carport. I called the school. You're not there. Where are you? Why don't you get one of those phones?"

"Who's Lola?" I asked.

"A gabby nurse—friend of Amá's. Keeps her misinformed about what's going on at the clinic."

Mrs. Salazar talked till the tape ran out.

"Are you sure you don't want me to give her your cell-phone number?" I teased.

"I'll give her yours too. As your future mother-in-law, it's something she needs to have."

"This might come as a shock, but my own mother was so—remote, I wouldn't mind having yours cluck over me—a little bit anyway."

Ryan brushed the hair back from my face and kissed me. "A little clucking goes a long way, but she'll love it. She already loves you."

The phone rang before he had a chance to rewind the tape. "Gosh," Ryan said, "I was scared we might have a minute between calls." He answered the phone, and as he listened his face became serious. All I could hear from my end was, "Um hmm," and "I see," and "okay."

"That was Leo," he said as he replaced the receiver. "He's with Erica. She's pretty upset. Tina went to see her earlier, and after she left, Erica called Leo. They want us to come over there."

* * *

It seemed strange to be at the Montoyas' old house once again. Mrs. López had redecorated inside so it was quite different, but outside was almost the same. Not exactly the same, but I couldn't put my finger on what had changed. Still, I had the eerie impression that I'd gone back in time.

Leo and Erica were in the back yard, sitting on the glider under the huisache tree. She'd obviously been crying, and began crying again as she came over and hugged me.

"Sharon, I can't believe I put you up with that crazy woman."

I hugged her back. "You didn't know. You thought it was safe, and so did I."

She continued crying. "It's all my fault."

"Honey, you might as well blame my parents. It's all their fault. If they'd been getting along, they'd have never sent me to Aunt Amanda's to begin with. We'd have never even known each other."

Leo and Ryan came and stood on either side of us, putting their arms around us.

"No musketeers," Leo said. "No clubhouse. No spaceship."

"No kissing behind the Dairy Queen," Ryan added.

We all started laughing, Erica brushing away her tears, and broke out of our little circle. Erica and I sat on the glider while Ryan and Leo drew up lawn chairs opposite us.

Now I realized what was missing. "Our clubhouse—it's gone. Now *that's* something to cry about."

I couldn't explain why it made me feel so sad, losing that familiar relic of my childhood. When did I become a grownup? And why was being a grownup so complicated? Suddenly, for one timeless moment, I had the mesmerizing sensation that Mrs. Montoya was embracing me again, saying, "Now, now, mijita. Everything will be all right. You'll see."

I ached to hear her musical voice, see her loving smile. I blinked back tears.

Erica held my hand and whispered, "It's Mami, isn't it."

I sometimes wondered if Erica and I were twins separated in the cosmos before birth—our bond, our telepathy so strong. For a while none of us said anything, all of us caught up in our shared memories.

Emma López broke the spell, coming outdoors with news from her husband, who'd gone over to meet Julio at Los Mareados. "You won't believe what happened when Julio questioned Mrs. Pirtle. She not only confessed, she BRAGGED about poisoning people." Mrs. López seemed as shaken as Erica over the realization that their apartment manager was deranged.

"Julio must have gotten quite an earful," I said.

Mrs. López nodded solemnly. "It was a little confusing at first. Ray said it sounded like she was involved in some middle-East anti-government conspiracy."

Oh that's right. I could see her now, ranting and raving about the invasion of Libyans.

"She saw herself as some kind of avenging angel—ridding the world of sinners," Mrs. López said. "You know, like those people who blow up things and think they're doing God's Will."

"Was there anyone else?" My voice faltered. How long had Mrs. Pirtle's vengeance been going on, and was Laura's Abuelita also one of her victims?

"So far there was only poor little Laura—but when no one connected her death to Mrs. Pirtle, she began planning more."

"Knowing her, she had quite a list." A list I used to be on. Exactly what sins she'd pegged on me, I could only guess; but no amount of reasoning would have changed her mind.

Erica shivered. "I hope her confession holds up."

Mrs. López nodded. "It should. Ray said Julio went strictly by the book, but Mrs. Pirtle couldn't wait to tell all."

"People like that usually stick to their stories," I said. "Either way, I think there's enough evidence to convict her."

I was opposed to the death penalty, but not for the reason many people give. To me, a quick death is *too* humane. I preferred to see Mrs. Pirtle spend the rest of her miserable existence locked away in prison for killing Laura. Dear Laura, guilty of nothing more than loving Tina. "We'll just have to keep our fingers crossed."

Mrs. López agreed and went back inside.

I turned to Erica. "All this has made me worry about Laura's grandmother. Didn't you tell me nobody's heard from her since she moved to Monterrey?"

"That's what Laura's mother said when I asked about her after the funeral."

"It's not true," Leo said. "Mrs. Velásquez didn't like Laura's 'lifestyle.' She blamed Abuelita for taking Laura's side, and it caused bad feelings. Maybe Mrs. Velásquez didn't hear from Abuelita after she moved, but Laura certainly did. In fact, I know Abuelita called Laura a day or two before she died. That was when Laura told me she'd found out something on Bernice."

"Hmm. I wonder if she told anyone what it was. Tina, or maybe Alana."

"I doubt it. She told me she wanted to check something out before she said anything else."

"We'll probably never know for sure, but I can guess." I told them what Patty had said about Bernice's brother dying

267

under suspicious circumstances. "In a town this small, if Marisa's mother heard rumors, I bet all the parents did."

Erica lowered her eyes. "I know I said I'd quit defending Bernice. But this is too much. Besides, I can't believe my mother would have let me hang out with her if she'd heard anything like that."

"Well, rumors do die down eventually. And like you, most people probably found them too far-fetched, if they listened at all. I doubt if the stories would have even resurfaced if Bernice hadn't been making trouble for Marisa. And for Laura."

"You said Patty said Marisa said her mother said. Leo said Laura said Abuelita said—and we don't even know *what* Abuelita said."

I didn't want to argue with Erica. "You're right. It's just a theory."

"Maybe." Ryan stood and stretched, then came over and squeezed in beside me on the glider. "Scoot over."

Erica and I wiggled over to make room for him. I was squashed in the middle, so Erica decided to go sit by Leo in the chair Ryan had just vacated.

"And maybe not," Ryan continued, putting his arm around me. "Now I understand why you got so upset when Bernice started talking about her brother when she was tormenting Carlos."

Erica frowned. "What are you talking about?"

She'd been so disturbed about Mrs. Pirtle's attempt to poison me, Leo hadn't gotten around to telling her about Carlos' encounter with Bernice. We took turns filling her in on the details.

"I changed my mind," Erica said angrily. "I believe everything."

"I've been thinking." I could sense Ryan and Leo getting ready to protest. Maybe we were all quadruplets separated in the cosmos. "Quit reading my mind and just wait a minute."

Erica spoke up. "Whatever it is, count me in."

"I could use your help. I'd like to meet with Bernice. Not one on one," I added quickly before Ryan and Leo could interrupt. "You, me, Alana. Bernice might be less suspicious if you were the one to arrange it, Erica."

"Maybe," Ryan relented. "If you're still determined to confront Bernice, maybe it would be better if we were all there, not just the three of you."

"I thought of that. And you might be right. But I'm afraid if you all are there, she'll try to shift attention to whatever nasty accusations she likes to throw around, and I'd like to keep her on the defensive instead."

"Go on," Erica said.

"Leo, before this goes any further, I need to know if there's any way Percy can finagle your books."

"Who's Percy?" Erica asked.

Leo looked at me warily, and I wished I'd thought to ask him while we were alone.

"He's a bigwig at the bank," I told Erica. "When we were brainstorming last night, Leo said he'd heard stories connecting Percy with Bernice, and I suspect Percy's the one who's been paying for Bernice's Porsche."

Erica raised her eyebrows. "And you think he might be what? Embezzling?"

I nodded. "Something like that. I know this is all guesswork. But suppose he's been juggling funds at the bank. He might find a way to lay the blame on someone else."

"Why pick on Leo?"

"It could be anyone—or no one. I just don't want to take any chances before I pull the rug out from under Bernice."

Leo shook his head, a half-grin on his face. "What the hell? Take a chance, Sharon. I've been thinking of losing that job anyway. Besides, I don't think Percy can do anything to my books—too many cross-checks and safeguards."

"Then how could he defraud the bank to begin with?" Erica asked. "I don't understand."

"Without getting technical," Leo said, "he could set up phony accounts that wouldn't come to light unless someone asked to look at *his* paperwork."

"One of these days there's bound to be a bona-fide audit," Ryan said.

Leo shrugged. "He probably thinks I owe him one—thinks I'll cover for him. Won't he be surprised!"

Erica looked puzzled. "Why would he think that?"

"It's a long story."

"No, it's not," I said. "Trust me. It's a short story."

Leo clasped his hands behind his head. "Okay, I trust you. You tell it."

"Leo didn't get Percy's signature on something, so now Percy can make a big deal about it."

Leo laughed. "You do have a creative way of explaining things."

"Well, let's see what creative things we can come up with for dealing with Lady Dracula." I ran a few ideas by them, but wanted to get Alana and Beto's input too. I gave Alana a call at work, and we agreed to meet at their house after supper.

CHAPTER 43

"I'm still not comfortable with the idea," Ryan said on the way to Alana and Beto's. "But Leo's right. You do have a way with words."

"If Leo wants to tell Erica anything else about his one-day loan, that's up to him. As far as I'm concerned there's nothing to tell, and no reason for Leo to keep feeling guilty over a stupid mistake. A mistake he corrected in record time."

"That mistake or any other," Ryan murmured.

Erica and Leo were already there for our brainstorming session when we arrived. We joined them at the kitchen table, along with Alana and Beto. The boys were supposed to be doing their homework, but the older ones kept coming in the room for one thing or another and caught enough of the conversation and the tension in the air to know what was going on.

"There's another reason it might be a good idea for just the three of us to show up." I said. "I'm going to bluff like hell—might even say some things that could get me disbarred. SO—the fewer people who have to pretend they never heard them, the better. okay?"

Alana put her hands over her ears. "You said something?"

The circles had reappeared under Erica's eyes. "Don't stick your neck out too far, Sharon. And don't underestimate Bernice."

"Best advice I've heard all evening," Ryan said.

We bounced around a few more ideas, then rose to leave. Miguel came into the kitchen and pulled me aside before we got to the door. "I hope you're not doing this because of stuff I said."

Someone else taking on unnecessary blame.

Evidently Ryan had the same thought. "Why don't you two talk this over. I'll wait in the living room."

The others left the kitchen too, Erica and Leo saying their goodbyes. Miguel and I sat at the kitchen table again, Miguel drumming his fingers on the tabletop.

"What is it you think you said?" I asked him.

He shifted in his seat. "Well, stuff about not trusting...the system. And now you're going to try something that could get you hurt."

"Miguel, believe me, I wouldn't do something that I thought could get *any* of us hurt. And it has nothing to do with anything you said."

"What if *la fea* brings a gun, or pepper spray, or something?"

"One of us will be close enough to grab her purse if we need to. Her reflexes can't be too fast with all that alcohol sloshing around in her brain. Besides, I don't think it'll come to that."

"What if she brings a tape recorder and gets you disbarred for something you say?"

My eyes widened. "It seems unlikely, but it's something to consider."

Miguel stopped drumming and cleared his throat. "Gabe told me about what you said at school. About the work you do. You're not the way I thought lawyers were."

I smiled at him. "I think you'd make a good attorney, Miguel."

He seemed unsure whether to be pleased or alarmed. "Why do you say that?"

"You're smart, and you think things through. And now that you know you don't have to chase ambulances, you might give it some thought."

He grinned and slid his chair back. "Maybe."

"See there? You're already coming up with good lawyerly answers."

We joined the others in the living room, Miguel still grinning. "Maybe," he repeated.

Ryan stood and put his arm around his nephew's shoulder. "What's this sweet-talking lady getting you into?"

Miguel chuckled. "She thinks I should be a lawyer."

Ryan winked at me. "Don't you think one attorney in our family is enough?"

"*Our* family? Is there something you haven't told us?" Alana demanded.

Gabe appeared in the doorway. "Am I missing something?"

"Yeah," Ryan said, laughing. He moved beside me and took my hand. "Where's Carlos? I don't want anyone left out of this important announcement."

Carlos was close on Gabe's heels. "What's going on?"

Ryan's eyes were full of mischief as he explained. "Sharon's promised to join 'The Salazar-hyphen-Eavesdropper Clan.'"

I laughed with him. "And I couldn't be happier."

"Me too!" Alana opened her arms wide and came over to hug us both.

Beto decided this called for a toast, and broke out a bottle of wine "we've been saving for a special occasion." There were more hugs, more laughing, and even the boys' grumbling about having to toast with apple juice was light-hearted.

* * *

I checked my cell phone the next morning after breakfast to discover a message from Dave Martínez. "Sharon, if Mac sent you off on vacation so I'd appreciate you, it worked. The Lovato kid won't talk to anyone but you. Call me."

"Well, I knew this was coming," Ryan said, his voice dull. "But I'm not ready."

"Neither am I."

"Is Dave married?" Ryan asked nonchalantly.

I bit my lip, then smiled. "Yes. Happily. I like his wife, Cynthia. After I was...attacked, Dave signed up the two of us—Cynthia and me—for karate, and we became good friends. She invites all us loose people over for Thanksgiving dinner every year."

Ryan raised one eyebrow. "'Loose' people?"

"Loose cannons? You know, unattached people who don't want to cook turkey for one. That's how I met Jeff."

Ryan grinned. "Guess she'll have to take your name off her list of loose women."

After Ryan left for school, I called my office and talked to our secretary.

"Sharon, I'll be so glad when you're back! Dave's been working with that nitwit Stacy. I haven't seen him this uptight in I-don't-know-when."

"Dave thought I was a nitwit when I started there."

"Oh. Well. If that's true, he's forgotten. Here, I'll put you on the line with him now."

"I don't want you to cut your vacation short," said the new appreciative Dave. "Maybe you could combine it with work."

"Wow! That sounds fun!"

He ignored the sarcasm. "Well, I need some depositions down in Starr County first of the week. If you'd handle those...."

I liked the idea. Starr was the next county to the south, close enough to give me some extra days in Zapata. We could wait till the middle of next week to get with the Lovatos, and by then I should be psyched for work. Plus, the weekend wouldn't seem so far away.

* * *

Erica called that evening to tell me that setting up a meeting with Bernice went as planned. As Leo had guessed, Bernice showed up at the bank that afternoon. Leo called Erica at Head Start right away, and she dashed over so she could run into Bernice "accidentally."

"I'm not used to all this subterfuge," Erica said. "And I almost felt guilty at how easy it was."

"If you have any doubts, we can scratch it."

"No. I'm still in. What happened, *she* was the one who suggested meeting at Eloy's. I said it would have to be tomorrow because I have to pack tonight. We'll see if she remembers."

We discussed our plans some more, then Erica changed the subject. "True confessions. I'm afraid I wasn't too sympathetic with Tina yesterday."

"Oh?"

"I told her I hoped she wasn't planning to keep on sponging off Leo."

"I can't picture you being that blunt."

"Well, Tina surprised me too. She's more perceptive than I'd given her credit for. She told me she realized Leo was 'too softhearted for his own good'—I think that's the way she put it. She also told me that up until a year ago, Leo played Santa Claus for some of the charitable organizations around here, and the kids loved him."

I smiled. "I *can* picture that."

"Me too. Tina said Leo missed his calling not working with kids, and that made her sad. Then we both got teary-eyed, and I felt ashamed for not being kinder to her."

"Poor Tina. I got to thinking about her making those anonymous calls. Given her personality, plus her distress over Laura, plus the fact that there really wasn't anyone she could talk to about it, I could understand."

"I know. And she was genuinely sorry."

"Is she moving back in with Johnny?"

"Yeah. She said what she really wanted to do was go back to Ohio, but she'd wait till the term was out because she knew it would put the school in a bind, especially with Laura gone. Apparently Johnny's not so noble. He teaches math at the mid school, but she figures he'll resign now that things are falling apart. No big loss from my point of view, but I suppose it'll take the school a while to get a replacement."

We ended our call, and I thought ahead to tomorrow's meeting with a mixture of apprehension, anticipation, and fatalism.

CHAPTER 44

As Alana and I headed for Eloy's Cantina the next morning I tried not to think about the butterflies in my stomach.

"Well, Sharon, maybe you'll get a chance to practice your karate."

"I hope not. To tell you the truth, I only learned it in hopes of never needing to use it."

"I repeat. If you don't use it on Bernice, you might have to use it on me if I decide to deck her."

Both Erica's rental car and Bernice's Porsche were already parked at Eloy's when we arrived. Per plan, Miguel had let the air out of the tires on the Porsche. I hadn't wanted the kids to be in on any of this, but Miguel and Gabe had talked the guys into letting them do something "constructive."

There weren't many cars this time of day, and I didn't see any others I recognized. I hoped the members of the "construction crew" weren't cooling their heels in jail. At least Carlos was safely tucked away with his grandparents.

Eloy's was definitely nicer than Hugo's, but lacked the class of the Purple Sage. I saw that Erica and Bernice had arrived early enough to get a booth along the far wall. I hoped we'd be out of earshot of any other early birds.

Alana and I ambled over to their table and asked if we could join them.

Bernice glared at us through slitted lids. "I'd like to say 'what a surprise,' but I have a feeling it isn't."

Erica's discomfort was genuine. "I hope you don't mind. We wanted to get everyone together before I leave town."

Alana and I sat down just as if Bernice had given us a lavish welcome. The bartender took our orders for ginger ale, and we settled in for our "little chat" with Bernice.

Alana came straight to the point. "My son told me you tried to force him into taking a ride with you even though he refused."

Bernice pretended to look amazed. "Did I give him a ride? Now that seems like something I'd remember."

Alana was ready to spring. She was right. I might have to sit on her.

"No, he didn't go with you, but you threatened him." Alana paused, then emphasized each word. "Stay away from my kids!"

"Really, Alana, you have no gratitude. It was just a friendly gesture on my part—offering him a ride on such a hot day. It's not like you and I are strangers. I hope he didn't tell you any lies."

I put my hand on Alana's arm. "It seems warm in here, or is it just me?"

"It seems warm in here" was the expression we'd agreed to use if one of us saw that we needed to move on. I was glad we'd discussed it beforehand. Logically we knew that pitting Bernice's word against anyone else's would deteriorate into a senseless "he said, she said" impasse. But we also knew it would be easy to get caught up in it. I also wondered momentarily if we should have strung garlic around our necks before this meeting.

The bartender brought Bernice another Manhattan and the rest of us ginger ale. I was glad he didn't offer to turn down the thermostat. Probably figured he wouldn't be getting a gigantic tip off our soft-drink orders.

Bernice was the one who wouldn't drop the subject. "Poor latch-key kid. No mother to come home to. His dad off fucking Marisa Rael while everyone thinks he's fixing computers."

I pressed down harder on Alana's arm and slung one ankle over hers.

"You're right," Erica said. "It is warm in here."

"Speaking of fucking and such." I hated that word and almost gagged getting it out. "Does Mrs. Smithers know about you and Percy?"

Bernice turned purple, and I knew we were on the right track. "Speaking of fucking and such," she mimicked. "Does Ryan know you were fucking half the football team when you came down for Erica's quinceañera?"

"Only half? Did I leave someone out?"

Bernice blinked, confused that I hadn't risen to the bait.

"Very warm," Alana said, as she disengaged her ankle.

My turn again in this loco version of blind-man's bluff. I swirled the straw lazily through the ice cubes in my ginger ale, hoping the gesture made me look more casual than I felt. "Mrs. Smithers might want that Porsche for her own."

Erica finally took up the cause. "Of course if Percy winds up in prison, that Porsche will wind up with nobody."

The look of hurt on Bernice's face, the bewilderment that Erica would side against her, revealed for the first time any vulnerability I'd ever seen in her. For a nanosecond, I felt sorry for her.

She rose from her chair, swaying slightly. "I don't need this."

"But the rest of us do," I said.

We were right behind her and surrounded her as she reached her car. I was glad to catch a glimpse of Beto's van in the far corner of the parking lot.

Bernice was livid when she saw the flattened tires. "Wait till my lawyer hears about this!"

Just what I'd been waiting for—my disbarment speech. "Really! You don't know much about the way we lawyers operate, do you?" So much for my bird-watching gig. "Talk about a close-knit group! All any of us has to do is say the word, and you'll never find a lawyer—or a judge—to listen to anything you say. I'll see to that."

"You wish." Her tone was uncertain, the sarcasm falling flat.

"And wait till they hear that tape Ryan made when you threatened him."

She smirked then. "Ryan didn't have a tape, and even if he did, it wouldn't help him. I'm the one with the tape."

I shrugged, though my heart sank. "I don't believe you."

I could only hope she was lying about that too. Even if such a tape never made it before the ethics committee, it could still be damaging in the wrong hands. She knew that, and she hadn't cracked the way I thought she would. I wondered how long we'd keep on trying to outmaneuver each other.

I gave it another stab. "If you did tape this—and that's a big 'if'—it can only be used against you. Do you really want everyone to know about you and Percy? Or...." Another connection clicked into place. Elmer Smithers—Bernice's goon, and most likely Laura's supplier. "Or is it about you and his son the drug-dealer?"

"You can't prove anything."

Bingo. The speech of the guilty. "Percy's protecting his son, isn't he."

"You're full of shit."

"It's warm out here," Alana said.

I had only one ace left—the biggest bluff of all. "Bernice, people have begun talking about your little brother again."

"What about it?"

"Back then, we didn't know so much about DNA. But if he were to be exhumed today...." Suddenly, thinking about that innocent little baby, I felt like crying. I'd been so rational. Now wasn't the time to lose it.

"I'm going to deck you, Sharon," Alana muttered under her breath, "if you botch this."

Erica stepped in. "Even if you don't know much about forensic medicine, Bernice, I'm sure you've heard about the discoveries they can make with the most minute particles of bone or hair."

We had avoided making a direct accusation. After all, we had only rumor to go on. That and a deep-seated intuition. But the implication finally hit a nerve. Maybe coming from Erica, it carried more weight than anything I could have said. Bernice stopped smirking and actually looked pale beneath all her makeup.

"What did your mother tell you, Erica?" Bernice whispered.

"I'd rather not say."

"It was common knowledge," Alana said.

Bernice sagged against her Porsche. "There's a statute of limitations."

I refocused. "Not on something like this."

"It would take a court order."

"Easy to get."

In reality, I thought it unlikely this would ever get to court, but apparently it was the only thing that had either shamed or frightened Bernice. And just as I'd promised Carlos, she seemed to shrivel up under the pressure.

With shaking hands, Bernice struggled to open her car door, then slid inside. Erica came around and opened the door on the passenger side. She reached in and picked up Bernice's purse, then rummaged through it. She held up a tiny tape recorder, then dropped the purse back in the car and closed the door.

Bernice didn't even rally, except to remember the flat tires. How am I going to get home?" she mumbled.

"Try walking," I said. "That Porsche is going to be repossessed pretty quick anyway, tires or no tires."

I was walking away myself when I heard Erica scream, "Look out, Sharon!"

Too late. Someone had come up behind me and thrown his arm across my neck in a choke-hold. This time I knew what to do. Almost reflexively I turned my head to one side so I could breathe, then crushed my heel into the top of his foot as hard as I could.

This time I was the one with the advantage of surprise. He loosened his grip, and I elbowed him in the stomach, then spun around to face him. I took a quick step back, then kicked him in the groin. He doubled over in agony, temporarily immobilized. It happened so fast, I think we were all stunned. At first I felt a sense of triumph that all my training had finally paid off.

But that initial sensation was quickly replaced by other emotions. Far from being elated, I was horrified to realize I actually relished the pain I'd inflicted on another person. Someone I didn't even know—a kid at that. And though I'd never seen his face before now, I realized it had to be Elmer.

The next thing I knew Ryan was at my side, his arm around my shoulders, his own face ashen. I leaned against him, grateful for his support.

"Did he hurt you?" Ryan asked in a strained voice.

I shook my head. "I'm okay," I lied.

We were quickly joined by the others, everyone talking at once. Seeing Elmer try to straighten up, Miguel pushed him to the ground, then sat on his back to make sure he couldn't get away.

"We started over here as soon as we realized he was following you, but I guess we weren't quick enough," Beto said.

I looked around for the maroon pickup. "I didn't see him drive up."

Miguel gave Elmer an extra shove. "He just got here a minute ago. Came in his dad's Lincoln and parked on the row behind *la fea's* Porsche. I guess he was pis...uh...ticked off when he saw it like that. Maybe he thought you'd done it."

The whole situation—and especially dealing with Bernice—had left me too emotionally drained to feel anything but depressed.

Physically shaky too. I slid from Ryan's embrace, sank to the ground, and pulled my knees up against my chest. I folded my arms across my knees, put my head on my arms, and began crying. Ryan sat down beside me, and silently gathered me in his comforting arms.

Alana had finally broken too and was sobbing in Beto's arms. "That precious baby. How could she?"

Leo was hugging Erica, who was weeping too.

My tears finally subsided. "I guess Elmer and Julio will have a lot to talk about."

Gabe, whose eyes were wide with awe, had been helping Miguel keep Elmer pinned down. "You really do know karate!"

"Yeah." I pulled a Kleenex out of my pocket and blew my nose, a loud unglamorous honk. "But Charlie's Angels we're not."

"Somebody's angels, I think," Beto said.

Ryan kissed me on the cheek. "Amen. Come on, let's go home."

CHAPTER 45

We learned later that Julio planned to arrest Bernice for her part in Elmer's drug trafficking—the only charge he had any hopes might stick. But her hotshot lawyer managed to run interference long enough for her to re-inflate her tires and flee into Mexico. Whether she was more afraid of prosecution or of losing the Porsche, we'll never know.

Erica took Bernice's "X-rated tape," as she called it, and cut it into little pieces. We made the unanimous decision that we couldn't let Erica leave town without a real going-away party. We met at Alana and Beto's again that evening for the sendoff, this time including the Salazar parents.

By now everyone was in a lighter mood. It was understood that no mention would be made of *la fea* or anything else to spoil the atmosphere. Leo seemed quiet around his parents, but not withdrawn the way he'd been before. Beto found another bottle of "special-occasion wine," and we toasted Erica and her success with her Head Start program.

Alana kissed Beto fondly. "Don't you have a 'special-occasion dicho' too?" she reminded him.

He smiled at her, his gray eyes twinkling. "Qué sí, corazón." He raised his glass. "Another toast."

We lifted our glasses with him as he quoted, "'*No hay mal, que por bien no venga*.' There's nothing so bad, that good doesn't come from it."

Although the words were simple, they had a profound effect on me. How dear all these people were to me. What if

I hadn't returned? The mood was too happy for me to get maudlin, so instead I kept my voice cheerful as I said to Erica, "Now aren't you glad you 'dragged me' into all this?"

She hugged me and laughed. We promised we'd call each other once a week, and I knew it was a promise we'd keep.

"I'm going to call your mom more often too," I told her. "I miss her."

"Good. She misses you."

I might even call my own mother. Although we still had things to iron out, I'd finally begun to understand her need to go back to Minnesota, back to the people she'd grown up with.

* * *

As Ryan and I were leaving, Leo and Erica joined us. We began chatting again, and Leo said, "I think we need another toast—one for the four musketeers. Stop by for a few minutes? It's still early."

The "few minutes" turned into another hour, and by the time we got home, the light on the answering machine was blinking insistently.

"Ho hum," Ryan said as he punched the button to listen to the messages.

"Honey, it's your sis. Just wanted to warn you. You'll probably be getting a call from Amá any minute. I didn't know you hadn't already told her. I would say I'm sorry I broke the news first, except she's so elated. Catch you later."

Ryan grinned. "Here it comes," he said as the second message began.

"Mijo! Alana tells me you and Sharon are getting married! I'm so happy! Have you talked to Father Lucero? I wouldn't let anyone but Norma Candelaria do the flowers. Now, about the mariachis...."

I smiled. "Cluck, cluck, cluck."

Ryan turned off both the machine and the ringer, then took me in his arms. The mariachis would have to wait.

TWO YEARS LATER

Whenever I drive the 410 loop around San Antonio at rush hour, I think of lemmings. I follow the car in front of me; someone is following me; there are cars on either side of me traveling in the same direction at the same pace; and I wonder if we're all racing to the edge.

I used to use this time to make phone calls, but I've found that—even with a hands-free cell phone—I need to focus all my attention on the traffic. All too often one of the lemmings—in a heady burst of freedom—swerves into my lane without signaling and with barely enough room to squeeze in.

Ryan and I did get married—with mariachis, the grand parade, the whole works. Norma Candelaria did the flowers. I found a lovely dress at Goodwill and wore the priceless "diamond" ring Ryan gave me when we were kids.

Ryan had wanted to buy me another ring until I explained my attachment to the one he'd bought for me so long ago with his last seven dollars and 58 cents, and all his love. "Doesn't it tell you something, Ryan, that even when I didn't think I'd ever see you again, I kept that ring?"

Mrs. Salazar was in her glory clucking and planning; all Ryan and I had to do was talk to Father Lucero and show up. Erica and Leo, as well as Alana and Beto, were our "best people" of course. My mother and stepfather came down from Minnesota; and to make the celebration complete, all the Montoyas were there.

We're more in love than ever, but I'll try not to get goopy about it. The only drawback is that, for now, I still live in San Antonio while Ryan still lives in Zapata. Summers we spend together in San Antonio. Ryan teaches summer school here, which keeps him from resorting to cellophane.

The rest of the year, we spend every weekend together, either here or there. Otherwise the telephone is our lifeline. That's the main reason I'm anxious to get off the freeway and onto the phone. The other reason of course is the lemmings.

Ironically, while Ryan stayed in Zapata, Leo moved to San Antonio about a year ago to start nursing school. I introduced him to my other best buddy, Jeff Valencia, and they're a couple now. They have me over every Wednesday for pizza and a movie they've rented. When Jeff and Leo start to get goopy, I go home.

Leo always calls the next day to apologize for running me off, and I always tell him the same thing: "I'm just glad you're finally happy, little bro. So it's okay." And I mean it. I get to call him my "little" brother, since I'm a couple of months older. I get an extra kick out of it since he's so big and burly. Leo tells me he loves me and I tell him I love him. I mean that too.

I reach the Jourdanton Exit, and turn toward Zapata and Ryan.

No hay mal, que por bien no venga.

(Mexican dicho)